MW00795437

TAKEN BEFORE DAWN

BOOKS BY B.R. SPANGLER

TAKEN BEFORE DAWN

B.R. SPANGLER

bookouture

Published by Bookouture in 2022

An imprint of Storyfire Ltd.
Carmelite House
50 Victoria Embankment
London EC4Y 0DZ

www.bookouture.com

Copyright © B.R. Spangler, 2022

B.R. Spangler has asserted his right to be identified as the author of this work.

All rights reserved. No part of this publication may be reproduced, stored in any retrieval system, or transmitted, in any form or by any means, electronic, mechanical, photocopying, recording or otherwise, without the prior written permission of the publishers.

ISBN: 978-1-80314-775-8
eBook ISBN: 978-1-80314-774-1

This book is a work of fiction. Names, characters, businesses, organizations, places and events other than those clearly in the public domain, are either the product of the author's imagination or are used fictitiously. Any resemblance to actual persons, living or dead, events or locales is entirely coincidental.

This book is dedicated to my family.
With much love, thank you for your support and patience.

PROLOGUE

The path she walked was bathed in moonlight. She placed one foot in front of the other, her head heavy, the disco music still ringing in her ears. The night was muggy but had thankfully come with a breeze. Nighttime bugs trilled and tree frogs called as the spark of fireflies flitted in the distance. She hesitated before turning left into the alley, a shortcut she'd taken before, her apartment on the other side. A hundred yards was all. Broken pieces of glass crumpled beneath her Doc Marten shoes, her step coming with a spin that forced her to close one eyelid. She held her place, fingers clutching brick, a rat stirring from behind a nearby dumpster, the smell making her gag.

Just a few drinks, she thought to herself, a sloppy chuckle slipping from her lips, the evening's fun ending. *They never have just a few.*

What had started as a memorial service for her aunt, much loved and much missed, had turned into a night out with the team. There were more drinks afterward. Her newest friends invited her for dancing and laughing and even some karaoke, which she did well, surprising them with her singing.

A scrape. A footstep, perhaps. Her friends coming to join

her? She whirled around, tipping sideways. She caught herself against the wall and tried to focus on the alleyway. There was a scatter of cardboard boxes, a pile of wood pallets next to them, along with trashcans and recycling bin.

"Nichelle?" she asked with a laugh. Thick clouds lumbered toward the ocean, and the moon reappeared to show her shadow on the wall. "Tracy? Is that you... guys?" She wagged a finger toward the sound, muttering, "Don't you guys try and scare me... I'm *imboxisated*!"

No answer. Surely it was drunkenness playing with her eyes and ears. Her smile waned as she turned back to face her apartment building. Thoughts of a hot shower and cold water replaced her concerns. She'd add a pile of ice in a frosty glass and top it with spring water. That'd fix the dry and sticky feeling in her mouth. Drinking always did that and she began to regret that last drink. The last few. It was a workday tomorrow and the clock had already struck midnight. Or was it later? Her phone's screen was black, an empty battery in the middle with a dead red line across the bottom. With her charger on the nightstand, she'd fix that too.

Tomorrow she'd blame Tracy. And why not. It was Nichelle and Tracy that insisted on staying late. Who was she to disappoint them? Her heart warmed with the thought of them as friends. With her move to the Outer Banks, she'd been skeptical about keeping company and wanted to isolate and concentrate on her studies. But her aunt Terri would hear none of it and insisted she invite them for a meal. One lunch turned into two, which turned into three, followed by late evenings, along with hard music and sweaty dancing. She never wanted the round table frolicking to end. Had she ever laughed so much? Another stir. A soda can this time. Aluminum crinkling as she froze. Samantha told herself that she was only hearing things again.

Behind her, fingernails scraped the brick wall. Samantha's heart jumped. Shock tingled in her spine as she moved to run, kicking a bottle, the glass skittering across the pavement. The sound of footsteps hitting the concrete, approaching faster, made the hairs on her arms rise.

She spun around, her balance rocked but staying intact. Nobody was there. Nobody was following her. Samantha steadied herself as she regarded it as more silliness.

"It was that vodka-something Nichelle ordered," she began, mumbling, her voice calming. It was that and the dark alleyway with the full moon and its light playing with her eyesight. Unable to shake the fear, she waved her arms and saw her shadow come alive and dance like they did in Peter Pan's story. "See! That's all it—"

She stopped dead when another shadow joined hers again. Samantha began to run, yelling, "Who's there?!"

The end of the alley was closer, her pace clumsy but moving forward. Instincts took over. She was eight years old again and running to leap onto her bed, terrified that the boogeyman's arm would shoot from beneath it. Relief slipped from her lips when she glimpsed her apartment door.

The boogeyman was real though, and it caught her foot as she reached the end of the alley. That's when the fall came, her knees striking concrete, her chest slamming against the ground, the impact squeezing the air from her body.

Head spinning and bile climbing the back of her throat, Samantha got to her hands and knees. She sucked in the humid night air. There were shoes in front of her face and confusion clouding her brain. She peered over her shoulder, certain someone had been following her. *Two people?* she wondered. "My friends are coming—"

"They're gone." A low, grating voice interrupted her, a hand extended to take hers. "A pretty girl like you shouldn't be out here alone."

Was it him? she asked herself, hope rising as she tried to see his face. The orange glow of a streetlight was behind his head and bleeding into her eyes. Samantha began to clean herself off and took his hand, believing he was the one who she'd been flirting with at the bar. He was a little older, but still cute and nice, and very tall with shoulders like a football player. He had the look that she liked, and a voice that could be on the radio. The flirting had been short-lived though, his seeming bitter over someone. They'd exchanged numbers, but her phone died shortly after. Squinting, she asked, "Jensen?"

"He's gone too," the man answered coldly and suddenly wrapped his arms around her body with a squeeze. The move was swift and took Samantha by surprise, her face crammed against his chest, breath gushing with a rasping wheeze. "It's just us now."

"Please—" she tried to beg but couldn't speak more than a word. With a hand pressed painfully against her mouth her teeth cut the insides of her lips. The taste of metal, of blood, touched her tongue as fear stabbed her heart. She dared to peer up at him, to see his gaze which was white with the moon's light and filled with evil. He was twice her size, his arms as thick as her thighs, the smell of him sour with sweat.

"Time for us to go," he said in a whisper as he hummed a tune she recognized. "I have work to do."

He held her still like a trapped animal. Tears ran down her face when her feet left the ground.

Fight, she heard in her head. Aunt Terri yelling at her from beyond the grave. *Fight for your life!*

Samantha ate the fright and shock and turned it into a maddening anger. Revolted by his assault, she kicked and squirmed, the soles of her Doc Marten shoes heavy and punishing. It didn't faze him though. Didn't slow him in the least as he carried her. He took his hand from her mouth to squeeze her body harder, the force silencing her instantly, forcing her to remain still as it crushed and ended her fight.

Her apartment building blinked in and out of her vision as

she began to lose consciousness. The stars in the night sky shone bright and began to move, began to sway back and forth as though the music inside the club was playing everywhere. Her lips were strangely cold and tingly. From the blood in her mouth there was a bitter taste and Samantha realized with fading alarm what he'd done.

"It will help you sleep," he told her in a deep voice. "It's easier this way."

And sleep she would, her gaze fixed on the end of the alley where Peter Pan's shadow continued to dance. It was there she saw it joined by others. Saw it joined by Nichelle and Tracy as they left the club and passed her by, their walking arm in arm the way they sometimes did. Samantha lifted her hand, silently screaming with her eyes, her wrist limp with a helpless hope that one of them might look in her direction. But they were gone as her eyelids closed and the night disappeared.

ONE

The sun was already becoming bright with rays shooting through our window when a call from the station arrived on my cell phone. I rubbed the sleep from my eyes as Jericho stirred and rolled toward me. The touch of his hand on my shoulder was warm and urged me to disappear into his embrace. But as the morning colors filled our apartment on the beach, I slipped one leg from beneath the bedsheet and brushed the cold floor with my toes. If the station was calling me, that meant there was a reason. Bleary eyed, I focused on the screen.

"Hey," I groaned and jumped back into bed to face Jericho, my chest against his, my cheek brushing the stubble on his face. He'd let his beard grow the last month, the whiskers a mix of grays that looked sexy but were terribly scratchy. His lips were still soft though and I placed mine against them in a kiss. "I gotta go."

"I figured as much." A long sigh. I sat up, the warm sunlight beaming onto my face and neck enough to make me squint. He ran his hand up and down my middle, his fingers moving with intentions. I narrowed my focus, giving him a look that promised time for us later. Jericho replied, "But I've got a late patrol today."

"Late?" I asked, taking his hand, my grin thinning as I considered his shift. Jericho was a major in the Outer Banks marine patrol. And as much as I'd rather see him behind a desk where he'd talk about the work and leave others to do it, I knew he loved the water and loved the patrol. Concern gnawed as I brought his hand close to my heart.

"I will," he answered without my having to ask. "I promise I'll be careful."

"You're driving?" I asked, his partner Tony having a penchant for reckless speed on the water and on land.

"I'm driving," he answered and tried to hide a smirk.

"You'll be extra careful," I insisted and thumped his chest. I glimpsed the black jewelry box sitting atop our dresser and felt an itch around my finger where there could have been an engagement ring. He'd proposed in a romantic gesture, but I'd answered with a *not yet*. At the time, I wasn't ready, but things had changed since then and I'd begun to question my decision. Jericho saw me looking but said nothing. A flurry of bittersweet nerves sprang like dandelions around a garden, along with a thought to tempt him. "Maybe you could ask again?"

He raised his brow as he grinned, sunlight on his dimpled chin and blue-green eyes. I raised a hand to put his face in shade as he answered, "Maybe you could ask me?"

"Maybe I will!" I grazed his lips with another pass and gave in to my phone's buzzer. When I read the message from Tracy, the delight of our pending engagement disappeared in a cold snap. "Samantha?"

"Dr. Swales' niece?" Jericho asked, a warm breath in my ear, his chin over my shoulder as I flicked the screen. "What's happened?"

"Tracy is saying that Samantha has been missing a few days." With my focus locked on the screen, I got up and grabbed for my clothes. The additional messages were from Tracy Fields, a young crime-scene technician on my team. She was also my daughter, but I hadn't known that until recently. Stolen from me when she was only three years old, I wanted to get to know my girl first before marriage to Jericho. "Tracy forwarded a description of a possible homicide—"

"What is it?!" Jericho asked. I could see his thoughts running wild.

"Female. Late twenties to early thirties. Caucasian with black hair and approximately five feet two... it matches Samantha."

Jericho swung his legs over the edge of the bed to join me, the mattress creaking. He'd gotten close to Samantha recently. Her aunt Terri had been a long-time family friend and had passed away a short time ago. Terri had been more than a friend though, she was also Dr. Terri Swales, our medical examiner and mentor to her niece, a medical examiner in training. Jericho helped Samantha navigate the complexities that came with her aunt's passing. From the legal pronouncement of death to closing Terri's accounts, and even donating her clothes, Jericho helped. "Mind if I tag along?" he asked.

"Tag along?" I asked, shoving a leg into my jeans. He ignored me, having heard the reservation in my voice. On almost any other call, I would have said yes. With one leg in my pants, and Jericho rushing to get dressed, I continued, "Do you think you might be too close to it? I mean, it's Terri's niece?"

He stopped what he was doing and dropped back to the bed. "I might be," he said, voice soft with a look of worry putting a crease between his eyes. "You'll text me—"

"The minute I am on the scene," I assured him.

"I didn't know she was missing," he said as he flipped through text messages. "My last text was to grab a coffee with her on Thursday."

"Did you see her?" I asked, feeling the brim of an investigation begin.

A nod. "We had coffee and split a cheese Danish. I helped her with some of Terri's estate paperwork."

"She seemed okay to you?" I asked. Another nod. We hadn't had any new homicide cases in weeks, no murders that required the service of a medical examiner. I stopped to lean over and tie my shoe, trying to recall the last time I'd seen Samantha. Had it been a month already since her aunt Terri's death? "I know Tracy and Nichelle have gotten close to her. I think they might have gone to a club Saturday night."

I grabbed my badge and station identification, cleaning a smudge from my name so it was clear, the letters spelling *Detective Casey White* in a way that seemed formal, serious. Jericho unlocked our gun safe, the metal lock clanking as it released, and retrieved both of our firearms. When he handed my revolver to me, he repeated what he's said every day since we moved in together. "You'll be careful."

"Always," I answered, gripping his arm briefly before leaving. I didn't show it, but my stomach was tight with knots. Learning someone from our team had been missing, the worry had come on strong and soured my insides. And with a call of a possible homicide and a matching description, the worry was mounting. I thought of Samantha's Aunt Terri, my friend, the only medical examiner I'd ever become close to. I imagined in some magnificent and mystifying way that Terri was with us, watching over us, protecting us. I'm a detective and investigating murders is what I do for a living. But when it's someone you know, the investigation rises to a different level, a frighteningly scary level. Perhaps because it hits home. It shows we're vulnerable to crime like everyone else.

I dropped in behind the steering wheel and pumped the gas while turning the key. In my mind, I saw Samantha's face, saw her standing next to Terri's casket. *Terri, if you're listening. Please don't let this be her.*

TWO

Concerns climbed and adrenaline pumped in my veins like water through a firehose. The drive from Corolla down to Kitty Hawk warranted a hot coffee to feed my early morning. The pot was full, and there was mention of it being fresh when I passed the cash register. The steam rising as I poured, my hand trembled slightly, heavy thoughts whirring errantly about one of our own in trouble. I kept telling myself that it couldn't be Samantha Watson the station had reported. I kept telling myself that it must be somebody else. A case of coincidence, the same age and description. But not Samantha.

I dismissed the wishful thoughts quickly. My wishful thoughts were a lie. They were a way to prepare for the possibility. With the carafe clunking back onto the hotplate, I cringed at the bitterness on my lips. The clerk's mention of a fresh pot had also been a lie, but I'd drink it anyway. I'd lie to myself, believing that it tasted good. I decided to do the same for Samantha too. I'd believe she was safe, that she'd taken to the road for some traveling was all and would be back soon. A sigh. Another taste. All I had was hope.

I jumped onto Route 12, the location of the body twenty

miles south of my apartment. From the latest station texts, I'd learned the body was discovered along the highway. They'd indicated a homicide. If this was a murder, then it was a body dumped. In my time living and working in the Outer Banks, I couldn't recall a single death reported along Route 12 that was a result of a homicide. They were all accidents. A vehicle, a car or truck, and an unlucky tourist riding a bicycle, or crossing without looking both ways first.

What if this was a homicide? Why Route 12? It was a hundred and fifty miles of highway which connected the barrier islands with two lanes of pavement. Having grown up in Philadelphia, I was familiar with the highways in and around the city. We had four or more lanes sitting side by side, except when there was construction, which seemed to be most of the time. But in the Outer Banks, Route 12 felt more like a backroad to me. It ran straight for the most, but wound tight around some bends, stealing the sight of oncoming traffic. It was scary the first time I drove it, especially when entering Carova. Even this morning, it was still a little scary, but I'd gotten used to it by now. I'd also gotten used to the heavily treelined shoulders that edged the north and the sand dunes on the shoulders in the south.

As I exited Corolla and then Duck, and entered the town of Southern Shores, it was the tall evergreens bordering the road that had me thinking like a killer. I hadn't seen it before, but passing by them this morning I recognized the opportunity he would have. For much of the northern barrier islands, Route 12 was hidden. The evergreens stood twenty feet, their bark a deep brown, their foliage a palette of colors that mapped the seasons. The sun had climbed above the horizon, brightening my drive. And at its brightest, the thick trees were able to keep the houses behind them hidden from the road. What was put in place for the purpose of privacy had also made the highway secluded. If this was a homicide, the killer would have known they were safe.

After the busy morning traffic of the Southern Shores, I closed in on Kitty Hawk and saw patrol lights flashing. A foot on the brakes, I slowed to a stop behind an old Buick, its trunk patchy, the faded red paint weathered thin enough to rust the metal. The two-lane road had been cut to one. There was standing traffic in front of me ten cars deep, my patience waning with a flutter of beats in my chest. With the adjacent lane empty, I lowered my visor and flipped a switch next to my steering wheel. A siren blared to alert the other cars as lights flashed from behind my visor and through my car's grill. A patrol officer managing the traffic saw my lights and waved me in, pointing to the road's shallow lip.

Tracy was already on scene, her car saddling the shoulder. She had her crime-scene kit in one hand and shielded her eyes with the other. When she saw me, she began to make her way around the officer's patrol car. She was friends with Samantha, and from the look on her face, I could tell she was fearing the worst. While she could have given the body a look, I think she was waiting for me to be there. I parked and opened the door as a motor roared and tires spun. The sound echoed in the back of my mind and struck a memory like a pickaxe hitting granite. Sparks ignited the dormant images that I'd only visited in my nightmares. My chest thumped and my throat closed around my heart.

I looked up in time to see white smoke rising and a minivan the color of seashells heading straight for Tracy. I punched my car's horn as the van veered around the scene and tried to exit the traffic jam. I couldn't breathe, blood rushing into my head as I waved to Tracy, my arms flailing. There was sudden alarm registering in her eyes, but she couldn't react fast enough. The driver saw me though as the side of the van clipped Tracy's arm, spinning her around, her hair flying about her head. She fell backward against the patrol car, the van easing off the gas, the driver realizing what had happened.

"Slow down!" I yelled into the passenger window when the van neared.

"I didn't see her," a man shouted, his face frozen behind the wheel as the woman in the passenger seat ranted at him.

I shouted to the patrol officer, gesturing him to go after the van, and made my badge clear. I ran to Tracy, the tips of my shoes kicking loose asphalt. The thought of losing her again hurt like the nightmares. Out of instinct, I brushed her arm and searched her body from head to toe. While I couldn't shake the fright, I nodded to her encouragingly, "Tracy, are you hurt?"

"Uh-uh," she half-answered while checking on her left arm. Beads of sweat gleamed on her upper lip. Her skin pale, she was panting and wide-eyed. Frantic, she made eye contact and said, "I think he hit me."

"Oh jeez! Are you okay though?" the officer asked. I faced the van thinking to get a plate number and saw it had already traveled a quarter mile. The rear plate was a dark blue with bright yellow indicating they were tourists. The officer followed my gaze, saying, "Leaving the scene of an accident. I'll pursue—"

"Nah, I'm fine!" Tracy shouted over another passing vehicle. "It wasn't intentional."

"Let's get this road closed!" I insisted, my voice stern, my breath hot. "Managing the traffic through the scene isn't working."

The patrol officer gave me a startled glance as though I'd slapped him. I gave him a hard look, questioning his reaction. He glanced over his shoulder toward the crime scene and then to me again. "You mean you want me to close the road? In both directions?"

I frowned, answering, "Yes, I do. Absolutely!" I knew the area well enough and continued, "Divert the northbound traffic toward the east a block or two. And divert southbound traffic west as well. They'll travel a half mile beyond the scene."

"And then back onto 12," he finished. "Do I have to call in to do that?"

"It's an order," I said, voice tight. I was uncertain if I had the authority, and uncertain that I cared if I didn't. From where we stood, I could see a woman's legs splayed across the white line, half her body lying in the road. He followed my gaze as I continued, "There are tourists, vehicles with children. They don't need to see that. Nobody does."

"Yes, ma'am," he answered, and took off toward the south, shoes slapping the pavement.

As another car passed, slower this time, I yelled, "And if anyone asks, you have them come to me, Detective Casey White!"

When he was out of sight, Tracy squeezed her eyelids and let out a moan. Hands trembling, she exclaimed in a shaky voice, "Shit! That was close."

"Are you sure you're okay?" I asked, swiping at the dirt on her arm and tucking a lock of light-brown hair behind her ear.

"I'm good," she answered. But I continued to poke and prod and inspect every inch of her the way a parent does when their child arrives home with a skinned knee. Annoyed, she took my hand. She lowered her chin and looked at me, her bright baby-blue eyes stinging my heart. "Casey, I am okay."

"Right," I said, fingers fumbling clumsily, forgetting my place.

Tracy was my baby once and had been kidnapped from my front lawn when she was only three years old. The memory of that day remained fresh like a cut. It was the van, its engine noise muscling the air that had got to me. The sound of it was like the sound of the car driven by the woman who'd snatched my girl from my clutching fingers. Though Tracy was gone from my life, my days had been filled with investigating what had happened to her. The torture of it lasted more than fifteen years. It was her kidnapping that led me to the Outer Banks, and to where we were finally reunited. It was also my reunion with her that had me turning down Jericho's proposal.

I cocked my head toward the body, shaking myself back to the present. "We've got work to do."

"Yeah—" she began, but stopped. Tracy held on to my fingers with a gentle pinch. "Maybe I should ask, Casey, are *you* okay?"

There was concern in her voice, but I forced a smile to ease her worry. She didn't know why I'd turned down Jericho's proposal, didn't know it was because I wanted to see who we were first now that I'd found her. Maybe we'd never be the mother and daughter we would have been if it hadn't been stolen from us. Maybe a deep friendship was enough. Maybe that would have to be.

"Hearing and then seeing that van gave me a fright is all."

"Work," she said. "That'll shake it from the both of us."

It did too. Almost at first glance of the body. But was this a victim of murder or an accidental death?

We needed to follow the procedures we'd been trained in. That meant waiting patiently to see who this really was, even when seeing the resemblance to our teammate and friend. Both of us held our breath, thinking of Samantha. The woman's skin was ivory white like Samantha's, save for the veins and arteries, which had already become pronounced in the early stages following death. Her hair was the same short crop and dyed a jet black, which Samantha maintained regularly. Although the woman was lying face down, her height was over five feet and half, but we'd get a better measure once she was transported.

"Injuries?" I asked, keeping my voice steady and noting the purple and black marks around the legs. "I've seen pedestrian versus vehicle before, and these are not from any accident. If I'm right, some of these are a few days old."

"Samantha was with me and Nichelle Saturday night." Tracy swung the crime-scene camera around and began recording. Each photograph would be viewed and reviewed two to three times by day's end. How must she be feeling, knowing the body in front of us could be her friend, a woman she'd danced and laughed with two days ago?

The woman had no shoes. She wore no socks either. Her feet were bare which Tracy framed with her camera, focusing on the soles of them first to take pictures. I leaned over to inspect the woman's toes and heels and knees. All were free of injury that would have indicated a struggle or running, perhaps. But there was dirt on the soles and between her toes. It was dusty and a gray-brown color, telling us she'd been without shoes when she was walking last. Her toenails were painted a lime green, an almost neon color, and blemished with the tips of them chipped. One hand was visible, her fingernails matching her toes.

"That's a good sign," I said, feeling awful even as I said it. Samantha might still be out there somewhere, but another woman was dead.

"Samantha never wore this color polish," Tracy agreed, flooding my ears with the camera's shutter.

"There's more injuries on her torso," I said, lifting the left side of the blouse with the tip of a pen. On the woman's waist and side, there were three more injuries, the ugly bruising as large as a half-dollar. Like the roar of the van's motor, the sight of the injuries raised a memory. Was it a coincidence?

"Casey, this skirt and the blouse, and that fishnet thing around her middle," Tracy said with emotion.

"Yeah, I know. The clothes could have come from Samantha's closet," I said, regarding the similarity while sleeving my fingers into a pair of latex gloves. On the woman's ankles, there were markings made from a rope or a metal chain. "Got the same on her wrist too."

"Tied up? Do you think she was in captivity?" Tracy asked, the camera flash turning the view white.

"Well, car accidents don't involve restraints," I said, imagining a car stopping, a killer opening the passenger door and dumping the body onto the road. I nudged my chin toward the victim's hand where there was dried blood that had run down her arm. "Killer used a different restraint on the victim's wrists. Look how raw her skin is, and how the blood traveled."

"Gravity?" Tracy asked, focusing on the wrists and blood trail, the picture appearing on the back of her camera. She zoomed in, showing me the injury. "Her hands must have been in the air?"

"Captivity. Physical harm—" I began to summarize as I held my arms over my head briefly, demonstrating the position the victim was in. "She was hung like this. From the coloration and depth of the open wound, she was in that position as long as a week." More ugly memories popped into my head with even uglier images of past victims from a case I hadn't thought about in years.

"Casey?" Tracy asked. "What is it?"

"Not sure yet," I answered and inspected the back of the victim's legs and her bottom where I found the same gray and brown dirt. "Hands restrained above her head, the victim was in a seated position." I sat back on my heels, interpreting the clues to see how the victim had been positioned. "That means she was against a wall, ankles tied, wrists in restraints above her head."

Tracy frowned, questioning, "A garage?"

I squished some of the dirt from her feet, pinching it between my fingers. It was fine and lacked moisture. "Or a basement," I offered. "We need to see more."

"Roll the body?" Tracy asked with hesitation in her voice.

"Yes, let's." The victim faced the ground and her hair hung

limp and covered the side of her face. "Did you get all the pictures?"

"Need to get a few more," Tracy said, continuing to move across the body as I got back to my feet. I stretched my legs and walked the scene to search the grounds. The patrol had already given the area a cursory look on our behalf, but as lead detective, I wouldn't sign-off on anything until I put eyes on the entire scene. My hands on my hips as I walked the site, I realized it had become eerily quiet, the traffic routed around us, the patrol officers guarding to give us space. In the absence of traffic, there was the faint roar of breaking waves, the beach near Route 12. There were gulls calling as well, a dozen lifting on a stiff breeze, along with colorful kites with tails a dozen yards long. "Find something?"

"Nothing unexpected," I answered, the top of my head warming from the sunlight. I stirred the loose gravel with my foot. There were no skid marks or tire impressions. Nothing to indicate an unusual activity that might have come with foul play. I also confirmed there was no sign of an accident involving a pedestrian and vehicle. But I knew that already. I knew it in an instant. The injuries on the woman's legs was the work of a killer. Not just a killer, but one of the worst kinds. A sadist who achieves sickening gratification when causing pain or when degrading others. So far, we'd seen evidence of both.

"Just about ready," Tracy said.

I returned to the scene, the tall grass close to the road brushing my legs. "Tracy." She lifted her head from the camera, heat shimmering from the pavement around her. "I think a car stopped exactly where you are, and the woman's body pushed from the passenger side."

Tracy rushed to get up and step aside as though she'd been standing on a grave. Scanning the road, she said, "I did grab a bunch of pictures around the body before we entered the scene." She went to the other side to assess the scene from a different angle. "They would have been traveling north?"

"That'd be my guess. The right side of the road. Passenger side. The question is, was the woman already dead?" I motioned to the south.

"I'm ready to take pictures of the front," Tracy said, the sun over her shoulder which put her figure in silhouette and turned her hair to gold. The sky was nearly cloudless, save for a pink fringe that was like cotton candy. Tracy went to the body, her face pale. The moment had come. "What if it is Samantha?"

"We can't think like that," I said and then bit my lip, hating my response. "But if it is, then we do what we always do."

"Uh-huh," she half-nodded, her commitment thin as she regarded the idea of a friend being murdered. "We were just out with her the other night."

"Let's do this first," I said gently. "I'll have questions for you and Nichelle later." Nichelle was an FBI agent who'd worked for me once. An IT specialist, she'd added crime-scene investigator to her title and after a few big cases, her talents were noticed by the FBI. An invitation to work with them came shortly after. Nichelle was also Tracy's roommate, the two becoming close friends with Samantha. In the clutter of traffic, there was the brim of red and blue, the lights tall, the vehicle a large white van used by the medical examiner. "We've got Derek and the medical examiner coming. I can do this with them—"

"No," Tracy blurted with a shake, taking to the position to help roll the body. "I'm okay."

It hurt to see her scared, but mothering wasn't what she wanted. "When we turn her, we'll check her eyelids for discoloration, as well as the neck area for signs of rigor mortis," I commented, offering instructions to help stick to the cadence of our duties. "We want to check for early signs."

With enough force, I was able to lift the woman's left shoulder, a joint popping, the odor of death rising. "The human body begins decomposing immediately upon death," Tracy said, reciting text from one of her books as she stared hard at the woman's face. I held my breath, waiting for Tracy's reaction. "It's not her! It's not Samantha."

I could have cried out in joyful relief, but held myself back, shutting my eyelids and breathing a sigh. "That answers that," I said, weakened by the relief even as I felt guilt. This was still somebody else's friend, colleague, daughter. "Let's continue the work."

"Casey?" Tracy blurted. There was a look of rigid fright mixed with disgust on her face.

I held the body upright, unable to see the woman's front, and asked, "What? What is it?"

She pointed at the woman's face as her nose wrinkled and her upper lip tightened. "I think... I think they were made to look like tears!" she answered with shock in her voice.

"What do you mean—" I began as my muscles quivered against the weight and the awkward angle.

"Here, let me." Tracy took hold of one arm and helped to lower the woman onto her back. "Take a look!"

"Tears," I said, the body facing up now. Another memory rose from its long sleep and left me to stare with disbelief as Tracy repositioned herself and continued working with the camera. "No. It can't be—"

"Can't be what?" Tracy asked as flashes sprang to life along with rolling shutter clicks. I couldn't answer though, staring instead at a face I hadn't seen in years.

While I'd never once seen this person before, never seen this victim, I had seen the work of her killer, a dangerous sadist I'd thought to be long gone from this earth. Below the victim's eyes there were tears. They'd been drawn into the skin with a smooth cut, deep and wide, reaching the middle of each cheek where they ended with a single teardrop, a gouge, the flesh torn open to make the shape.

I searched the woman's face, desperately looking for a difference that would indicate this was only a morbid coincidence and nothing more. Beneath the left eye there was an additional tear, a superficial first cut that the killer made days before he finished what was started. It was the same. It was the same from a case I'd never been able to solve. The final tears were made permanent, carved into the flesh, the killer using his blade just before death so the body could never heal.

"Casey?" Tracy asked again, her voice distant. Without looking, I knew there would be a single stab wound to the victim's heart. A puncture wound was a better description of the injury. It was applied torture. After the killer's pleasure was satisfied.

"One second," I said, my tongue feeling thick and my mouth watering with nausea. I dared to lower my focus to the victim's chest, and slammed my eyelids shut when seeing that it was there. I covered my mouth with the crook of my arm and stood up in a rush. The victim's white cotton shirt had been soiled by a red stain between her breasts. And at the center was a small hole where the killer entered. A single stab wound to pierce the victim's heart. My own heart cramped—the killer I once knew had returned and claimed a new victim. I gently touched her arm, knowing this poor woman had met the same violent fate as the victims whom I'd never been able to bring justice. "This can't be."

Tracy saw the shock on my face, saw me jump up as though I was going to run. She stopped taking pictures to stand, the hot asphalt and bright sky slamming into my mind with the images of five women who'd died in the same tragic manner ten years earlier. Tracy clutched my arm to steady me, worry mounting in her eyes. "What is it?"

"It's the Midnight Killer," I answered coldly. "He's back."

THREE

Tires crunched stone as a medical examiner van parked along the side of the road. A fleeting wish came to mind: to see Dr. Terri Swales again. But she was gone, and it continued to hurt. I mourned her loss and probably would for a long time. Since Terri's passing, we'd had three temporary medical examiners, including the most recent, Bob Roth, who'd come out of retirement to fill the position. Doc Bob was what he wanted us to call him. As Tracy and Nichelle had slightly rudely described him to me, he was old when the earth was still young. But in the few short interactions, I found that he was sharp and had a great eye for detail. I gave the crime scene a hard look, thinking of the past victims I'd seen years ago, their murders unsolved. I'd need Doc Bob's skills now. I'd need the same from everyone if it truly was the killer from past cases I believed we were dealing with.

As for a permanent medical examiner to replace Dr. Swales? From what we were told by the mayor and the council, our part of the Outer Banks was in rotation. Meaning, we got what we got until there was someone available. From me to Jericho and everyone in between, we were rooting for Samantha Watson. The temporary placements, relying on retirees like

Doc Bob, these could work in her favor. She was in her last year of a fellowship Dr. Swales had wanted to be a part of. When finished, Samantha could be our next medical examiner, the job offer made. But none of that was going to happen while she was missing. While we had no identification, we knew for certain that the dead body straddling the edge of the northbound lane of Route 12 was not our associate medical examiner.

From the medical examiner van, Derek exited the driver side. His thinning blond hair caught a breeze, sunlight bleeding through to make it look like yellow flames. He gave us a short wave and got up on his toes to try and see the body. I shook my head fervently, letting him know that it wasn't Samantha. His eyelids closing slowly, he covered his heart with a meaty hand. Like the rest of the team, he'd also grown close to Samantha. A long-time assistant to Dr. Swales, Derek stepped into the role of Doc Bob's right-hand with ease. It helped that he was a giant next to everyone and was as strong as a bull.

Derek helped Doc Bob down from the passenger seat and then to our crime scene. The old-time doctor did his best to look the part. It didn't matter the time of day, or what day of the week it was, or even what the weather was like, Doc Bob always wore a suit jacket and slacks. He also wore some of the ugliest ties I think I'd ever seen. Next to the flat colors of his suit, the clashing ties, the brightness of them an understatement. But given his white hair, his steel-gray eyes and pale skin, the colors actually worked.

"Missy," he said politely, addressing me with a term I hadn't heard since my early years on the force. He dropped a black medical bag onto the ground. It was like something I'd seen in a movie, or maybe it was the old *Quincy, M.E.* show. Next to the bag, Derek placed a blue gardener's mat for Doc Bob to kneel on. When he was in position, he opened his medical bag, the hinges creaking, retrieving a penlight and a couple of the instruments I recognized for measuring body temperature.

"Hi, Doc," I replied, moving to give him room. "Fairly certain the cause of death is a single stab wound to the chest." I didn't tell him yet that I recognized the wound.

"Uhm," he grunted as he slipped on a pair of gloves. I'd expected to see his hands shaking with age, but they were rock-steady while he inspected the wound. He put a small tape recorder up to his mouth, a red light blinking, and spoke into it. He had a thick, wiry mustache that bounced with his words. "The victim has a single puncture wound above the heart, off center. Made by a round instrument, which may have compromised the victim's sternum—"

He stopped speaking, a frown forming when his eyes caught the bruises on the victim's legs and middle. Creases etched into his forehead when his sight locked onto the tears cut into the victim's face. When he frowned with a question, I offered, "They were made to appear like tears."

"Tears?" he asked, bushy eyebrows rising again. He leaned back, Derek's hand on his shoulder to support him. "When a killer marks a victim like that..." a pause, mustache moving as he chewed on what he wanted to say "...you can eliminate most of the common causes of murder. Greed. Passion. Jealousy—"

"Agreed," I said, his understanding what it was we were looking at. "I had an unsolved case in Philadelphia, same MO, bruising on the thighs and teardrops cut into the victim's face."

"Unsolved... so it could be the same guy?" he asked without looking at me, busily studying the marks. "The first marking looks days' old and superficial. The second is a more severe laceration and appears to be post-mortem."

"See how the cut on the left cheek is already healing?" Heads nodded. "In the past case, we believed that cut was made first, inflicted at the time of the abduction."

"And the second tear was done just before death?" he asked, straightening, giving me a hard look. "This is a killer's ritual?"

"That was our thinking, that we were dealing with a killer

who followed a ceremony, a clear pattern." My stomach turned at the thought of the killer's return. "But as I mentioned, the previous case remains open, the murders unsolved."

A car door slammed and stole our focus. The distraction was a woman rushing toward us which put me on alert, muscles tensing. The tips of her biggish shoes kicked pebbles in the road, scattering them as she waved. I relaxed when I saw her bag, saw that she was here to help Doc Bob.

"Sorry I'm late," the woman said, panting. She was in her late twenties, possibly early thirties, her face close enough for me to do a double take, blinking fast to make sure of what I was seeing. She had purple hair, almost a light magenta color that touched her shoulders, the highlights catching the sun behind her. A pair of thick glasses sat at the tip of her nose, the lenses making her eyes look small. I couldn't help but stare as she pushed against them, the gesture eerily like something Dr. Terri Swales used to do. Her height was like Terri's too, the top of her head reaching my shoulder. There was no relation to Terri. None that I knew of. I was probably seeing what I wanted to see. I'd done the same after my daughter had been kidnapped, especially in the years I searched for her. It was all in my mind, tricking me, helping to ease the loss of someone I loved.

"Carla?" Tracy asked, shaking her head. "I had no idea this was the job you were talking about."

Her voice bubbly, she opened her hands and wiggled her fingers, and shouted a whisper, "Surprise!"

"Traffic?" Doc Bob asked, annoyed she was late to the crime scene. She bowed her head, looking down and away. "You can ride with us next time. We'll make room."

"Detective Casey White," I said, introducing myself. Carla's green eyes jumped from me to Tracy, and then returned. She adjusted her glasses, the frame teetering and sliding again. When her eyes came into focus, I could see that she recognized me from the news. That she recognized the story of me and Tracy, its having been circulated at a national level at one time. "I'm the lead detective. And you already know Tracy?"

"Carla Reynolds. I'm here helping Doc Bob," she said shyly. "I met Tracy the other night."

"Nichelle and Samantha too?" I asked, tipping my chin, adding her name to the list of those I'd interview. She flashed a brief smile with a nod before her focus shifted to the body. "We're just about to discuss the bruising."

"Okay," she replied. Her hands were bare, which had me thinking first day jitters, that she forgot to put on a pair.

"Gloves?" I offered, latex fingers swaying.

She shook her hands. "Allergic to latex." From her pocket, she brought out a non-latex pair, the same color as her purple hair. "I bring my own."

"Noted," I said. "What's your role with Doc Bob?"

"I'm the new assistant medical examiner," she answered without looking at us.

Carla got straight to work, kneeling next to Doc Bob and taking the instrument for measuring body temperature. The group went quiet, Derek pressing his lips tight. He said nothing. None of us did. But we all thought of Samantha's role in the medical examiner's office and regarded the idea of it being replaced already. Carla must have sensed the awkwardness and added, "I'm just a temp though, like Doc Bob."

"Welcome to the team," I said, trying to sound encouraging. In my experience, it was those temporary things that became permanent. For Samantha's sake, I hoped that wasn't the case. I returned to the body, speaking to Doc Bob. "With the unsolved case, we'd also had thoughts the killer might mark his victims like this as a process of selection and to show ownership."

"Yes, it would," he agreed, tracing his fingers around one of the bruises. "These may not be for the sake of ritual or ceremony alone, but could be him branding what he believes is his."

Tracy turned to Carla, explaining, "There may be a connection to a previous case."

"Perhaps," Doc Bob said flatly. The bloodshot whites of his eyes appeared from beneath his brow. I saw his interest was piqued. "Perhaps not. We won't know until we know."

"Well..." Tracy began to say. She held her phone, swiping the screen until it showed a news release of my old unsolved cases. I saw the old cases I'd told her to look up, the black-and-white picture of the Philadelphia newspaper's headline, *Midnight Killer Strikes Again*. With the sight of it, I felt the return of the same regret and angst that dogged me years earlier. "It says here that ten years ago, there were five murders. All of them women. All around the same age, the same profile. And that all of them were believed to have been tortured before they were killed."

"What about those?" Carla asked Tracy, snapping a pair of gloves, cornstarch shimmering in a powdery cloud. "Is there any mention of the cuts on the face?"

Tracy's lips moved as she read the article to herself, searching the column for mention of the teardrop marks. I'd worked the case with my partner, Detective Steve Sholes, and answered, "That information was never released."

"Ten years ago? And now today?" Doc Bob grunted while continuing with his examination. He held up his hand and lifted the tape recorder, speaking softly into it, "Measuring the intrahepatic temperature." We turned away as he performed the temperature check, returning our focus as he read the numbers, "The victim's body temperature is 82.5 degrees."

"That would put death as having occurred sometime yesterday," I said, noting it, along with the temperature reading and the time of day.

"You said ten years ago? Five women and same circumstance?" Carla asked, swinging her head, her hair flopping to one side.

"Ten years almost to the day," Tracy answered, flicking her finger across the phone's screen. "Wow, according to this, the five victims occurred in a short span of five weeks."

"One victim a week," I added, recalling the victims' faces, their names on the tip of my tongue like names on a grave's headstone.

"What happened?" Carla asked.

"Yeah? Did you have a suspect?" Tracy added.

"I'll fill you in later," I answered and knelt next to the victim and pointed to the tears. I gave the order, "As for these. There's no mentioning outside of the investigation. We don't want this made public."

"Agreed. Tell me more about the wound in the chest," Doc Bob asked.

"Other than being fatal, we kept that detail from the press as well."

A look of understanding brightened the old man's eyes. "The cases remain unsolved?"

"Still unsolved," I said, remembering the craziness of the case, the local newspapers and television reporters. "The press called him the Midnight Killer and it put the city into a state of panic. We kept the details of the murders from the press. Otherwise, we'd risk the few good leads we had becoming a hundred nonsense leads."

Doc Bob held his tape recorder in one hand as he hushed us with the other. "Previous case may be related. Request autopsy findings to confirm likeness."

When he pressed stop on the tape recorder, his gaze hung absently and he said nothing. "Doctor?" I asked, concerned.

"If it is like the past cases, there's going to be more," the doctor answered, shoulders slumping. "Can you get me the autopsy findings from the previous victims?"

"That's what I have in mind," I answered him. I showed him the left hand, the wrist with the injury and the blood that had traveled down the victim's arm before it dried. "We believe these are from restraints."

"Same as the past cases?" he asked, assessing the marks around the wrists, a flap of skin opened just beneath the left hand. "Could be a handcuff, or makeshift restraint with an edge sharp enough to cut."

"It's new," I warned, seeing it as an escalation in the killer's behavior toward his victims. "Previous cases, there were burns from rope."

"And these too?" Carla asked, pointing to the bruises across the victim's torso as she plotted them on a sketch book with a figure of a human body. "Do you see anything different with them?"

My breathing was ragged now. "Although she's clothed, there's more of them." Gripping one arm, I waited for Doc Bob to give the okay before lifting her shirt. On the right side of the victim's chest there were four more marks, the bruises older, the edges of them an ugly green that came with injury. "He started here. These were the first."

"Do you mean this victim has more bruises?" Tracy asked, picking up on the difference from the previous cases. A nod. Tracy frowned, asking, "Why is that?"

I stood up and faced the sun, the heat of it on my face and making me sweat. If only it could bleach the stain of what this killer forced me to witness. I sucked in the humid air and turned around to face the team. "I believe he's making up for lost time."

FOUR

We were nearly finished with the victim's field assessment and our gathering of evidence and photographs. A search of the victim produced no workable identification. We forwarded a description to the station for comparison with any recent missing person reports. From there, it would be distributed to our immediate sister stations and then up and down the Outer Banks and to the mainland of North Carolina. Crime-scene tape fluttered, a breeze lifting it with a snap, ocean waves a distant roar. The sun had climbed to the noon hour, our figures without shadow, the heat shimmering on the road. I handed out bottles of water from the back of my car, the plastic caps snapping, the officers thanking me as they guzzled them empty.

Tracy's arms had begun to pink, her cheeks turning ruddy with color, the day cloudless. I found myself pausing with a memory of her father. He only had to think of sunlight to get a burn started with sweat gleaming on his forehead. She was like that. And why wouldn't she be? After all, she shared half of his DNA. We'd split up years ago, but to see her working made me think of him, had me missing his voice and wishing he'd been alive to know his daughter, and for her to know him. He'd been murdered, the case made more tragic with Tracy having worked it. I shook with the sadness of it, but now wasn't the time.

Doc Bob produced a mobile fingerprint scanner, a brand I'd never seen. The machine was a black box with a screen on top, the display a turquoise color with lists of options. He surprised us with his knack for technology, setting it up while quietly talking to himself. We watched with keen interest until he noticed.

"What?" he asked, chin up, hunched over the body. When he saw what we were looking at, he tilted the machine for us to see. "I'm one of their beta testers."

"I thought you were retired?" Tracy asked while taking to a knee on the other side of the device. Her eyes devoured the technology, drinking it in like she had come from a twenty-mile walk in the desert.

The doctor scrunched his nose, answering, "We never really retire."

"Any good?" I asked, familiar with field scanners, and having found their performance to be spotty. "In my experience, they're only as good as the data on their servers."

"True. Alone, it's just a mobile fingerprint scanner," he answered with a shrug and placed the victim's hand on the reader, using the index finger and thumb.

"This thing is cool," Tracy said, reading her phone. "Cloud based identification. A constant update of all missing persons around the country."

"We'll see. It could be good tech," he said, tilting his head, and giving the reader an approving tap.

"Here, let me," I said and gently eased the victim's head from the asphalt. The sight of her face tugged at my heart as I carefully moved her, taking care not to disturb her hair, a forensic combing planned. Tracy saw me, eyes becoming sympathetic as she helped turn the victim's shoulders for Doc Bob to frame the face and take a picture.

"Got it," he said, the unit buzzing, the display showing it was connecting and sending the data.

"Looks like you're doing more than writing a paper on it." The screen flashed to display the words, *waiting for a response*.

"When I got the call about Dr. Swales," he began to say and paused to read the screen, "I thought to bring this along."

"Is it working?" Tracy asked, shifting with every beep and whir and change in display. "What's it say?"

"Pauline Rydel?" Doc Bob answered, his tone questioning the accuracy. At once we began the process of validation, texting in the name, reconciling the fingerprint read taken in the field with the name. Doc Bob warned, "Remember, it's new, it's—"

"Look at that. It's accurate," I said, interrupting and showing them a picture of Pauline Rydel on my phone. "She's been missing for eight days."

"Her parents reported her missing this past Monday," Tracy went on to say, showing the same picture on her phone.

"Good to see this thing is working," Doc Bob commented while Tracy added the victim's name and the initial missing person's report. "They told me they were working the data feeds, that they might not be ready."

"They were ready," I commented, reviewing a picture of Pauline Rydel's fingerprints. "It's a school card, from when she was in school."

"That's one," Doc Bob said, his words a surprise. He held the victim's hand up, placing her gray fingers into the sunlight and brought them within an inch of his face. "We need a sample."

"One!?" I exclaimed, understanding. "The backend also links to criminal databases too, like CODIS. How many?"

He peered over his glasses, answering without inflection, "I think it's all of them."

"What kind of samples?" I asked, thinking through the

myriad of what could be used. Carla opened a box, the logo on it the same as the unit. Inside it, there was a bag of swabs and plastic cartridges, and another with fluid. With this unit, they could prepare a sample in the field for DNA testing, cross-check nationally, identify a suspect while we processed the body. "Tissue beneath the fingernails?"

"Absent," he answered, shaking his head. His gaze shifted to below the victim's waist and then to the surrounding officers. "It might be best that we continue this in the morgue."

"Might be," I agreed, unable to imagine their taking the next steps on the road where this poor girl was dumped. "We have a name, a missing person's case, and her parents to visit."

"Detective," Doc Bob began, pausing to eye the sample preparation kit. Carla acknowledged and repacked it. "I don't envy that part of the job."

"I sent you her home address and parents' phone numbers," Tracy said, my phone buzzing with the text. As she packed her camera gear, she asked, "Should we go?"

"Doctor?" I asked, his being the medical examiner on duty and having responsibility of formally confirming the victim's identification. He shaded his eyes, the whites broken by thin veins. "Would you confirm the victim's identification for us?"

He patted the top of the identification unit like he was petting a dog. "I do like my technology, but"—he motioned to Tracy's phone which showed a driver's license picture of Pauline Rydel—"I'll want a second metric to confirm. A picture will do."

I brushed the victim's hair away from her face as Doc Bob held the phone, placing it next to it. I couldn't look away from the teardrops cut into her skin, the depth of the one that was making the open skin sag and which made the facial identification a challenge. "Doc?" I asked, his study seemingly long.

"I can confirm," he answered, lips tight. He handed Tracy her phone, muttering, "There's never getting used to it."

"You're right about that," I replied, easing the victim's head onto the pavement. "When it comes to murder, there never should be."

There was no getting used to it. My insides twisted and had wound into knots as we parked outside the Rydels' residence. While Doc Bob and Carla accompanied Pauline Rydel's body to the morgue, I visited with her parents. Tracy joined me, our going in pairs as a normal part of the police procedure we practiced. But there was nothing normal about telling a mother and father that their child was dead. Even worse, having to explain that their loved one had fallen victim to foul play.

"You have her!" a man shouted from the front stoop as the bottom of my shoes touched the driveway. He wasn't much older than me, a full head of brown hair without a strand of gray. His eyes narrowed with expectation when Tracy's car door opened, and then sprang wide when she stood up. He braced the doorframe, fingernail digging into the paint, his jaw clenching tight. His gaze was locked onto my badge, his voice rising through gritted teeth. "Where is my daughter?"

"Sir," I began to say as his wife appeared in the doorway. She had a dishtowel in hand and was drying a casserole dish, her dark blond hair hung limp, her face shiny and without makeup. A stray thought came to mind, an image of their refrigerator, the shelves piling high with casserole dishes covered in foil. Surely, the neighbors were flooding the couple with food during these desperate days when their daughter was missing. That's what people did when they didn't know what else to do. They brought meals. They brought a lot of them. I remember. There was no appetite when a child had gone missing though. How many casseroles had gone uneaten when my daughter was kidnapped? "If we could go inside?"

"Ma'am?" the woman asked, her eyes glassy, hands beginning to tremble. Her gaze shifted to Tracy then. When Tracy turned to me, Pauline Rydel's mother knew in an instant. In my experience, I'd come to learn that mothers always knew. The casserole dish crashed onto their patio, the glass smashing against stone pavers, chunks skittering toward our feet as her dishtowel flopped atop the remains. "She's dead. Pauline is dead."

"We'll get that," I said as glass crunched beneath our shoes, and we escorted Jack and Sharon Rydel into their home. Tracy held one arm while I held the other, Sharon Rydel's legs had become grossly weak, every step a challenge. I followed the hallway into the kitchen, a family room to our right with a couch and loveseat, and a red-brick fireplace that climbed to the top of the vaulted ceiling. "Water?"

"Please," she replied. Her husband's face had turned as white as a ghost, his jaw slack while he busied himself in a closet, a dustpan and broom in his hands. "In the refrigerator."

"I got it," Tracy said, her words soft while she tended to the task of catering and helping clean up the shattered casserole dish.

"Sir," I asked, my voice rising to get his attention. He stood stone-faced and unblinking, his eyes blank and as round as coins. Tracy removed the dustpan and broom from his clenched hands, his forfeiting them, though I wasn't at all certain he was aware of what he was doing. Like his wife, he was in shock. "If you could sit, please."

"Yeah," he answered, eyelids fluttering with acknowledgment. I nudged my chin at Tracy; she took his arm and helped him to the couch, the cushions wheezing as he plopped into the seat. "You... you said that you found our daughter?"

"Yes, sir. Mr. and Mrs. Rydel, your daughter was found this morning along Route 12. Paramedics were called to the scene, but discovered that Pauline was unresponsive—"

"Was she already dead?" Sharon Rydel asked, brow

furrowed, her stare fixed on a family portrait above the fireplace. I answered with a brief nod. "How did she die? You know, Pauline is allergic to shellfish. Was it a reaction?"

"Did she have her epinephrine shot?" Pauline's father added. He faced his wife, continuing, "Before she left, we asked if she had it on her. Didn't we?"

They seemed to forget their daughter had been missing for days as they discussed the epinephrine, calling it an EpiPen, and the dangers of living on an island abundant with seafood. How often had their daughter left the house with her parents worrying? I raised my hand to get their attention, but the conversation went sideways about the lethalness of their daughter's allergy. "I'm afraid your daughter was killed," I stated, their mouths snapping shut. The room fell silent, save for the distant clinking, glass on stone, as Tracy broomed it into a dustpan. "I am sorry to inform you, but your daughter's death was at the hands of a murderer."

"Murder?" Jack Rydel asked with a sob, arms extended, reaching for his wife.

"My girl?" Sharon Rydel shook her head harshly, casting the news from her ears to avoid the truth of it. She put on a smile then, her cheeks glistening. "I'm sorry, but that's impossible. Nobody would ever want to hurt Pauline."

"Detective White?" a patrol officer asked, footsteps approaching as he entered the home. Tracy followed, a bag in hand with the broom and dustpan.

I turned back to Pauline Rydel's parents. "We were able to make a positive identification. However, this officer is here to escort you to the morgue if you choose to meet with the medical examiner."

"We'll do that," Sharon Rydel answered, mouth in a defiant pout, her disbelief continuing. "Right now."

"Thank you," I said. "The officer is here for you."

Jack Rydel stood up and took my hand and then Tracy's. "If you could lock the door afterward, when you're done here."

"Of course," I said and eyed a hallway exiting the far side of the kitchen. When he noticed, he gave an approving look to search Pauline's room.

"You won't find much though," he muttered while taking his wife's arm. "Pauline has it all packed to move to a new apartment. It would have been her first."

FIVE

As Jack Rydel told us, his daughter's room was packed, the sight of it dashing ideas of our finding an immediate clue to Pauline's life before her death. There were cardboard boxes labeled with cream-colored masking tape lined along the bedroom walls, climbing almost to the ceiling on two of them. The room's corners were stacked with furniture, a bed frame in pieces, the parts disassembled and standing upright. With the strong likeness to unsolved cases from my past, I decided to leave the room as it was. If determined necessary, we'd send a team to revisit and dig into them, unpack her life one box at a time. For now, we needed to review the past cases—the only cases in my career that had gone unsolved.

It wasn't every day that I had Tracy and Nichelle driving with me, but it was the second time in recent cases that they'd accompanied me to Philadelphia, my hometown. It was also Tracy's birthplace and home before her kidnapping. Not that she remembered that time.

I'd been a uniformed cop several years when the kidnapping occurred. Despite an obsession to find her, my career continued to rise. There were promotions and bigger cases, along with a gold shield and homicide detective title. But it came at the cost of my marriage to Tracy's father. I'd put a thousand percent of myself into the cases that crossed my desk, including my search for our daughter. I was working homicide in the city of brotherly love during one of the city's worst heatwaves ten years ago when I'd come across a notoriously dangerous criminal. In the press, the newspapers and television, he'd become known as the Midnight Killer due to his selecting victims between the midnight and dawn hours. As Tracy and Nichelle noted, the name given to the killer was cheesy. That wasn't our doing. The press sensationalized the murders, following in the likeness to famous cases like the Lady Killer Ted Bundy, and the unsolved cases of the Zodiac Killer. I always thought it a sad state when murder was used to sell the news.

Nichelle sat in the front passenger seat, her gaze fixed on the traffic passing in the next lane to us. Her laptop was closed and tucked into her backpack, which was out of the norm for her. I said nothing but saw her expression changing. First a frown, followed by a slight rise of her brow. She was debating something. She wasn't new to the FBI anymore, but they'd called her for an in-person meeting back to Philadelphia's FBI offices on Arch Street. She'd told us it was to pick up a new identification badge, something she called a PIV card to authenticate her computer. I sensed there was more though. That it wasn't good.

Tracy sat behind Nichelle, her laptop's keyboard sounding the clicks and clacks of a report I would read tonight or tomorrow morning. She'd supply the first report, the initial findings filed in a new case I'd open. The paperwork rolled up from there. I'd join my report with hers, and then marry them with the medical examiner's preliminary findings report, along with notes from Derek and also Samantha's temporary replacement. It was the same process worked ten years earlier where five files with my notes were created. Five folders, each thick like the new one, but each of them a cold case that had collected dust and was stuffed inside a dark desk drawer.

"Thanks for letting me hitch a ride," Nichelle said, turning down the radio, the eastern sun bright and making her skin glow a beautiful bronze color, her hair curly and shining like strands of copper. She put her hand behind the seat's headrest and dangled her fingers until Tracy reciprocated with an affectionate squeeze. The two were good together, but I worried for them. I couldn't help it. I loved them both. But Tracy was my daughter, and I didn't want to see her hurt if something happened to Nichelle. "Would you mind dropping me off at this address?"

"Where?" I asked as she handed me a note. The address was a couple blocks away from the Arch Street building where the FBI was headquartered. "What is it?"

"It's an apartment building," Tracy answered from behind us.

"We're just looking," Nichelle said, her voice swift, but the words impactful. It must have been what she was contemplating. Perhaps some news she wasn't sure how to share. From the rearview mirror, I could see Tracy looking at me with a mix of excitement and reserve. I shook my head, saying, "I'm confused. What's going on?"

"I've been asked about a move in the bureau to become a field agent," Nichelle answered. The car filled with the sound of tires on the road. "I just have to pass the physical fitness tests and be available to report to a field office."

"A field agent?" I asked, realizing her career in law enforcement was shifting beyond the technical professional she'd been. They were calling her to Philadelphia's office to discuss her training, which included all the rewards, the risks, and the dangers of the job. My mouth went dry as I spoke the right words, the rehearsed words we learn for these situations, "That's exciting news. Congratulations."

"I'm going with her," Tracy said, her face appearing between the seats. There was guilt on Nichelle's face as though she were stealing from me. In that moment, I felt my body racked with the thought of losing my girl again. I said nothing and concentrated on the drive. A hand on my shoulder, Tracy seeing it on my face. "It'll be like I was returning home."

"Isn't the Outer Banks your home?" I said without thinking. They reeled back and I clapped my lips tight, finding composure before I continued. "Tracy, you've only been certified a short time—"

"I'm going to finish my master's degree in criminology," she answered, interrupting. "I still have another two semesters."

"You'll be a full-time student?" I asked, feeling the sting of a tear, the loss sounding imminent. I'd lost Nichelle to a new career in the FBI, but she'd stayed in my life through her relationship with Tracy. But now they'd both be gone. My throat was thick with emotion as we crossed the bridge toward the shores of North Carolina's mainland. They were looking at an apartment, which meant the plans had been in motion for some time. "You already found a school and registered?"

"University of Pennsylvania," she replied softly as though she'd been scolded.

"Casey?" Nichelle asked, brushing her hand on my arm. "This wasn't an easy decision."

"Moving up in the world," I said, chin quivering. I rubbed the back of my hand across my face to dry my eyes, fixing a gaze on a decrepit water park, abandoned, the joyful colors of a giant water slide faded by the elements. Was that what I was feeling? Abandoned. This was their life, not mine. This was an amazing opportunity for both. "You two will do wonderful."

"We have your support?" Tracy asked. There was hope in her voice. I glanced in the rearview mirror, her eyes big.

"Of course," I said, fibbing, and wishing I was home with Jericho and tucked beneath the covers where he'd hold me and tell me things would be alright.

"Now, can we talk about something that's really pressing?" Nichelle asked, her tone scary.

"More news?" I scoffed, trying not to sound sarcastic. "I don't know if I can handle more news this morning."

"It's not about us," Tracy said. The two went silent then, exchanging glances.

"What is it?" I asked, curious and a little afraid.

"When are you going to marry that hunk of man?" she asked, a hungry smile appearing.

"Yeah! When?" Tracy joined in. "You really need to land that fish!"

"Land that fish!?" I repeated with an ugly cry and a laugh. There was a tornado stirring, a regard for my home in the Outer Banks and for Jericho. Full circle? If Nichelle and Tracy made a new home in Philadelphia, then would I consider moving back to the city? I wanted to be with my daughter. I'd just found her and didn't want to let her go. But I loved Jericho. I cleared my throat and stuffed the emotions into the pit of my gut, filing them away for another time. "Well, it just so happens that the other day I brought up the proposal. I think the ball is in my court now."

"Oh, Casey, you have to ask him!" Nichelle said with a bounce in her seat.

"Can we help?" Tracy asked.

"Sure," I said, sounding uncertain, a bit nervous. A slight eye roll. I shrugged, and admitted, "Just as soon as I figure out what to do."

The girls started to chat, speaking fast to each other the way they did sometimes. The news, and how I felt about it seemed to be lost on them. That hurt a little. But they were young, in love, and planning a life together. Plans at any age are exciting. But they're never as exciting as when you're setting out on your own. I eyed Tracy through the rearview mirror, a smile brimming as she spouted romantic ideas of proposal and wedding ceremonies.

"What about a wedding on the beach?" they asked in unison. Tracy adding, "Breaking waves, outside your apartment, the two of you facing west. It's an amazing view when the sun is setting."

"I could see that," I said as I imagined the scene. We needed to discuss the case, but I decided to leave the business of murder and other atrocities outside for now. I'd been robbed a lifetime of memories with Tracy. We had a couple of hours to enjoy together and make new memories. "I think Jericho would love it."

* * *

We'd rolled across the last of the state lines, entering Pennsylvania around noon. We'd left the Outer Banks at five in the morning, the sun just a hot bump on the horizon. Leaving before daybreak was a struggle, but the timing worked out so we could get to my old station by midday. We'd have the afternoon to dig through my desk drawers and comb through case files and my old notes. In them, we'd find the five unsolved murders that I'd never forgotten but hadn't thought of until seeing the wounds on Pauline Rydel.

"I can pitch in a few dollars for gas?" Nichelle said as she leaned forward, dipping her head low enough to read the street signs. "We're coming up on North 3rd Street?"

"A couple of blocks. And nonsense about the gas," I said, scoffing at the thought. Ulterior motives. It wasn't just

Nichelle's delightful company I was interested in. "You didn't think this ride was coming without a favor, did you?"

"Ah-ha! Become a fed and the favors start to pile." She laughed and snapped her fingers as I made a right turn and put Race Street in my rearview. She turned serious then and faced me. "What can I do to help with the recent murder? You're thinking it's the same guy?"

"I'm sure of it," I answered, and glanced at my phone as a text message popped onto the screen.

"It's been ten years though?" Tracy questioned, her face appearing between the seats again, her initial report completed, emailed, and received.

I clutched the air as if snatching a bug from it, saying, "That close! I was that close to getting him the last time." I brushed back my hair to reveal a ragged scar that traveled my hairline in front of my ear. "That's how I got this little gem."

Tracy touched the scar, the raised skin had a strange numbness to it, an oddly disconnected tingle. "That looks like it was bad."

"When you say that you almost had him, you mean an arrest?" Nichelle asked and inched closer. I nodded. "Then you've seen him?"

"It was dark," I answered and slowed the car to park it.

"What happened?" Nichelle asked, checking her phone. "I've got another fifteen minutes."

I rolled down my car window to breathe in the city that I'd called home most of my life. The breeze was already humid and carried the smell of a coming summer shower along with the muted scent of garden flowers and fumes from a passing bus. But in my head, I smelled the strong acrid stench of new tarpaper, and saw flat rooftops, and felt my feet running in the darkness as Detective Steve Sholes followed me close behind.

I had been in pursuit of the suspect for two city blocks, the time well past midnight when the chase led to ascending a fire escape. The suspect took to it like an animal, climbing the wet iron with a spryness that put distance between us. I holstered my gun and gripped the ladder as Steve shouted at the suspect from over my shoulder, "Halt!"

"Stop!" I yelled, the last of the killer's legs disappearing as he exited the fire escape. The rungs were slick, the metal gleaming from a heavy downpour. A storm sat above us, spitting lightning and hollering thunder relentlessly. When I reached the rooftop, I could see the Benjamin Franklin Bridge to my right, electricity spreading across the sky around it. Our target was already at the center of the roof, standing next to a skylight, glass panes perched open. My hands dripping, I stood the way we'd been trained and pointed my gun at him. "Halt! Get down onto your knees."

I could hear Steve climbing, his boots striking metal, ringing up the fire escape. But the suspect wasn't going to wait. He'd made us in the parking lot outside the nightclub, our stakeout flawed with one too many cars sitting in a tow-zone. Truth was, I might have jumped early, advancing on him as he put his arm around the bait. She was twenty-one and a rookie cop. She had the look, the same build and the height we believed the killer wanted. I should have waited though. One more minute and I wouldn't be on this rooftop near the Delaware River. I wouldn't be daring our lives with a chase four-stories above the street.

Steve climbed onto the roof, breathing hard and asking, "Where—" The suspect gave us a wave and took off running. I ran after him, holstering my gun, shoes slapping the wet tarpaper. A round of lightning brightened the chase with Steve screaming, "Wait!"

"I got him!" I yelled behind me and saw the suspect jump from the roof as thunder boomed, its voice deep and reverberating through me. I felt it in my chest, felt it coming, the distance of the strike giving me concern. But we couldn't lose him. There were five women who'd been tortured and then murdered. And I was convinced there were going to be more. I was breathing fast, chest pounding. But that stopped when the suspect jumped from the roof, his legs and arms pinwheeling mid-flight before he crashed into a tumble onto the next roof. How far was it?

"Stop, Detective!" Steve ordered, his voice drowned by the storm as I tuned him out, tuned out the world, and concentrated on the pursuit. I was going to jump. As my steps came to the lip of the roof, my pulse joined the thunder booming in my ears. Rainwater ran down my face and sprayed from my lips. The jump was eight feet, maybe ten across to reach the next building. Blood rushed through my veins like it never had, and I fed on the bitter taste as the commitment to the leap grew clear. "Casey! No!"

I planted my back foot near the edge of the roof, muscles throughout becoming taut. I glimpsed the suspect once more, and saw the reflection of lightning in his eyes, the rest of his face dark while he pulled a hood over his head. He was waiting for me. And it was the waiting that put a hesitation in my step as my front foot touched the air between the buildings. Steve screamed again as I started to fly, my arms spinning wildly, the alleyway beneath looking impossibly small. Impossibly far away.

I struck the other building with a thud. A crash is more like it. My body slammed the brick wall, squeezing my lungs dry and cutting my head open before I slipped down. I missed the landing by one foot. Twelve inches more and I might have had our suspect. Twelve inches more, and I could have saved face for having jumped the gun during the stakeout.

"What happened to him?" Tracy asked, the memory fading with the excited shrill in her voice. "What happened to you!?"

"Did the killer save you?" Nichelle added. She shook her head, eyeing my body. "You couldn't have fallen."

"There was another landing beneath me. The second building had a fire escape too and I was able drop onto it."

"Oh my God!" Nichelle said. "An actual rooftop chase."

"That's like in the movies," Tracy said with awe.

"Well, maybe not so glamorous. I scared a family half to death when I knocked on their window."

Nichelle opened the car door, saying, "The FBI building is a couple blocks from here. I'll head over after I meet the realtor."

Tracy exited too, switching places, and planted a kiss on Nichelle before she jumped into the passenger seat. "Text me the details," she said, eyeing the red-brick building. The front window was cracked, the glass mended with duct tape, a black-and-white poster on the other side with the words: *Available Space.*

"Casey, what was the favor?" Nichelle asked.

I told her, "I need a nationwide search of any open murder cases that share in similarity to this one. And include the five previous going back ten years."

"I can do that," she said, closing the car door. Tracy rolled the window down to look at the place that might be her new home. Nichelle leaned in, asking, "Do you think he's been active the last ten years?"

A shrug was all I could muster, answering, "For the sake of victims, I can only hope you find nothing."

SIX

I opened the door to enter my old workplace, catching a musty smell that came with the place. It didn't matter how many times they'd rearrange the floor plan, or how often they'd switch between the open seating concept and cubicles and offices, the smell was always the same. It was age. It was layers of paint and decades-old vents and floors with traces of everything that was ever spilled on them. And if there was one thing Philadelphia had a lot of, it was old buildings. Tracy followed behind me, her hands clasped together, dimples shining from a smile that was fixed in place with an eagerness to see where I used to work. I could tell she was excited about the plan to move north too, and especially excited to live in a big city. I only wish I could share in it. Maybe I could move back? Maybe Jericho would consider a move with me?

We were in luck, the floor plan was the same as it had been during my last trip. There was a half-attempt at the concept of open seating, pooling all the desks into an open area, but makeshift partitions had been erected, building the cubical walls the staff wanted. My old boss was one of the few who still had an office, the walls made of glass, his ancient oak

monstrosity of a desk sitting in the middle with pitted filing
cabinets behind it. Like my desk, his was empty, his chair was
tucked away. It did my heart good to see it was the captain's. I
recognized the worn leather and the yellowed stuffing where it
needed mending.

In the middle of the floor, where sat the remaining desks
that had gone unclaimed, I spotted what had once been mine. I
hoped that the drawers still contained my old notes and case
files. If not, there were the archives we could tap into too. The
days of pen and paper notes were gone. The station had shifted
to online bits and bytes, a digital wave of detective scribbles that
were indexed with keywords to create a kind of Google for
murder investigations across the city of brotherly love.

I waved Tracy to follow as passing officers did a double take,
their names a memory that was out of reach while their faces
stayed familiar. We passed the kitchenette, the vinyl replaced,
the new counters a loud orange color, with a toaster and
microwave oven, along with a K-Cup machine, the old-build
smell mixing with fresh coffee.

"This was my desk," I told Tracy, pulling out the chair and
sitting in it. I ran my hands along the armrests, fingers gliding
across old grooves in old wood where my nails had whittled at it
over years of investigations. The computer was gone, but that
didn't matter. "If we are lucky, they'll be here."

"What will?" Tracy said, her voice hitching when another
detective stopped and began to stare. It was Detective Steve
Sholes. His sandy hair was longer than before and sported some
grays above the ears. But his face was the same, a smile
appearing with a spark in his eyes when he saw me.

"These will," I answered Tracy, sliding the desk drawers
open, my past case files appearing, my pages of handwritten
notes untouched since I'd worked at the station. There were the
archives of the words stored elsewhere on the city's servers, but
I preferred the hands-on with my work. I scooped up as many as

I could hold and plopped them onto the desk with a slap. "Get busy."

Steve rolled a chair from another desk and offered it to Tracy, his gaze fixed on her like she was a miracle. She grew cautious by the look, concern rising as she looked to me for help. "Can I help you?"

"I'm sorry. I don't mean to stare," Steve said, offering the chair again. Tracy accepted it, his adding, "You know, your mom and me go back a lot of years."

"Hi, Steve," I said, getting up to give him a hug.

"Sunny," he said with a broad smile. "It's so good to see you."

"Sunny?" Tracy asked.

"Old nickname. Started with Sun something," I said with a laugh. I mussed my hair, explaining, "A very bad attempt at adding highlights."

"Sun-In," he continued to laugh. "Which eventually became Sunny."

"Sunny," Tracy repeated, eyeing my hair. "I could see that."

"Sit, please," he said. He faced Tracy and extended his arms, hand on hers. "It is so good to meet you... to actually meet you in person."

She shook his hand, asking, "You were there when Casey jumped across the building?"

Steve's face drained as he instantly recognized the reference to the Midnight Killer case. He eyed the cases on top of my desk, asking, "This isn't a social visit?"

"I think he's back," I answered and split the tall stack with Tracy and started sifting through the folders. There was no need for me to explain who.

"I need a seat," he said, cupping his mouth as he grabbed a chair and leaned back, chair legs creaking, and asked, "We thought he was dead. What changed?"

My nose wrinkled with dust rising from the old papers, and

I shoved some of the stack in Steve's direction, asking, "Help us out while I fill you in on the details?"

"Sure. It's not like I don't have my own work to do," he said sarcastically, Tracy's holding in a laugh. I fixed him with a hard stare, uncertain if it would work. A moment later, he opened a folder, checked the header, and moved on to the next one.

"Speaking of work, are you a lawyer yet?" I asked, recalling his decision to attend night school after having been shot.

"You riding me, White?" he asked with a frown. His expression eased, and he answered, "Getting there. Taking care of the kids and going to night school. That's been tough."

I put my hand on his arm. "A single father while in night school and doing all of this! It's freaking amazing."

"Thank you," he said and then looked back to Tracy and put on the same doting look as he had earlier. "But seeing you two finally together. I mean, wow!"

"That was all Casey's doing," Tracy said, cheeks turning with some color. "That was all my mom. She found me."

My heart swelled with her comment. It was small, but she'd referred to me as mom. I didn't say anything more and continued searching the folders. When I found the second of the victims, Joline Schumer, I saw her face as I had remembered it last.

I was at the morgue for a review of her autopsy with the medical examiner. The overhead lights were bright and made her skin eerily gray, turning her light blond hair almost white. Baseball stitches crossed her chest, and her eyelids were open with death appearing in her frozen stare. The image snapped me back to why we were here, and I shoved a folder in Steve's direction. "We sure could use some help with this case."

Steve placed the folder beneath his face, standing, a hand resting on the edge of the desk as he spread the papers and pictures, fanning them out for a broader view. "You really think he's back?"

Tracy opened her laptop, answering, "Now that we've got those, let's compare them." On her screen, she showed the recent victim's legs, the inside of her thighs where the bruises were more gruesome, the suspected torture extensive. "From the preliminary findings, there was no sign of sexual assault," Tracy said as Steve made room for her to work, his gaze jumping from me to Tracy.

He raised a finger, "While there was no sexual assault with our five cases, we did have bruises on the inside of the thighs."

"It's the pain level," I said, assessing what the killer's motives were. "He's a sadist, and the greater the pain, the higher its intensity—"

"The better the satisfaction for him," Steve said. "Sick fuck."

"Yes he is," I commented. "And still is."

"Where did he go? I mean, we searched city block after city block and came up with nothing." Steve leaned back again, chair legs wobbly. "Regardless, after the rooftop chase, the killing stopped."

"They might have never stopped," I said, breaking the news to him. "I've got a friend in the FBI."

"You're searching nationally?" he asked. From the corner of my eye, Tracy slid a folder away from the pile, taking it to the far corner of the desk. "Let's hope nothing turns up."

"That's what I said," I told him. "I thought he was dead all this time." I shoved a picture of the recent victim forward. "Not that we have to."

He pawed at his chest, tapping the center with a finger. "Same cause of death?"

"A single wound piercing the heart," I answered as an ache surfaced. A painful reminder from the past sitting in front of Tracy. My handwriting was on the folder's jacket, her birth name written in bold letters, HANNAH. Steve followed my gaze, seeing what Tracy had picked to read, a picture of my old house with the front lawn where she'd been abducted from.

"Non-stop," Steve said, knocking on the desk's wood surface until he had Tracy's attention. "Your mom never stopped searching for you. Even when everyone told her she should."

Her eyes were wet and her mouth downturned as she closed the folder cover. "May I take this with us?" she asked with a sniff.

"I think that'd be okay?" I managed to say, voice tearful. "Detective?"

Tracy held the case folder close to her chest as Steve answered, "It's a closed case. I don't think anyone here has a need for it."

"Thank you," Tracy said, stuffing the folder into her backpack.

"As for these—" Steve began, picking through the folders we'd set aside, the cold cases about the Midnight Killer. He spun around in his chair to see if anyone else was around. "They're on loan."

"Thanks," I replied, pleased. I closed one of the drawers, wood sliding on wood as I commented, "I was a bit surprised to see my desk still here. Even more surprised my files were as I'd left them. I thought I'd have to hunt for them."

Steve crossed his arms and looked at the pool of empty desks. "Yeah, we're still remodeling."

"This place is always remodeling," I scoffed. And with seriousness, I asked, "Why were my files still here?"

"Well," he began to say and pitched the tip of his shoe against the side of my desk, his mouth twitching as he chewed on the words. He looked at me then, answering, "I made sure they kept a seat for you. Ya know, in case you come back."

I didn't know what to say, the sentiment striking deep for some reason. Maybe it was Tracy's talk of moving to Philly.

"Thank you," I managed to tell him and wiped the corner of my eye.

"Come on, Sunny," he snapped and did his best to hide his face. "Shit, don't you start doing that."

I grabbed his hand and held the moment with him. When he nodded, I did us a favor and changed the subject. "You never answered me about our using your help."

"I would if I wasn't already swamped here," he said and shoved his fingers through his hair. He stood to leave, clearing his throat before leaning over and pecking my cheek. When he saw the look of disappointment, he added, "I'll tell you what. How's about I shuffle things around. Give me a couple days."

"Really?" I asked, excited by the idea of having him join the team. Tracy gathered the folders and continued searching the remaining pile.

"I think I'd have to come anyway." He picked up the case file for the first victim, the name on the jacket written in black marker, ANDREA BEVIN. "This is victim number one. It was my case. You joined me with the third victim."

"Patricia Slate?" Tracy asked, thumbing a folder, and turning it in my direction.

"Yeah, that's her," I answered, crime-scene pictures falling from it. I picked one up, the bruising around the legs and torso the same, dark memories of her autopsy showing in my mind. "She was only twenty-two."

He scanned the pictures, cringing as he asked, "And the latest victim?"

"The same," I assured him. "Remember how there were seven days between the night of the victim's kidnapping and the discovery of their body?"

"Course I do," he answered in an anguished tone. His eyelids fluttered. "Shit, that was the same too?"

"Uh-huh," I answered, feeling emotional about Samantha's

disappearance, the urgency growing like heat from a fire. "And now I think he's got one of our own—"

"Shit!" Steve braced the desk with a steep slouch. "How many days?"

"A couple now," Tracy answered while I tried to compose myself and clear my thoughts. Emotions cloud an investigation. I couldn't allow that to happen. "Her name is Samantha. She's our assistant medical examiner."

"I suppose this means a trip," Steve said, looking to me and Tracy. "I'll see you in the Outer Banks?"

"Yeah, I think we could use every available body on this one." His attention shifted to a patrol officer and detective entering the station and turned to leave. "How can you be sure it was him?"

"Remember how he always took his victims after midnight? And how they'd been at a nightclub, after last call?"

"You got evidence she was abducted from a club?" he asked, needling into the details.

"She was with me," Tracy answered, rising in her chair, her voice loud.

"With you?" Steve asked, his attention turning to Tracy. "You know her?"

"We're friends—" Tracy answered, looking to me for approval. I nodded as she continued, "It was a karaoke club. Samantha left a little after midnight."

"One victim, same MO, and the potential of a second... damn." Steve straightened himself, pawing at his chin the way he did when thinking. He looked at Tracy, lowering his head, "I wish I'd gotten to meet you under better circumstances."

"Yeah," she said, a dimple showing as she twisted her mouth. "Me too."

"Steve!" a patrol officer yelled.

"Listen, it was really good seeing you, Sunny," he exclaimed with a rush as he waved to the uniformed officer. He gripped our shoulders with a squeeze, hands warm, the touch brief. "That's my cue to go, but I'll call with a schedule."

"Soonest!" I yelled after him, the clock ticking.

"Nice guy," Tracy said when he was gone. "You mentioned he was single and raising kids on his own? That might make it tough for him to get away."

"I hope not," I answered, wanting to make sure I was doing absolutely everything within my ability. "If I know Steve, know him to be the detective he was, then he'll make it work."

Tracy leaned forward, curious to know more, her elbows perched to cradle her chin as she closed the distance across my old desk. "Divorced?"

"Something like that," I answered, referring to Steve's wife. I could tell Tracy wanted more, but it wasn't my story to tell. I gripped her fingers in mine, proud to show her where I'd once worked. Across the station I sought the whiteboard I'd used over the years, the writing on it erased, some of the letters still faint enough to read. How many cases had been solved on it? "See that?"

"The whiteboard?"

"Uh-huh," I answered, eyeing the folder about her kidnapping. "Hours and hours. Probably days in front of that thing."

Tracy gave it a hard look, and then the station, the two of us saying nothing until her phone sounded a ding. She held it up, showing me the text from Nichelle. "Ready?"

"Time to go home," I said, grabbing the pile of what we'd come for. "We need to find Samantha."

It was close to midnight by the time we'd returned to the Outer Banks. Nichelle and Tracy followed me inside where we discovered Jericho in the kitchen, the long day showing on his face, a spoon sticking out of his mouth. In his hand we saw a pint of ice cream, his favorite flavor, espresso bean and caramel.

"What?" he said, mouth full. "It's in season."

"Yes," I agreed, dropping my bag on the table, and grabbing a spoon from the drawer. "It's Ben and Jerry's season, now hand it over."

"That does look good," Nichelle said as Tracy opened the freezer where Jericho kept his stash. She pulled a pint of banana and walnut ice cream, Nichelle handing her a spoon.

"Tell the truth," Tracy said, "they're all your favorites."

"They are," he answered, teeth crunching on a chunk of chocolate. "How was the trip?"

"Much progress," Tracy said, hoisting her bag, case files sticking out of the top.

"Got to see the Arch Street office too," Nichelle commented.

"Arch Street?" he asked, while I dug deeper into the pint.

"They're moving to Philadelphia," I told him, emotion adding a hitch in my voice, the sound of it unintentional. "Sorry, I didn't mean to sound sad. I am very happy for you guys."

Jericho rubbed my back, drawing me closer, the look on his face telling me he was at a loss for words. "Guys, congratulations on the move. Nichelle, the FBI is lucky to have you."

"Move back with us?" Nichelle burst out, the whites of her eyes growing enormous. She looked at me then, adding, "Tracy said your desk is still at your old station, and that Detective Sholes made sure to keep it around for you. He would love to work with you again."

I had planned to talk to Jericho, but I'd wanted to talk to him about it privately, Nichelle asking put me in an awkward position. I looked at him, tried to read what he might be thinking, but couldn't. "Definitely something I'll think about." I put my hand on his chest, turning to face Nichelle and Tracy. "But it wouldn't be a decision I'd make alone."

Their eyes shifted, fixing on Jericho, Tracy asking, "Would you ever consider city life?"

Their faces were bright with the idea of us all putting down roots in the city. "Soft pretzels. Hoagies, tomato pie," Nichelle said, her hands cupped around her mouth to make like a megaphone, an omnipotent voice speaking directly to his mind.

"Tempting me with food?" he said, spoon scraping the last of the ice cream. "Jericho Flynn in Philadelphia. It's a thought."

"Really!?" Nichelle squeed, covering her mouth with her hands.

"Really?" I said, following Nichelle's excitement with surprise.

"Well," he started to say and threaded an arm through mine. I rubbed the bristles on his chin, his continuing, "Casey, home is wherever you are."

With his words, my insides melted. I leaned against him, unable to say anything. How do you respond to something so perfect? Nichelle's eyes watered as she fanned the air. "You guys are just too romantic."

SEVEN

Every picture we'd ever taken of every Midnight Killer crime scene was placed on our conference room table. We were back in the Outer Banks, the day new, the morning warm, the window open to rid the stuffiness with a stiff ocean breeze. Nichelle circled the table, taking notes, offering a promise to take them to her manager at the FBI. Ten years were missing. Ten years without a victim. Until recently, that is. We had to know what happened during those missing years.

Nichelle joined us, offering to help. She took to her usual seat, even though she wasn't on the team anymore. Not directly anyway, but she'd gratefully accept an assignment if I handed her one. I think she wanted to help too. I could tell she was excited about her new role with the FBI, but also sensed some reluctance, maybe some homesickness. If it were up to me, she'd stay on my team forever, but I knew that was impossible. I'd take anything she had to give.

Tracy had an assignment too. A nearly impossible one. Determine the instrument used to create the bruises. The bruises around the legs, arms and torso were unique enough to tell us the instrument used was the same type the killer had used before. At the center there was a deep black and blue. Around the middle there were points, the shape reminding me of a starfish, the legs a faded yellowing green. In the cold cases, we were never able to determine what the killer used. But the placements, the sizes, those were eerily similar. There was the hole in the victim's chest too. The exactness of it. An icepick perhaps. That's what was thought of before and was fresh on my mind of what might be the weapon used in Pauline Rydel's murder.

"Hardware store?" Tracy asked, suggesting a trip to browse the tool aisles.

"That's a good idea, seeing all the tools on display," I answered, but then thought again of the star shape. I tapped my keyboard to display Pauline Rydel's body, zooming in on her torso with the larger collection of bruises. I mirrored my laptop onto the conference room's monitor, the dimness suddenly brightened by the screen. The typing slowed as attentions shifted.

"Is there something different with that one?" Nichelle asked, holding up a picture of a victim's thigh, eyeing the bruise, comparing it to what was on the screen.

"The smallest of details," I told her. And there was a difference. An easy one to have overlooked. "See the points around the bruising?"

"Uh-huh," Tracy said, sifting through the pictures, comparing them to the screen, to one another. "Huh," she said, sweeping her hand across her forehead. She dropped the pictures onto the table, pegging her fists on her hips. "They're not all the same?"

"They are not," I said, voice flat with disappointment.

"That sucks," Nichelle grunted bitterly. "Damn, I thought there was a lead there."

I pinched the tips of my fingers together, asking, "Human strength? Can an injury like this be inflicted without a tool?"

Tracy and Nichelle both tested the idea, picking areas of their body to try. "Tender areas. Sensitive skin. I'm sure he selected the areas where the bruises are for a reason."

"I'll keep searching tools too?" Tracy asked.

"Yeah," I said, turning back to the pictures on the table. We had only ideas to work with, and I threw another out there for us to explore. "Could the killer be telling us something?" I asked, holding up victim number four's picture, spinning it around to find similarity in the placement of the bruises.

Tracy did the same, flipping the picture upside down, and then sideways. While there was no mistaking the likeness in the bruises, the placements looked to be random. She flipped over the picture, reading the back of it, "This is the first victim. Andrea Bevin."

"Twenty-one. She was Caucasian with chestnut brown hair and green eyes. A slim, physical build, she stood five feet and an inch."

"Andrea Bevin's injuries are consistent with the recent victim. Torso, arms, the oldest bruises on the inside of her thighs," Nichelle said, grimacing.

I went to the next victim's picture, repeating the exercise. It was like searching the stars for a pattern, turning the pictures around and around until the constellations appeared like the Little Dipper or the Aquarius. "Victim number three's body was discovered in an alley two miles from the nightclub she'd been to with her friends the night she disappeared."

"How long was she missing?" Jericho asked, arriving in the doorway. He had a stopover to see the sheriff before his shift on the water began.

"Seven days," I answered his question as he made his way to the screen, the smell of sunblock following. He hung his hands from his utility belt, the leather creaking. I sensed concern weighing heavy on him, the reason he was here today. I touched his shoulder lightly, assuring him that we were working the case with utmost urgency. He was visiting us because of Samantha, and I couldn't show him the panic that was mounting. It'd serve no purpose. My voice caught on an unexpected emotion, forcing me to clear my throat. I had to stifle them for the sake of the case, for the sake of Samantha. As much as I wanted to canvas the Outer Banks with an army, flip every seedy night-stop, turn over every abandoned house, we couldn't do that. We had to work this case like it was any other. "With the previous cases, there were seven days that passed between the kidnapping and the discovery of a body."

Jericho read his phone, counting. "Samantha has been missing since late Saturday evening, after midnight." He went to the table, arms crossing as he studied the pictures, the horridness of them. Picking up a photograph and comparing it to what was on the screen. His lips thinned when he didn't see any similarities to Samantha. "Have you found anything?"

"We just started," I answered, wishing I had better news to share.

"It's a countdown," he said as he carefully placed the picture back onto the table. His gaze traveled from victim to victim, their pictures showing a grim outcome if we didn't find Samantha. "Like the killer is playing a game with you."

"That's possible," I said, hating that I'd been on the losing side if this was a morbid game.

"Today is Wednesday." Jericho frowned and shook his head. "That doesn't leave much time."

"It was the evening of," I answered, the earlier panic clearing as I opened the calendar on my computer, recalling the killer's timeliness. "The killer always took his victims after midnight. That means Sunday would be the first of the seven days. If he holds to the same pattern, then we'll have until Sunday night. Midnight."

"How about the time between the abductions?" Jericho asked, flipping through the old case file notes.

"We tracked those too," I answered, thinking back to a wall-size calendar I'd constructed with Steve Sholes. "There were no substantial findings. Nothing to map to. No major events or position of the stars or seasonal changes."

"Just random?" he asked, questioning it.

"I'm reviewing the old cases," Tracy said, patting the top of the pile we brought back from Philadelphia. "I'll make sure to check that too."

"It was opportunity," I said, my tone defensive and feeling sensitive about the previous work. It wasn't about Jericho's question though. We'd almost had the killer once before and he got away. "We concluded that he struck on opportunity. The victims had always been alone."

"It's already Wednesday," Jericho said beneath his breath. It wasn't directed at us though. He was scared, rigid concern across his face, his brow creasing as he pawed at his chin. Hearing him say it made my chest tight.

"We're working it," I told him, my voice soft. Wanting to help, he grabbed crime-scene photos from a pile and went back to the screen, holding them up. "And you guys haven't found anything that matches?" he asked, and then spun it around like we'd done once already. "Just random?"

"You know, even with something random, there could be a pattern?" Tracy offered, her suggestion sounding like a riddle. She shrugged, adding, "We talked about it in my data analytics class."

"Data analytics," I repeated with a flitting glance at her and then the screen.

When we gave her a look to elaborate, she offered, "What if it isn't a pattern we can see?"

I closed my eyelids thinking of the details that existed. The data in the data we didn't have to see. When it hit me, I blurted, "The number of them," I said and grabbed a spool of tape from the table to help tack them to the front whiteboard.

Jericho counted and exclaimed, "Some victims have four bruises below the torso, others have three."

Disappointed, I said, "There's nothing that stands out, other than the killer being a sadist."

"Hmm," Tracy grunted, pulling the tape and spinning the picture.

"What about the bruises on the legs?" Nichelle offered, adding those pictures too, matching the legs to the torso and filling the whiteboard.

"Let's put some organization into this," I suggested, believing it might show us more to see it all. I began by adding the names of the victims across the top. Beneath those, I placed the pictures of their faces with the teardrops cut into the skin. Tracy worked the next row, adding the pictures showing the injury to the chest that resulted in death. Jericho helped too, his eagerness eating into his work shift, the room filling with the sounds of paper shuffling, of sticky tape being dispensed, the pace gaining with the murmur of a team reworking the whiteboard to see all the murders. When we were done, I raised my hands asking, "What do we have?"

"A very macabre scene," Nichelle answered grimly. Only, she wasn't being sarcastic. The sight was morbid, the punishing torment of the killer sickening. She came around the front, pants swishing, a hand cradling her chin as she studied the photographs like they were data.

"We have a killer who is desperate to dominate and control," I commented as I added pictures of the ankles and wrists. "Victims are tortured while held captive."

"There doesn't seem to be anything consistent here," Jericho said, pacing back and forth, hungry to pick up a detail we could use.

"Nichelle? Anything stick out to you?" I asked, knowing her ability to see patterns and how to find the smallest of clues, working them into something tangible. Her mouth and eyebrows, and even her nose, were fixed like a statue, frozen. There were none of the twitches or half-smiles that would come when she was onto something usable. "Is it pure violence? No thought to the injuries inflicted?"

"There are the teardrops, but they weren't made at the same time. The age of one is new around the time of death, while the other looks a few days old?" Tracy questioned.

"If I recall—" I began to say as I fished through my notes from ten years ago, leafing through the pages with a vague recollection of what was written. "Here it is! The medical examiner at the time had determined the initial injury on the left cheek had occurred the evening of the kidnapping, possibly the next morning."

"And the right cheek was injured the day of their murder?" Tracy asked.

"Correct," I answered. An old sting of disappointment came with reading the report. "We never concluded why. The teardrops sliced into the face aren't consistent with the age of the bruising on the legs. We never found any patterns."

Pegging her laptop screen, Tracy reading from it, "What about punishment for pleasure? It says here that it can be verbal and emotional."

"And physical. A sadist. That's always been our assumption," I answered as I regarded the bruises. "I'd always thought of sadistic behaviors as motive, but what if I was wrong?"

"I don't follow," Jericho said as plump raindrops pelted the windowsill, a passing shower and distant rumble warning of the wet day to come.

"In the original investigation, we'd worked the case around sadism, the bruises evidence like bite marks that we'd seen in other cases, along with signs of bondage on the ankles and wrists. We must have interviewed dozens and visited every sex club there was in and around the city." I dropped to an office chair, elbows perched, face cradled while I looked over the pictures we didn't tape to the board. "If these aren't a product of sadistic behavior, then what are they?"

"How about injuries with structure," Nichelle said, her face turning a bright orange with the screen's reflection, the panel inches from her nose as she studied the most recent victim. She went to the whiteboard, the taped photographs. "Since the teardrop marks are inflicted at different times, we could use that."

I was following where Nichelle was going, and said, "The bruises seem random. However, the teardrops exhibit a beginning and an end, they're showing intent," I said, elaborating on the mention of structure. She moved to the right, a short side-step to the second victim. Her fingers splayed as she waved over the bruises. "I agree. Unlike the teardrops, there's no pattern in these." She shrugged and shook her head, continuing, "And I'm good at finding continuity or meaning, but these are random."

"Which takes us back to the killer inflicting punishment to watch them suffer," Jericho commented with a huff, the idea of what might be happening to Samantha was a silent torture. I could see it on his face.

Nichelle sidestepped again, moving to the third victim. "Let's look at the teardrops again," she said and ran her fingers down the victim's face. "I think with some better calculations, we could measure when the first one was inflicted—"

"If we know the timing, it might help us identify a motive," I said, summarizing, yet confused and growing frustrated.

"It's like he's two people," Tracy said while working around the whiteboard to place the victims' names across the top.

"Maybe not." I got up and suggested, "If we made a profile, we could be looking for an individual that is highly structured, time oriented, regimented. And who has the personality warranting the behaviors we're seeing exhibited between the beginning and the end."

"Those poor women," Jericho said, taking to lean against the wall. I tilted my head toward the exit, suggesting he leave, thinking this might be too much for him. He shook it off, scratching at his neck, prickly heat he'd called it. It sparked something in my brain.

"There was a rash," I said, thinking of the preliminary findings. I showed my phone's screen, a text message from the medical examiner. "Doc Bob commented in his initial findings about the victim having a rash."

"He sent pictures," Tracy said. I tapped my laptop keyboard, finding them and displayed them on the screen.

"What are you looking for?" Jericho asked. I felt the frustration heard in his tone.

"Nothing and everything," I said, unable to come up with anything else. Tapping the touchpad with a thump, I zoomed in on the victim's skin. "Just covering every detail—"

"Where is that?" Nichelle asked.

"Doc Bob found it on the small of her back," Tracy answered, approaching the screen, her step slowing as she began to see what it was I was seeing. Her voice trailing, she added, "We didn't see it in the field."

"It's clearly structured in some way," Jericho said, his brow a hard furrow. "Zoom in all the way."

I set the zoom to maximum, telling Tracy, "Call down to the morgue, have them take more pictures, increased magnification with a macro lens on the camera."

"What is that?" Jericho said as we made our way to the screen, leaning forward, straining to see it. "They're dots. Are you thinking Morse code or something?"

"What would have made those? The tip of a knife? A needle? Too big to be made by a needle. Right?" Nichelle asked and ran her hands across her head to pull her hair tight.

"Whatever it was, it was done repeatedly," Jericho answered and made a jabbing motion. "Like tattoos, the old kind."

"Did I ever tell you guys about the documentaries I like to watch?" I asked, speaking casually, trying not to raise my hope.

"Only all the time," Tracy answered sarcastically. "There was the one about the recycling. And the other about the honeybees—"

"Okay, okay," I said, my voice short as I opened a web page and searched for evidence to support my idea. Was it possible the killer had intentionally created what I was seeing. "The latest I watched was about this young woman named Grace. A writer."

"I remember that one," Jericho said, half listening as he was joined by Tracy, the two staring at the screen like it was a stubborn puzzle. "That was last week? I think I fell asleep."

"That's the one," I commented. "You always fall asleep."

"True," he admitted with a shrug. A chuckle, Nichelle covering her mouth.

"Anyway," I said. "The novelist, she went blind by the time she was a young adult. Pediatric glaucoma, I think it was called."

"A message only the blind can see!" Nichelle blurted. She jumped back into her chair, fingers tackling her keyboard with ideas.

I went to the screen, touching the pinpricks on the latest victim's lower back. "In the documentary, the writer described learning how to read again, learning how to read Braille."

"No way," Tracy said. "You think the rash is Braille?"

"Look at this," I said and displayed the Braille alphabet on the adjacent monitor, filling the screen with a table of Braille letters and numbers, showing the three-by-two pattern that made up six dots.

"I think I see a possible match," Jericho said, the two of us moving closer to the screen.

"It *must* be Braille," I said, running my hand over the dots.

"Look at this one here. It could be a number four, assuming the orientation is correct."

"The orientation? That's a lot of assuming," Nichelle said, her jaw clenched with concentration. She spun the image of the victim, rotating it. "Where do we start?"

"You'll fill me in later?" Jericho asked as he went to the door, tapping his watch with his finger.

"Thanks," I mouthed. And continued, "For starters, how about we begin without an orientation."

"Like we were reading it, top down and left to right?" Tracy questioned.

"Still, there isn't a way to avoid interpreting the wrong letters and numbers," Nichelle said, focusing on her screen.

I regarded her comment, saying, "Upside down, flipped around, when oriented incorrectly then Braille is gibberish." I thought back to the documentary. "Because otherwise how does a blind person know when a book, or pages, is upside down or sideways?"

"Come again?" Nichelle asked.

From the desk, I grabbed a book and showed it. "Just like we read, a blind person relies on the Braille being upright and written from the left to right. Otherwise, they wouldn't be able to read it at all."

"Right!" Nichelle snapped her fingers, understanding. "If this *is* Braille, then we need to look at the rash from the top to the bottom."

"Top down," Tracy said, joining her at the computer, adding, "And from the left to the right."

"If there is something, we'll see it," I said. I made room on the whiteboard and created a Braille cell with six circles, filling them in to match the leftmost holes. I compared it with the table we'd put on the monitor. "It's a number."

"A number four?" Nichelle questioned.

I jumped to what would be the next set of pinpricks,

clearing and resetting the whiteboard Braille cell, filling in the circles that best matched the injury. "That's a number five."

"Is he numbering his victims?" Tracy said, asking while we hurried through what remained, repeating the effort of clearing the Braille cell and matching it to the chart on the monitor. "There's a four, five and eight."

"And a seven," Nichelle added.

"There's a couple more," Tracy said, optimistic the numbers would make sense if we continued.

"I know what those two say already," I said, stepping back to sit down.

"What is it?" they asked, eyes big and round.

"That's the street number of the building where I lost the killer ten years ago," I told them as I wiped my lips, the touch of them dry, the back of my throat closing with an itch. I faced Tracy and Nichelle, the cold case from yesterday's past like a hot stone in my stomach. "Those last two Braille cells are my initials. C. W. This is a message to me."

EIGHT

The afternoon slipped away from us before we knew the sun had dropped from the sky. When I was outside again, it had already sunk below the horizon and turned the brim of tomorrow into a fiery glow. I had to put my visor down, my car tires rumbling as I crossed Wright Memorial Bridge a second time in as many days, driving east to the club and the location where Samantha was last seen. It was where I believe she'd been abducted, the pattern fitting for the Midnight Killer with his stalking the woman like prey, and then pouncing when they were alone.

Samantha's apartment had been searched and her neighbors questioned. And while the club had also been searched, its employees questioned, I felt compelled to come here. Maybe it was the relationship I'd had with Samantha's aunt. Or maybe I thought I would find something the patrol had overlooked? Before the drive, I looked up the club's webpage and then checked its location against Samantha's address. If I was right, there might have been a shortcut between buildings that she could have taken. What if she'd walked home that night, never reaching her apartment?

Tracy and Nichelle had been dancing late into the evening with Samantha, having discovered a small karaoke bar somewhere on Route 158, a couple of miles from the bridge. From one of Jericho's texts, I learned it was also close to where Samantha called home. She'd been in the process of moving to her aunt Terri's house on the beach but hadn't finalized the move yet. Having seen the pinpricks, the Braille, a message to me that had been confirmed, I couldn't help but wonder if the Midnight Killer knew who Samantha was, selecting her because of her work with me and the team. Was he targeting us?

Guilt roiled in me with the thought of the Midnight Killer in the Outer Banks. While I searched for the cross street I needed, the sunset directly ahead, there were shops and hotels to my left and right. There were women young and old, a lot of them matching his profile. They were in their twenties to early thirties. Fair skin and light-colored eyes, their hair color didn't seem to matter, nor did its length. He liked taller woman, five feet seven or more, though one of his victims had been a few inches shorter. They dressed well, trendy clothes that cost more than average, and nothing cheap.

They were sisters and daughters and girlfriends. They were loved by their friends and family, but to him they were fodder, a plaything to devour, to discard, and then move on to the next. All of them had been alone when he abducted them. And it was that single piece of evidence that had me question the profile we'd developed for him. The killer's selection could be completely based on opportunity, leaving everything else to coincidence.

I drove beneath powerlines that were strung across the road, industrial parks on both sides of me. I tried to take a deep breath, tried to let go of the flashing guilt. I had to if I was going to do my job. I was terrified for Samantha. Mortified by the idea of what he might be doing to her. Her life depended on me. I could never forget that.

After passing a personal storage site with a gravel parking lot filled with boats, I drove by an abandoned water park with the faded waterslides and a chain-link fence guarding the property. Tracy had said that the turn would come up after the water park. It didn't though. There were corn fields and a golf course, and post office. I thumped the steering wheel with the heel of my hand, grumbling as I second guessed the directions. Jericho was on patrol, and I should have insisted Tracy or Nichelle come with me. But they had a meeting with the realtor in Philadelphia, a video walkthrough and to review the lease. I didn't want to get in the way of it.

I'd slowed to turn around and backtrack when the name of the cross street appeared, the strip of buildings a hundred yards from the road, the name of the club, in blooming letters, pale orange and red. K-Beatz. The parking lot was almost empty, but I suspected that had more to do with the early evening, and expected it'd fill with the night. I got out of the car, accidentally finding a puddle, the rains from early in the day soaking into the bottom of my shoe. There were five shops in the strip, the red-brick building stained one- and two-stories tall, two of them separated by the tight alley I'd seen on the map.

I began with a retrace of Samantha's steps as an SUV pulled into the parking lot, tires grinding on loose stone, stopping in front of me while I approached the club's entrance. The windows were tinted dark, the fading daylight reflecting into my eyes and causing me to squint. The motor rumbled, the driver gunning, the vibration racing through me.

"You want to move it!" I warned, already feeling on edge. I tapped the dark window with my badge. It wasn't often I used it to get my way, but the coercion worked. The driver obliged and drifted into a parking spot. "Thank you."

Night clubs were curiously different in the day. The disco blitz of lights and music muted by the daylight. It bled through the edges of the covered windows, the sound system turned down and playing the soft beat of a tune you could move to while enjoying a cocktail at the bar. The K-Beatz dance floor was empty of patrons, two barstools saddling an older couple, the remainder empty as a bartender busily prepped for the night. I sat next to the woman as she gave me a look which ended with a courteous nod when her bleary gaze fell to my badge. She held a sweaty glass in one hand and a cigarette in the other, its ashes growing precariously long. I gave the rising smoke a hard look, certain the laws about it, including dance clubs, had not been rescinded. But this woman's affairs were not my concern. I was here for Samantha.

"Ma'am," the bartender said, placing a white napkin in front of me. He was no older than a college student, his hair cropped in a buzz cut, his chin unshaven while his cheeks were newborn smooth. His clothes were a size too small, which was the style, the buttons on the dress shirt strained, a black vest bulging. "What can I get you?"

"Seltzer and lime," I asked, lifting my badge for him to see.

"Officer," he answered as chunks of ice tumbled into a glass, and he filled it with club soda while sliding a lime around the lip and dropping it inside for me. "Nothing stronger with that?"

"On duty," I answered, cigarette smoke drifting as a song from the seventies began to play. At the far end of the dance floor there was a stage with large monitors, a pair of microphone stands. I hung my thumb over my shoulder, asking, "Karaoke?"

"It's what keeps this place afloat," the bartender answered. He whipped a towel from his shoulder to wipe the bar, the wood grain shining as he cleaned. "That and the younger crowd, mostly tourists looking for cheap beer."

I showed him my phone with a picture of Samantha and her aunt Terri. "Does this woman look familiar?"

He stopped cleaning long enough to glance at the screen, asking, "The younger one?" I tipped my chin. He took a closer look, focusing, and began to shake his head. "To be honest, between the dancing and karaoke, we do get a lot of people in here."

"Any security cameras?" I asked, searching the corners of the bar, finding red lights in the ceiling for smoke detectors.

"There's the one over by the entrance," he answered, raising his hand, the towel hanging limp. In the ceiling there was a silver dome the size of a softball. "Not sure it still works or if anyone has done anything with it."

"Where's the feed go?" I asked as the bartender went to the built-in shelves against the wall and knelt. He slid open a cabinet door where there was an old VCR, a pile of video cassette tapes sitting on top of it. "Haven't seen one of those in years."

"This thing is older than me." He laughed. I put on a grim smile, knowing he was probably right.

I was old enough to remember the technology though, and asked, "Is anyone changing the tapes?" He picked up the top video cassette, wiping it free of dust. There was a 9-inch monitor next to it, the kind with a picture tube. I got up on my elbows, telling him, "Turn that on, the switch is beneath the screen."

His fingers moved around, feeling for the controls. "I've never even seen this turned on—" he stopped when he found the switch and brought the screen to life. There was a hum and the sound of static as a grainy black and white began to show, the club's door and the bar in the view. "Look at that! It works!"

"The VCR," I said, wanting to see if they had anything recorded. If so, then we might see if anyone followed Samantha out of the club. "Is the recording light on?"

He searched the face of the old technology, finding the record button and shaking his head. "It's not on. I'll eject the tape." The motors inside whirred, but nothing happened. When he flipped the door, poking his finger inside, his brow rose. "It's empty."

"Might explain the dust on the tapes. Nobody is rotating them." I sat back down, glass in hand as I cooled my throat and thought of my next steps. "Thanks for looking."

When he stood back up, he showed me his watch, saying, "It's almost six thirty. You sure you don't want something stronger. It's on the house."

I let out a sigh, thinking the trip was becoming a bust. "Thank you. As much as I'd love one, I've got to work." I turned toward the club, seeking out the next place to search. With the day getting late, I wanted to finish my search of the inside and leave as soon as possible. There was an alleyway I'd seen when I parked, and it was where I believed Samantha had been taken.

The sun was gone and I'd already searched the dance floor, the bar, and the karaoke stage. I'd found nothing but dusty corners and the shadows of curious patrons who'd been hovering close by. Even the bathroom stalls, including the men's room, had been searched. Finding anything was hopeful, and maybe more than I should have expected, but I couldn't leave until satisfying the checklist in my brain.

Music was thumping too. Loud and with a heavy beat that shook my hair. From the poster on the stage, it was the night of Metal Mayhem, a celebration of 80s rock bands. I snapped a picture of the stage, sending it to Jericho with an invite for next Wednesday. He loved his hair bands from the time.

The day's earlier storms had blown out to sea, leaving the sky cloudless with a full moon rising. It was bright enough to help me see as I stopped in front of the alleyway, a narrow path between the buildings. I opened a map's app and plotted Samantha's address, the pin sticking out of the building a block south of K-Beatz. From where I stood, it put her apartment within view. I suspected Samantha had walked home, using the alley as a shortcut?

Cautious, I entered the ally, the moonlight casting a harsh shadow in front of me. There was a short dumpster to my right with a dingy green recycling bin next to it. Broken glass littered the ground, fine bits of it crunching with each step. A loud clack thumped above me, the noise raising the hair on the back of my neck. It was a streetlight, the gases inside it energized, turning an amber color, warming until it was a hot white. The added light helped while I made my way through what I was assuming was a shortcut Samantha had taken.

My thigh vibrated with a text message. The sudden interruption making me jumpy. I stopped in the middle of the path, assessing the distance while I replied to Jericho, his accepting the rock band invite.

He texted,

I'll wear one of my metal-head concert shirts

I'd bought him twelve vintage concert shirts after he'd lost his collection in a fire.

The gnarliest one I have!

I texted back.

Sounds great. Maybe I'll borrow one—

The shuffle of feet. I stopped typing and turned on my phone's flashlight. The alley wasn't wide, maybe fitting three people across. But it was long, the length of the club and shop on both sides. Water dripped from a rainspout, the rhythm matching a thumping in my chest. Paper scratching pavement, I flashed my light, seeing a naked tail beneath a crumpled newspaper, the sight making me tense. I'd seen rats before, but never one so big. A breeze picked up the paper and revealed a pink nose, long whiskers, and a pair of black eyes on a white face. It wasn't a rat, but an opossum, which I'd been told were harmless.

"Looking for something to eat?" I asked. I backed away, turning to face Samantha's building. I wanted to finish the walk she would have taken, finish it at her apartment door and leave no chance of missing a clue. Her building was two-stories tall, maybe three, a red-brick face, and windows painted white. Yellow light and moving shadows showed in all of them, except one. It must have been Samantha's apartment, her neighbor appearing next door, an older woman wearing an evening robe, the material green colored and thin. Leaning onto the windowsill, she lit the end of a cigarette. She couldn't see me from where I stood, but I could see everything, including how revealing her clothes were. Could the killer have been watching Samantha's apartment? Was he stalking her?

Breathing. For a moment, I was sure someone was breathing. The muscles in my arms and legs stiffened with a cold shock rifling through my body. Softly turning to the entrance, I squinted to the change in light, to try and see in the dark. There were no shapes, no steps, nothing. Picking up my feet, I moved to leave, passing another dumpster, a second recycling bin, the pair for the adjacent store. A car's motor turned over, the engine revving, the tailpipe belching as tires cut into pavement. The noise bounced around my head, striking the brick, the origin of it lying, giving me no idea where it was coming from.

When I reached the end of the alley, I eyed the woman in the window as she snuffed out her cigarette and a car screeched to a stop in front of me. The passenger door swung open. I recognized the SUV and the tinted windows, remembering it had followed me into the parking lot earlier.

Before I could move, I felt arms around me. The strongest I'd ever felt in my life. Hot breath on the back of my neck. I tried to scream, tried to kick, but the attack was paralyzing, the man squeezing me with enough force to snuff my voice like the woman's cigarette.

Unable to breathe, I was losing consciousness. And for a second, I thought I felt the touch of a hand on my mouth, followed by the taste of something bitter on my tongue. My fingers tingled, my toes turned numb, and my eyesight went dim as a faint image of a pale hand appeared. The driver snapping their fingers at my attacker, urging him to put me inside the car. There *was* someone behind me. He'd followed me from the station. For all I knew, he'd been following me all along. Just like he'd followed Samantha. A text. I'd sent Jericho a text. My phone slipped from my fingers, the flashlight disappearing like the moon and the night, my eyelids shutting as my body turned to jelly and the only voice heard was a whisper in my ear.

"Finally," he said.

NINE

A hollow plunk, a drip into a bucket. I opened one eyelid, my lashes batting against a cover. Frightened, I opened both as wide as I could, finding blackness, my face covered with a scratchy cloth, the material coarse and tied tight enough to filter any light. I was made blind, the idea of it piercing my heart with an icy fright, a kind I hadn't felt since I was a child.

There was a faint odor that I struggled to put a name to. Was it from my childhood? From a swim team practice perhaps? I tried to concentrate, but my brain felt heavy. It felt like it was swelling beyond the boundaries of my skull, splitting painfully whenever I moved. A wave of nausea kicked up the back of my throat, threatening a heave. I braced for it to come but was able to hold it at bay. It was like ten hangovers lumped into one. Only it wasn't a hangover. I'd been abducted and had no idea where he'd taken me.

Up and down. I rubbed the back of my head against the wall, hoping the knot might catch. It didn't though. I'd keep at it, needing my eyes to escape. When I moved, metal clanked against stone. My arms were pinned above my head, shackled, the restraints cutting into thin skin. There was no bend in my elbows, which left me in a near hang with my back flattened against a wall and my bottom barely touching the floor. From the pain in my sides, the strain in my shoulders, I could only guess how long I'd been there, and that it was nearing the morning.

I bit back the urge to cry, knowing how crazy worried Jericho must be. Didn't I text him? My memory of the dance club and the alley were faded, the details lost. The images were stuck in a muck of mindless thoughts. A draft crossed my toes, my shoes gone, my socks too, leaving my feet cold in the damp air. There was a rope wrapped around my ankles, the material like nylon that scraped my skin when I wrestled the restraint. My knees were tied too, locked together, painfully knocking bone on bone whenever I wriggled or squirmed. I needed them, needed to bend my legs so I could put my feet beneath me. That'd give me leverage and put slack into my arms to rest my shoulders. I froze before moving. There was motion next to me, a short groan, a shallow breath. I wasn't alone.

"Hello?" I asked, trying to find the strength to raise my voice. A fire rose in my throat, the ache bad enough to hush my words. I heard someone's lips smacking, their mouth parched. I had no spit either, nothing to douse the heat, but dared to scrape more words. "I can hear you!"

"Shh!" A woman's voice. Soft and high-pitched. She might be young maybe. For certain, I didn't recognize it. Five feet, maybe eight. They were close.

Before I could reply, there were legs rubbing against the floor and metal clanking against metal, another pair of shackles ringing out from across the room. "He'll come."

How many were there? "My name is Detective Casey White," I said, panting, chest thumping wildly, my voice carrying.

More motion, the voice across the room a dry rasp, "Whisper!"

"How many are you?" I asked, trying to keep my voice low.

"I'm Jenni," the voice next to me said. "Jenni Levor."

"How long?" I asked, cringing against the raw burn that came with each word. "How long have you been here?"

She began to weep. The muffled cries tired. "Almost a week I think?" she said, questioning in a voice that sounded beaten and exhausted.

"Casey?" the voice across from me asked. It was hoarse and with only faint recognition. But I could tell it was Samantha. "God! What are you doing here?"

There were teardrops bleeding into my blindfold. "It's good —" I began, stopping when wood slammed against wood, chains rattled and tumbled onto the floor above us. The girls screeched and began to cry, their voices whimpering, their fright contagious like a disease. There was motion, fright gaining, metal clanking, bodies rubbing against the floor and wall. My insides tensed, unsure of what was coming. "What is that?"

"Me!" a voice said with a hot breath on my face. I screamed, terrified to learn he had been with us the entire time. His hands were like giant clubs, a palm swallowing my face whole, pinning my head against the wall.

"Leave her," Samantha cried, her pleas ignored.

"What do—" I tried to ask, but couldn't breathe, couldn't speak. He freed me from the wall, my arms falling like dead weight, hands numb, shoulders shouting with a deep ache. "— want with me?"

"Water," he answered, his reply laced with the Philadelphia accent I shared, his pronunciation of water sounding more like "wooder."

"Yeah," I said, my mouth like paper. My fingers tingled, blood coming back to them as I felt around my face to remove the blindfold.

When I touched his hand, a white light flashed with a hard strike, my head bouncing against the wall.

"Stays on!" he demanded as a dizzying spin took hold while he dragged me across the floor. There was a swoosh of air through plumbing, and a whining sound that I knew to be a faucet, the kind used in a basement or outside. There was a cold gush, a splash on my face, the taste of it like water from a garden hose. "Drink."

My head and chest were soaked as I held up my dead arms for balance and for direction. He squeezed my scalp clumsily and shoved my face into the stream where I could put my mouth to it. I needed the water and gulped three mouthfuls, the rush of it hard to swallow without choking. When I couldn't drink anything more, I backed away. I moved slow, his grip on my head loosening. I sensed he was distracted, maybe looking to Samantha or Jenni. It was a chance, and I took it. Gripping my hands into a single fist, I flailed wildly, throwing my arms upward, breaking his hold. I was free of him and yanked the blindfold from my scalp to see gray light, the killer's body a ghostly silhouette. "Samantha!"

I couldn't wait for a reply and scurried in the other direction, away from the hose and the killer. But my knees and ankles, the bindings, left me slithering like a broken snake, unable to get anywhere. He was on me before I could break free, his breath returning to my ear, his stubbled cheek next to mine. I peered up from beneath his crushing weight to see where we were, to see him. A single light bulb hung from the ceiling, his face blackened by silhouette. Escape. I had to escape and searched the room. There were four walls made of cinder block, a concrete floor, and a wooden staircase to the left. Next to us, there was the faucet he'd turned on, a hose partially coiled on the wall, the unraveled end gushing wildly, a rusted bucket perched against the wall.

"Casey," he said playfully, seeming to enjoy himself as a crushing blow struck, the weight of it like an elephant jumping on my chest. It was powerful and collapsed my insides. I wheezed and coughed and choked until he touched my face. I froze, frightened and sickened at the same time. He felt my nose and my lips, calloused fingertips rubbing my mouth and then my ears before he finally wrapped the blindfold back around my head. He'd blinded me to the place where he held us captive. The water I so desperately needed came up in a billowing gush as he warned me, "Casey, you're not going anywhere."

"Who—" I began to ask, another strike coming with the blindness. I saw nothing. Heard nothing. I felt nothing either.

TEN

Thirst. It was the first thought I had when I regained consciousness. Pain was the second. My head was heavy and felt as big as a balloon. My ears were tortured by an endless ringing as light flashes splintered behind my covered eyelids. There was a chemical smell filling my nostrils and irritating my eyes. Chlorine. I'd seen a crate of it in the furthest corner before the killer pummeled me for having removed the blindfold from my eyes. I'd seen where we were being held too.

For the brief moments when I'd regained my sight, my training as a detective kicked in and I recorded everything within view. It was a room beneath the ground to act as a conduit for municipal water or a sewer system. The floor was a solid concrete, the slab cracked down the middle, with one side sinking into the earth. Nothing grew from the wide crack though, the absence of light dousing any chance of life. The walls were made up of cinder block, and it was what the killer used to secure us to. Samantha sat across from me, her legs naked like mine were now, her feet bare, her eyes covered by a dark-colored blindfold. Next to her, there was a short staircase, the wood rotten in some parts, a black mold growing on its surface.

The other kidnapped victim, Jenni, was on the same wall as me, held captive in the far corner. With flowing blond hair that was made frizzy by the damp air, there were bruises on both arms, her clothes gone except for her underwear and a T-shirt. I understood then that it wasn't just fright that put a shake in her voice. She was cold, her teeth chattering. In the fading dim light, I saw the same grotesque welts that had been found on the Midnight Killer's victims. Some of them were fresh-looking, some older, the morbid splotches showing the torture of her stay. My heart broke for her, for what she was going through.

Along the ceiling, there were pipes running the length of the room. They were made up of different colors, which had me thinking there was a distinction with them. The largest of them were the size of a car tire, while others were like the plumbing in a house. This was a hub of sorts. Maybe a pump room to distribute the water to residential homes. With the pipes overhead, the room was short, less than six feet from the floor. It was cramped and made me feel claustrophobic.

I didn't have a chance to see where the pipes were coming from, or where the pumps might be. But I could see where they were heading, and the image of them was locked in my brain. It was going to save us. The wall across from the staircase was open near the ceiling, the pipes snaking through to the outside. The largest of them was the green-colored one, and a section of it was missing. I could fit through the opening. I'd only need to get free first.

"Samantha?" I whispered, hoarseness biting my throat. A stir. A whimper. They were frightened. I felt the memory of his last visit, felt the bruising on my body, and understood. When I moved, a fire bloomed in my shoulders, the burn deepening, traveling to the muscles in my back. My arms were pinned high up on the wall again. My legs were tied tight, giving me no room to move. The girls were too quiet, and I asked, "Tell me you're okay?"

"Casey," Samantha said in a low voice. "Please. You have to be quiet."

"We have to get out of here—" I started, but then shut my mouth when the footsteps above came.

"He's here," Jenni said in a voice I could barely hear.

More footsteps, leading away this time. There was a bump, a hip or shin walking into furniture. The sound of a door opening came, a spring creaking like the kind with a storm door. It slammed shut a moment later, leaving the three of us alone. I tempted what I thought had happened, asking, "Is it safe?"

"Wait," Jenni said with warning. We heard a car door close, and then a motor come alive, a transmission shifting into gear before tires crunched stone as it drove away. "Okay, he's gone."

"How long does he normally leave for?" I asked in a full voice, wriggling my legs around. "I think I know how to get out of here."

"The door is locked," Samantha said tearfully, her voice an echo of the voice I'd worked with. "I can hear him unlocking the chains on the other side when he comes down to—" She didn't finish though, a cry desperate of being heard rising inside her as she bellowed a scream.

"Samantha!" I said in a flat tone. "We're leaving this place."

A laugh. It wasn't hearty or sarcastic or mean. Jenny laughed with a sense of sheer defeat that was more frightening than anything. When the laugh stopped, she said, "I've already tried. And he cut me."

I stopped moving, images of the victims appearing one by one. "Your face?"

"Uh-huh," she answered, confirming it was him. "Beneath my eye and down my cheek."

"Samantha," I asked, "has he—" afraid of what she'd say.

"No. Not that." Her voice was shaking horribly. "But he's been hurting me."

"He'll come for you soon," Jenny warned. "He took your pants?"

"Yeah. My pants are gone." I moved my bare legs, vulnerability washing over me. "As for his touching me? Not if I can help it," I exclaimed and hoisted myself, raising my body an inch. It was just high enough to shift onto my side.

"What... what are you doing?" Samantha asked, alarm in her voice.

"If I can lift myself," I said, struggling to move my feet, "then I can get some slack and work on these restraints."

Shackles rattled as Samantha answered, "I tried that."

"Could be mine are different?" I said, half asking, paying more attention to my feet and legs. "I just need to get some lift."

"Mine's too tight," Jenni said, metal scraping the wall while she tried again. "It's hard to do anything."

"Put your feet under you," I directed. But it was easier said than done. With my ankles and knees tied tightly together, bending and moving them wasn't happening easily. I rolled to my side as much as I could, finding it gave me a bit of slack, but came at the cost of a sharp pain in my arms. That's when I felt it. There was movement in whatever the wrist bindings were attached to. "Guys! I felt it move."

"Felt the wall mount move?" Samantha asked excitedly, the idea of it spurring her into moving too. "When I tried before, I felt two lag bolts in the wall. They're about a half-inch thick."

"I think I understand," I said with a short gasp, the strain on my arms threatening to rip them from their joints. But I kept inching my feet closer. "Okay. Let's talk this through. Two lag bolts. They're fastened to the wall. What are they holding?"

"You'll feel a metal plate with a half loop thing that's about a quarter inch of metal," Jenni said with relief. "I was able to get onto my knees and lift my blindfold. I can see you guys. There's a padlock attached to it."

"That's a lock-loop. It's a steel loop welded to a thick plate. That's what is mounted to the wall," I explained, probing with my finger. "The restraints on our wrists. What are they?"

"Umm," she began, restraints jangling as she inspected. "Like it's some kind of medieval thing. They're an inch or two and cover the wrists."

"Shackles," I answered and tried to visualize her description in my head. "The padlock, it goes through the shackles?"

"Uh-huh," Jenni said, fiddling with them to try and free herself. "One padlock for all of it."

"The padlock goes through both shackles, and through the lock-loop plate on the wall," I said, summarizing our predicament.

"If I had a little room," Jenni said, jerking her hands, "I'd be able to slip my hands through."

"It isn't just the padlock," I warned, afraid she'd hurt herself. "The shackles have to be opened. We need to remove the padlock to release them."

"When he comes to us, I sometimes hear a keychain," Samantha offered. "I think he carries them on his belt."

"You hear them rattle?"

"Uh-huh," Jenni answered. "But you'll never get them from him. He's too big."

"I don't plan to," I said with a cry, my legs folded, my heels finally beneath me. I brought my face close to the wall, to where my hands and fingers were trapped, and lifted the blindfold. Squinting to get my eyes to adjust, I said, "I can see!"

"I can see you too," Jenni cried, her face filthy, her body coated in the same grime that reminded me of a coal miner. Her lips were cracked and bloodied where the skin had split, dark bags sagged beneath her eyes. She wore only underwear and a thin T-shirt, both soiled like her skin. The blindfold sat atop her head as she gave me a wave with her fingers. There were old tearstains on her cheeks, along with a fresh cut beneath one eye, the first half of the killer's insignia, marking her as his next victim. I think she sensed what I saw, or maybe saw it on my face, her voice quaking as she asked, "Can you get us out of here?"

"Right through there," I said, motioning toward the ceiling to where a green pipe ended, leaving a gaping hole to the outside. "That hole gets us to the other side of this room."

Jenni looked to the far wall as though she could see through it. "How do you know it leads to the outside?"

I regarded the question as water dripped into a bucket. "I... I have to think it does," I answered, assessing the pipes.

"And these?" she asked, jerking her arms, slamming metal against metal. Stretching her fingers, she reached the bottom of the padlock, barely touching it. "Can you reach yours and pick the lock?"

I shook my head. "Not that way," I said, and shook the metal plate, gripping the lock-loop and padlock firmly. Dust fell from behind the metal plate, pebbles ticking off the concrete floor. The whites of Jenni's eyes blazed. "The lag bolts are loose on mine."

"Oh shit!" she said, turning to face the wall, driving her fingertips into the edge of the backplate. "Samantha? What about yours?"

Samantha's head was cocked, tilted with an ear toward the top of the steps. "Shhh!"

We stopped moving. Stopped breathing. A motor was driving nearby. Blood began to rush in my veins as my heart sped up and my mouth went dry. Stones crunching beneath tires. A car was approaching. "Get back down!" I shouted with a whisper. Jenni began to cry while she forced her legs out from beneath her as I pulled my blindfold back down. I sucked in a breath, afraid of the painful movement to get back to sitting on the floor. My heartbeat rapped relentlessly, pounding in my chest as I unfolded my legs, a spasm locking in my thigh. I pushed with everything I had, stretching my legs and hanging myself from my wrists.

The slam of a car door quieted us like mice. I could feel myself shrinking into the shadows, trying to make myself invisible as chains tumbled to the floor. Jenni whimpered when the door hinges creaked, and then cried the muttering words that crushed my insides, "I forgot to put back my blindfold." He was going to see she'd been moving.

"Hurry!" I said, my heart battling to keep up with the mounting fear as her legs scraped against the floor and the metal restraints banged the wall.

But it was too late. His footsteps slammed the aged staircase, the wood steps complaining with thinly veiled threats as the smell of the killer filled the space in front of me. The sound of his movements had me thinking he was crawling across the floor, elbows and knees dragging. He stopped and grunted when he reached Jenni, her screams piercing. I shoved my face into the side of my arm as though I could hide. We had to get out of this place. We had to. Or die trying.

ELEVEN

Was this where he'd brought Pauline Rydel? There was a fourth
spot across from Jenni. On the wall, I saw a metal backplate and
lock-loop, along with an open padlock and empty shackles for
her wrists. They were the components that defined our predicament, our captivity. In the sickness of our dilemma, I am sure, if
given the choice, Pauline would rather be here with us, alive,
than to be lying dead in the morgue. When facing demise, it's a
wonder how little we'd settle for.

This had to be where he'd brought her. Where he had
carved one teardrop on the left cheek in the day or evening after
he'd taken her. A sinister teardrop for her right cheek made in
the moment of her murder. In Philadelphia, we'd never found a
location, only the bodies. With the investigation, we'd have the
last known whereabouts, a nightclub or bar, and then later, the
discovery of a body on an empty road or found in a vacant lot.
Where did he keep them in the city? Had he driven them all the
way down here or was there another hiding place? I felt my
thoughts wander aimlessly while I tried to think through the old
case. Maybe now wasn't the time. I should be thinking about
survival and escape.

There was no sleep in this place. No food either, which spoke of his intentions. We could live for a while without food, but we'd die without water. And the only water we got was from the garden hose, a few minutes each. I'd come to find out what the bucket was for too. The three of us using it before the evening consumed the day. When we were restrained again, I listened to him take the bucket up the stairs. There was no sink or kitchen that I could make sense of from the motions. But there was a front door he used to leave the building and then come back. This wasn't a house. Not in the traditional sense anyway. But it had running water. For the pipes above my head, they were connected to pumps, the big kind. If there were pumps then that meant there had to be electricity as well. Even with my blindfold on, I should have seen some light seeping through it. But I didn't. I never saw a thing. We were below ground level, in a bunker or cellar. I wouldn't have known it was dark or bright outside anyway.

My thoughts were slipping. They were becoming disconnected. Had it been a day already? Two? The worry Jericho must have been going through was its own torture. And Tracy. How they must be feeling. They were smart. They'd find my cell phone in the alleyway shortcut between the buildings. When they noticed I was at Samantha's apartment building, they'd figure out what happened to me.

After we each had a turn with the pail and drank some water, the car door closed and the motor faded as the killer left this place. It was time to get to work. My fingertips were raw and every muscle ached, I was exhausted. But if we were going to live, we needed to escape. Ignoring the pain, I got my legs beneath me to put slack into my arms and rest my shoulders. I shoved the blindfold onto my forehead, my eyelids crusty and sticky, an itch settling in them from the dirt. The room was darker than before, the far wall and staircase only shadows of their former self.

"Jenni?" I asked. Her body hung limp, her head lying on its side, the sight making my stomach burn. I dared a shout, a scream even, believing we were alone. "Jenni! Wake up!"

"Huh?" Her foot moved. And then the other. She lifted her head, searching blindly. When she began to cry, I realized she'd been asleep, that she'd been dreaming. It was the only form of escape we had. "What?"

"Keep working the lock-loop," I told her, lifting my voice to sound encouraging. "I think the mortar between the cinder blocks is loose."

"Mine won't move," Samantha answered. She jerked her arms, the padlock striking the lock-loop. "Nothing!"

"Feel around the floor for anything you can use as a tool," I said, lowering myself. The ropes around my knees had loosened enough for me to bend my legs. I felt around the floor, sweeping it with the soles of my feet. But it was smooth with a layer of dust.

"I got a stick!" Samantha yelled. "It's a broken piece of wood."

"The staircase," I told her. "It must have come from the stairs."

"I need to get it to my hands." With my eyesight adjusted to the late daylight, and her skin like ivory, I watched her move like a contortionist.

"Can you kneel?" I asked.

"I think so," Samantha answered and turned her body around enough to rest on her toes and knees.

"Good," I said, seeing Jenni moving too, the progress catching her attention. "Try and pinch the piece of wood between your knees—"

"Right! I can use my teeth from there." Like a game of pick-up sticks, Samantha held the stick between her knees, and moved back to a seated position. The stick dropped, the sound of it hitting the floor heart-wrenching. Maybe she'd get it. Maybe not. For now, it was keeping her busy.

"Jenni, you do the same. Search around you for anything that might help dig out the old mortar." I returned to my lock, the backplate loosening an eighth of an inch. Soft chunks of mortar dropped onto the concrete when I shook it, the lag bolt lifting. It was only a single thread, but it was enough. "Guys! I got one loose."

"Really!?" Jenni yelled, pulling her arms in a tug-o-war, the wall unmoving. "Maybe mine is too?"

"Is the mortar loose?" I asked.

"Dunno," she replied calmly. Her focus and attention were on the wall as she slid forward until her knees were planted against it. I didn't understand what she was doing until seeing she'd given herself leverage. Leaning back with all her strength, she jerked the restraints, tugging on them, throwing her head back with the strain.

"Take it easy, Jenni," I warned. She didn't stop. A crazed look appeared on her face as she pulled even harder.

"He won't take me," she grunted, ignoring me.

An animal trapped will do anything to escape. I'd read that once and was seeing it first-hand. Her legs began to shake from the strain. She climbed the wall, gaining more leverage with the shift. Her arms were thin, muscles straining as she let out a moan. "Jesus, Jenni! Stop!"

"I'm breaking free!" she yelled in a maniacal voice. "He won't take me!"

"Please, Jenni!" Samantha cried, sliding back to her bottom, the whites of her eyes enormous. "Casey, make her stop!"

"I'm getting out," Jenni cried, muscles taut, corded like sinew.

"Sit down!" I commanded. The louder we got, the harder Jenni jerked her arms. My words ignored. There was nothing I could do except watch, and listen, cringing, waiting, and then flinching when a bone snapped. Her wrist? Her forearm perhaps?

When the pain struck, Jenni's voice filled the room with a blood-curdling shrill. She didn't slow though. She didn't stop. She kept going, her left arm hanging limp as she repeated, "I'm getting out. I'm getting out."

"Keep working," I told Samantha, having no idea how much time we had. There was nothing we could do for Jenni. As much as it pained me, and as much as I wanted, there was nothing anyone could do for her. Samantha sat on her legs, wide-eyed and overcome by Jenni's breakdown. "Samantha! That's an order!"

"Okay," she said, moving to work the stick she'd found. "I will."

I worked the lag bolt, pinching the galvanized steel, squeezing hard enough to make the blood rise into my fingertips. A quarter inch turn. I paused when Jenni gave up and collapsed into a heap. She lowered her head without a word. In the darkness, I couldn't see her face. But I hoped the pain took her to a place that forced her to rest. I hoped she passed out from it and returned to that dream she'd been having before I woke her.

TWELVE

He came to me in the night. It was a soft touch first. A brush of a hand over my thigh. Light enough to let me sleep, let me steal the few minutes I could. In my mind, I was back home and under the covers with Jericho. The bedroom windows were wide open, the ocean waves lapping the coast as a breeze swirled around our bed, paddled by the ceiling fan. When the pain came, I woke with a start, a cry, a scream that took me to a place I'd never been.

My abductor spoke in whispers. His voice fast as he consumed the torture he delivered. His touch wasn't sexual. That's not what he wanted from me. It was my pain that he craved, drinking it in as if he'd suffered from an insatiable thirst. I wasn't in my dream anymore and reared up to get away from the cold metal gripping my skin. Pliers were my first thought, the tool like a mouth with teeth, holding until I cried out.

With dire understanding, I knew the bruises on his victims. He clawed at my leg, biting with the tool, the pain too much. I screamed out and heard him savor the sound, heard him relish in it. He was desperate to dominate and control. If he fed on the pain, then I could starve him. I just needed to contain it. I shoved myself against the wall and challenged him with my silence. The moment grew long, my lungs on fire, a sweat turning my body cold, the quiet dissuading him.

"What's the matter?" I asked, testing him.

"Detective Casey White," he answered. My blindfold hid his face from me, but I heard him licking his lips. I'd started shaking, the motion uncontrollable, his face close to mine. "You almost had me that night."

"A couple inches more," I said, gritting my teeth and remembering the rooftop and the leap from the other building. I could barely breathe, the injuries to my skin like a red-hot blade slicing through the bone. "A couple inches more and I would have had you!"

A chuckle. He released the instrument and waited for me to cry out, to thank him. I stayed silent by embracing the pain, biting my lips to keep my mouth shut. He sniffed at the air, grunting with disappointment. My muscles were tight with the tension, but relaxed when he eased back and sat on the floor, resting with a sigh. "I waited for you that night," he exclaimed, metal clanking, my legs untouched.

"What do you mean?" I asked, unsure of his meaning.

"I was coming for you," he answered, his words striking as deep as the physical torture. "I had it all planned. You were going to be mine."

"You *knew* we were watching!" I said, sickened by the idea. For years I'd thought I had blown our cover that night. I hadn't though. "You knew we were waiting."

"Of course I knew," he said, his body shifting, settling between my legs like we were old friends cozying for a chat. I thought of an attack, but he was too big and I couldn't trust my legs which were becoming stiff with pins and needles. "I'd been watching you for a while by then. Would have had you to—"

"What happened?" I asked and heard Samantha stirring. She was listening to us. "We searched for you."

He put his hand on my face as though trying to close my eyelids. "Another time," he answered and resumed the torture, his appetite unsatisfied, his needing more.

I tried to starve him again with my silence, but it only extended his visit with me. At the height of torment, I found a place back in bed with Jericho. I found Jericho's arms around me, his voice in my ear telling me that he loved me. That's where I stayed. It's where I put myself to separate my mind from the physical. I couldn't dare acknowledge what was happening to me. If I had, I would have lost my mind.

* * *

Chains. The rattle of them sliding across the door, locking us in this hellhole. I was down to my underwear and wearing the bra I'd put on the morning I'd last been free. And even without my clothes, I was drenched in a cold sweat, reeling from the injuries he'd inflicted. Would they heal?

Ten years in the making. I'd been in his sights for ten years. What happened to him on that roof? Where did he go? Why did he disappear? The questions bounced around my head, sharpening my thoughts, saving me from certain insanity that comes with torture and captivity.

"Casey?" Samantha asked in a whimper. I gulped the air, tongue fat and dry. "It'll stop hurting soon."

"Will it?" I asked, needing to see what he'd done to me.

"It will," she answered. She was back to working the stick, wood grinding against the wall.

"Shh!" I warned quietly, fearing his return. "He's still up there."

"He won't come back for a while," Jenni commented. It was the first we'd heard from her since she tried ripping the restraint from the wall. Movement came from my right, a low cry joining it. "When he finishes like that, he's kind of done."

"That means we have time?" I asked, forcing movement into my legs. I made my way back to the escape plan, asking Jenni, "Your arm?"

"I think it's broken," she said and then surprised us with a short laugh. "Didn't know I had it in me. And wow does it hurt."

"Oh, Jenni," Samantha said.

Jenni wept then. But not from the break in her arm. From our predicament. "I don't know how much more of this I can take."

"You've still got one good arm," I began, intentionally harsh, Samantha pausing. "Use it to start digging around the lag bolts."

"Uh-huh," Jenni replied, sniffling and swallowing a cry. "You're right."

When I was on my knees and able to reach my blindfold, I uncovered my damp eyes and rubbed the itchy grime from them. Jenni was in motion, a dark patch on her arm raising alarm.

"Is it a compound fracture?" I asked, afraid that if the bone had splintered, it would hasten our abductor's decision. She stared at me, unsure of my meaning. "Is the bone sticking out? Did it break through your skin?"

"Uh-uh," she answered and carefully moved to show me and Samantha. I'd only seen a shadow, the gray light playing with my eyes.

"Good. You can't let him know about it either," I warned, and rubbed the itch in my eyes, certain they were becoming infected. "Girls, we're going to get out of here."

"You promise?" Jenni asked, her question stealing my breath.

"I promise," I answered, praying to myself that it wasn't a lie.

* * *

There was a second visit that night. I'd been somewhere between dreams, somewhere between the sheets with Jericho's warm body pressed hard against mine. In my dream, there was the hot glow of after, and the soft pillow-talk that came so easily with us. With the interruption, my dream changed then. An old nightmare visited me, the images grainy and broken like an ancient reel-to-reel film. It was about a witchy woman driving the car with toothy fangs in the grill. She'd arrived at my house to steal my baby. She lured her to the car, fighting me and winning. But that was a long time ago, I had my daughter back now. When the blade touched my skin, I woke with a shake, this new nightmare never ending.

My eyelids fluttered behind the blindfold. There were insects trilling and tree frogs singing. If not for their song, I wouldn't have known the time of day. It was colder than earlier, telling me we must have been in the gut of the night, the hour around three, maybe four in the morning. There was a hand on my leg, gloved with latex caressing my bare skin. The metal edge beneath my eye was thin like a scalpel, the idea of what was about to happen making me shudder. It was the teardrop to my left cheek. It was like the one on the others, on Pauline Rydel.

"Please don't do this," I pleaded, body trembling with a voice that sounded like someone else was speaking. "Please—"

Before the cut came, there was a touch on my face. It was tender, almost gentle, a finger gliding down my cheek as if marking where to cut. Not a word was said as the grimy stains on my skin began to part and blood spilled to my chin. I winced and tried to move but couldn't. Fingers dug into my hair, squeezing with such force I thought my scalp would peel off my skull. I couldn't fight it. Wouldn't fight it for fear of his cutting more. Cutting deeper. I knew this was the first of two cuts. This was the superficial one, a mark of the beginning, an indoctrination into his maddening world. It also meant that my time was coming to an end soon.

THIRTEEN

There was no torture involved in the mornings, only the maintenance of taking us to the spigot and pail. Our blindfolds were kept on and the killer remained close to the ground like a wrestler, his thick fingers between my ankles, jerking with a harsh grunt and sliding me across the floor like I was a sack. He sounded intentions instead of speaking words, working us like we were a morning chore.

We'd become pets to him. Like a hamster or a lizard or goldfish in a concrete fish tank. We were living things to collect and admire and play with when he fancied it, when the craving hit him. We were also his burden. I kept my eyes shut to stave off the gray light of my blindfold, and to try and arrest the burn and itch of an infection I'd begun to regard as dangerous. It was sleep I was after. Even if it was only a few minutes. It was a temporary escape, and any escape was welcome.

His step was heavy and slow as he ascended the staircase. From Jenni's direction, she cried quietly to herself. Our abductor stopped. Shoes scraping with his movement, the stairs creaking. A moment later, he continued, and when the chains were threaded to lock us inside once again, I felt the weight of his presence lift.

"Casey, he cut me too," Samantha said. I rolled onto one side, swinging my feet around and forcing myself up. "My left cheek, but it's not deep."

"It's what he does," I told her, coughing, my lungs burning like my eyes. I sat on my feet and kept still to listen. I waited for floorboards to creak. Waited for the rattle of keys, a car motor or door. I only heard the wind, the clacking of branches, the brush of their leaves against other trees. He was gone. The temperature was a few degrees warmer too. It was morning and the humidity was already building. In the other cases, the teardrops indicated time. But that was then. Between the three of us, the timing wasn't the same. With a gut-wrenching thought, I believed it meant he was going to kill one of us tonight. "Okay, guys! Let's get moving!"

"I can't," Jenni said while I strained to bring my face to my hands and raise the blindfold from my eyes.

"Come on, Jenni—" I started to say, but then stopped. I couldn't see, my eyelids were glued shut. Though the skin on my fingertips was raw, I prodded and poked my eyelids. "Shit."

"What's the matter?" Jenni said, her concern putting her into motion.

"What is it, Casey?" Samantha asked.

"Seems I have an eye infection," I said, my words wavering with embarrassment.

"You have pink eye?" Jenni said with disgust. "Like, how does that even happen?"

"I don't know the answer to that," I said, grimacing while I pried an eyelid free. "I think it started with that old chlorine in the corner. It irritated me."

"That's what the smell is," Samantha said. "Can you see now?"

"Couple that with the dirt around the floor and I guess it got in my blindfold," I added.

"Ew," Jenni continued. "Hope it's not contagious."

I blinked through the sticky grit, picking at the crust until I could see, the girl's figures coming into focus. "Nope. This is all mine," I assured her. Jenni was on her knees and using her good hand to scratch at the wall. "I see it got you up and working though."

"Yeah," she said, crouching and adding, "I have to pee soon. He's usually here to let us go and give us water."

"We'll stop when we hear the car," I told them, shoving the tip of my finger into the loose mortar, a chunk falling. "I think I can get this lag bolt out. The mortar is really crumbly."

"The stick isn't helping much," Samantha said as she scraped around the backplate. "It looks like he put the lag bolts directly into the cinder block."

"Dig what you can," I said without revealing disappointment. While I had a chance because of the failing mortar, a lag bolt buried in the cinder block would need a lot more than a piece of splintered wood. It'd keep her busy, keep her mind off what was coming. And maybe that was the best we could do.

At some point during the night, the head of the lag bolt bloomed like a flower. Only its petals were made of glass, the sharp edges cutting my fingers with every touch. I knew that was a ridiculous thought but looked at my thumb and forefinger. The tips of them had peeled open, the skin blood red beneath, oozing and rife with sharp pain. If I could take off my bra, I would have. I could use the materials, maybe even develop a tool with it.

We were on the verge of hysteria while trying to ignore a mental and physical anguish that was beyond most anyone's comprehension. There was nothing from my training that would help, except the idea of distraction, anything to keep us occupied. I found it in a song that had gotten stuck in my head, a song that had played on the radio while I was driving to the night club. I hummed the popular tune from my childhood, the words loose on my lips as I sang the chorus about blessing the rains down in Africa. Jenni began singing along, joining in and smiling before Samantha did too.

I stopped what I was doing to laugh as we sang the rest of the chorus together.

"Great song," Jenni said. "Love Weezer."

"Weezer?" I asked, egging them into the conversation. "You mean Toto."

"Who?" she countered. "Never heard of them."

I hid a smile, seeing her expression lift. But the moment was gone as a car door slammed shut, turning the air in the stone room as still as in an empty church. We never finished the debate over the name of the rock band. And never finished singing it together or completing our escape. There were footsteps as we scurried to put ourselves back into position, covering our eyes and lowering our bodies against the floor, arms hitched up above our heads, mounted to the wall. And just as the first of the chain-links rattled, there was something that had escaped me until now. I couldn't be certain of it, but it was a second pair of shoes, another set of footsteps. Our abductor wasn't alone.

FOURTEEN

Hours passed without his return, the water dripping like a clock ticking. It was our only measure of time as we worked through the day and into the night. The strain on our bodies was severe, the lack of food and water an intentional design by our abductor. By limiting our intake, he was making us dependent on him, putting our welfare squarely in his hands. But there was one thing he didn't have. Our willpower. With each quarter inch turn of the lag bolt, and each drip of perfused sand and cement that had once made up the mortar, I could feel the strength of my will gaining, warming my insides like the sun on my skin. If I didn't know any better, I'd say I was getting stronger.

"I'm almost there," I told the girls, the tips of my fingers without feeling, the head of the bolt covered in dried blood. Sweat dripped into my goopy eyes, our hole in the ground becoming an oven as the day grew muggy and late.

"I can't do anymore," Jenni complained, sliding to the floor, her fingertips raw like mine. "I lost three of my fingernails."

"That's better than losing your life!" I snarked, needing her to continue. "Come on, Jenni!"

"I'm not getting very far either," Samantha said, holding the remains of the stick she'd found, more than half of it gone.

"Did you make any progress?" I asked.

"Not like yours," she answered, sliding onto the floor, her head dipping. When she raised her chin, I could see the wear of captivity in her sunken eyes and hollowed cheeks. "I'm too tired."

"This might make you guys feel better," I said, but they didn't budge, remaining still. The girls had gone days without food. And had only had enough water rations to keep them alive. While they lacked the energy, there came a joy-filled holler when the sound of a lag bolt struck the concrete floor. It rang like a victory bell, my yelling, "Got it!"

"Oh my God!" Jenni exclaimed, climbing back to her knees, leaning toward me as much as she could. "Can you get free?"

I jiggled the backplate, swinging it from the second lag bolt, answering, "Not yet."

"What!?" she cried, asking. "Then what?"

My hands went cold. And then my arms. The touch of defeat filling my body as the remaining bolt held me in place. "Give me a minute!"

"He used the same hardware on all these," Samantha said, inspecting hers to help. "What if you apply leverage?"

"Right," I said. I stopped spinning the plate and lifted to free a corner. "I've got the plate for leverage. If the other bolt is loose enough, it might come out."

"Try it!" Jenni yelled, returning to the wall and jerking the hardware.

To my surprise, prying the backplate from the wall came easy, the opposite corner digging into the cinder block like a hot knife slicing into butter. I could hardly contain myself, giddiness making my voice warble while I rocked the restraints back and forth. "It's coming loose!"

"Break it free!" Jenni shouted excitedly, the prospect of escape hitting a peak with sounds of stone crunching.

"Almost..." I said, the effort cramping my arms and legs. "Just a few more."

"Pull it!" Samantha shouted.

"A little more," I said, wiggling the metal, the crumbled wall dripping to the floor like blood from an infected tooth, the roots barely holding. Breath quivering, I put everything I had into yanking the bolt's last hold. I was flying then. My body sprang backward, the lock-loop with its metal plate still in my hands, the girls went silent as I slammed onto the concrete floor. Nothing was said while I tried to breathe, my lungs filling slowly. When I was ready, I held my prize above me and cried as Samantha and Jenni cheered.

"Me next!" Jenni begged as I stood up and stretched my legs. A dizzying wave hit me, blood rushing into my lower body. It was my first time standing since being taken, the time kneeling close to the floor taking a toll. "Please!"

"Okay," I said, going to Jenni, the sight of her touching my heart. She was smaller than I could tell before, her frame crouched, face grimy with filth, deep tearstains streaked on her cheeks. I checked her broken arm first, the bone jutting beneath her skin to create a black and purple bruise.

"Never mind that!" she demanded and jerked the restraints hard enough to make the padlock jump, metal jangling. "Get me free!"

"Take it easy!" I told her, fearing she'd break one of my fingers. "If you do that again while my hands are close—"

"Sorry," she wept, head shaking, a sheen forming on her skin. "I gotta get out of here!"

"We all do," Samantha said in an even voice.

Before I touched anything I could see there was no hope in freeing Jenni without the key to the padlock. The lag bolts were secured to the cinder block, which meant no movement to give by the backplate. I didn't want to chance an injury, and though it broke my heart to do it, I backed away and searched the floor.

"What are you doing?" Jenni shrieked. She raised her hands, blood oozing from beneath the shackles on her wrists. "Get me out of—"

"I'm looking for anything I can use. Anything that'd add leverage." I returned to inspecting the restraints on my arms to see if there was anything I'd overlooked before. There wasn't. Only the padlock key would remove them.

"Casey! Where are you going?!" Jenni yelled as I went to Samantha. I could inspect the lock-loop and backplate holding Jenni's restraints for days, but the truth remained I'd need heavy tools to break her free. She wailed then, her cries ripping my heart open. "Casey!"

"Go!" Samantha said, her glassy eyes blazing, the dim light showing fresh tears. She nudged her chin to the hole above the pipes, urging me. "I know you won't be able to free me. Go!"

"Just let me take a look—" I could barely see, the eye infection clouding and teardrops sitting. There was no hope.

"Oh, hon. Samantha?" Chains rattled, the links thumping across wood, the sound turning my blood cold. At the top of the staircase there was a door, a light beneath it, a shadow lingering on the other side. I cupped Samantha's chin in my bound hands, telling her, "I'll get help!"

"Go!" she cried and stirred like a trapped animal as the chains toppled to the floor above us.

"Casey!" Jenni yowled, her cry piercing. I didn't wait though and made my way beneath the pipes.

The room was low-ceilinged, which might explain why the killer stayed low to the ground. It helped now, my height tall enough to reach up, letting me leap and take hold of a strut the pipes saddled. The door was opening, rusty hinges calling to say he was coming. I shoved my legs into the hole, having no idea what was on the other side of the wall. When my bare feet touched gravel, I climbed the rest of the way inside, disappearing behind the cinder block and into the blackness.

"Please, no!" Samantha cried when the crushing footfall came, the killer entering the room. I cringed at the torturing sounds of his hands and legs sweeping across the floor, his inspecting each of us.

"Casey!" he shouted, taking hold of the broken lock-loop, the metal colliding with the wall when he threw it. I didn't look back, didn't dare let him see where I'd gone. But for a moment, I thought I would have to. I was in complete darkness, the cavity behind the wall leading nowhere. I braced the gravel and crawled straight, keeping to the opposite direction, finding the pipes and following them. The yells and tortured cries echoed behind me, the sounds crushing. A hand. Fingers snatching my foot and squeezing my toes like a vice. He'd found me! Stomach in my throat, I screamed and kicked furiously, getting free and crawling faster. "Come back, Casey!"

Boards. There was a wood panel with nails sticking through. It was a crawlspace that I was in, the edge of it boarded. I punched through, finding the outside, seeing that it was nighttime already, our hours of working the escape taking the full day. Behind me, the girls were screaming, Samantha yelling, "He's coming, Casey! Run!"

And run I did. Or so my mind said I'd do. My legs failed twice when I went to stand. The lack of light, the absence of a moon and its stars not helping. My eyes were half shut with infection as I felt around like the blind, adjusting to the outside. Tall grass struck my legs as his footsteps touched my ears, the sound driving me to run faster. I couldn't tell where I was, the gray light revealing little more than odd shapes that towered above me. When I ran into a fence, I fell to my knees, certain I was going to die.

Listen, I thought, collapsing into a heap and catching a breath. I was hiding from the killer, but felt he was near. From the other side of the fence, the other side of the woods, there was traffic. It was far, but I recognized what it was, cars on a highway. A siren passed, bending the way it does when moving away. *Climb!* I took hold of the fence and looped my fingers and toes onto the metal, ignoring the pain of each step, reaching the top where I rolled over the top and fell. I didn't know how high I'd climbed, but landed with a crash, branches breaking, twigs and stones digging into my skin.

"Casey!" he shouted and slammed into the fence like a caged animal. I didn't turn to look, didn't dare, and ran into the dense woods. It was thick with foliage, tree branches whipping my skin, my feet tortured by the terrain as I scrabbled over sticks and stones. I was in the home of the insects, their trilling peacefully, and with tree frogs, their song telling me that it was night. The rattle of metal, the killer was at the fence, screaming from behind it, "I'm coming, Casey!"

It was the traffic that ended his chase, the woods opening to the highway. My eyes couldn't adjust, wouldn't adjust, the sickness in them turning the oncoming headlights into floating orbs, their blobby luminescence flying by me and carrying a wind that buffeted my body. When I struck the pavement, I raised my arms, waving frantically for a car to stop. I couldn't see the edge of the lane or see where the road's shoulder began and where it ended. One of the oncoming cars found me though, brushing my hip and spinning me sideways, their tires screeching as brake lights filled my sight blood red.

"Are you okay!?" the driver yelled, shoes slapping the road as he ran from his car. I could see a face, the details muted. He had slicked black hair and a manicured beard. When he knelt near me, I could smell the soap he'd used, along with his after-shave, mixing with car exhaust. "Oh my God! What happened to you?!"

"Is she okay?" a woman asked, appearing from the passenger side. She cupped her mouth when she saw me, and then raised her hands to show she meant no harm. When she was closer, her focus shifted to assess my injuries. I clutched her arms, pulling her closer, her voice sounding heartsick concern. "We're here to help."

"Call... call the police." I choked out the words before everything went black.

FIFTEEN

I was in the nightmare. The evening noises filling my ears. The forest beneath my feet. There were leafy tree branches clutching my arms, and the killer's hand wrapped around my ankle, a distant car engine rumbling. A ghostly hand curled its witchy finger with a come-hither motion, their voice saying, *It's time.* I woke with a start, face sweaty and panting, a voiceless scream on my lips.

"It's okay, Casey," Jericho said, his stubbled face hovering over mine, a loving touch on my chin. He pulled a sheet over my chest, tucking me in. But I'd never sleep again, not while the killer still had Jenni and Samantha. When I went to touch my eyes, the feel of them strange, he took hold, clutching my fingers in his, saying, "It's the medicine. Conjunctivitis. One of the docs said it's the worst—"

"I need to go!" I tried to say, interrupting with a voice that was a dry rasp. Tracy was on the other side of the bed, a worried look fixed on her face as she handed me some water. It was a clear plastic jug with measurements on the side, an intravenous tube rising and falling with my hand. I was in the hospital. The floral-patterned curtains around the bed, and the bustling activities on the other, had me thinking we were in an emergency room. I must have passed out when the ambulance arrived. "How long!?"

"A couple hours," Tracy answered and swiped a tear from her cheek. She leaned over the edge of the bed, running her fingers through my hair. The anguish of my abduction had exhausted her, the look of it showing with dark pouches beneath weepy bloodshot eyes. "I'm so glad you're okay."

"I'll be fine," I said and patted her arm. But there wasn't time for sentiment, and I kicked my feet clear of the bedsheet. "Did they find Jenni and Samantha?"

"You saw Samantha?" Nichelle asked, appearing from behind Jericho. Her hair was unbraided and standing big, her eyes wide with shock. Shaking her head, she said, "Casey, we had no idea what happened to you."

"Abducted," I answered, sipping the water, the iced touch cooling the burn in my throat. "The Midnight Killer. He has Samantha and another girl."

"Samantha is alive?" Tracy asked and swiped errantly at her cheeks. "Thank God!"

"A second girl?" Nichelle asked.

"Her name is Jenni Levor. Dirty blond hair, around five-four. She's thin, early twenties, but it was tough to say down there—"

"Down there?" Jericho asked, voice breaking. I waved it off, unable to talk about it yet. He cupped my hand, kissing my fingers. "When you're ready."

"Jenni Levor. I'll notify the team." Nichelle held her phone to report the name, to confirm what had happened and add another victim to the list.

"The woods," I told them. "I escaped through them. Maybe a mile or two from the road."

"There's a team there now," Tracy answered, trading

glances with Jericho. "They've been trying to figure out where you came from."

"Babe," Jericho said with a squeeze, my focus returning to him. "The nurse—"

I frowned as he struggled to speak. "What... what is it?"

He swiped at his mouth, answering, "The nurse has a sexual assault kit and is asking to do an exam."

I shook my head and slowly closed my eyelids. "No, it was only the torture, the same he'd inflicted on Pauline Rydel and the others," I answered. Machines beeped, an alarm ringing, the sharpness making me flinch. I looked at Tracy and Jericho more alert than I'd been in days. I jumped up, voice ratcheted, "I gotta get out of here!"

"Casey," Jericho objected as I pulled my hand free of his. "We've already got a team out there searching."

"You don't understand!" Tears stung my eyes, the words of my promise gripping my heart. I swung my arm, removing the rest of the hospital sheet. I yanked the tube free of my arm and then froze at the sight of my pale legs, the hospital lights showing everything. The skin on my feet were torn from the run in the woods, some of the toenails blackened and split. There were ribbon-thin cuts, raised and puffy across my shins. My knees were bruised and grossly swollen from having knelt so long on the concrete floor. It was the injuries he'd inflicted that stole my breath. There were ten marks on my thighs, the pain of them, the memory of what he'd done sickened me and made me want to scream. "Guys, I have to go back."

"Oh, Casey!" Tracy exhaled sharply, voice shaking as she glared at my legs. She swallowed dryly and returned her gaze at me, saying, "We'll go for you."

I grabbed her arm, squeezing. "I made a promise to them!" When she reeled back, hurt registering on her face, I let go. "I... I'm sorry. But I promised I'd get them."

"Then we'll help," Nichelle said, closing the curtain behind her. She slung a backpack from her shoulder, letting it plop onto the end of the bed. "Tell us what to do."

I realized then, I only had a hospital gown on, and tried to cover my bare legs. Jericho held the end of the sheet. I took the offer, wrapping myself in it. I grabbed his hand too, pulling him into my arms, the need to weep and to have him hold me coming on strong. "I'm so sorry."

"This wasn't your fault, Casey," he said, choking up. He cleared his throat, adding, "Tell me how to help."

"For starters, I could use some clothes," I told him. "And my car."

"Clothes, I can get. Your car, we found it, along with your gun too," he answered, sitting on the bed. He brushed his fingers across my hair, picking out a piece of green leaf, the dimple on his chin jumping as he held back the emotion. "What else?"

"A map," I answered, motioning to the laptop as Steve Sholes joined us. He glanced at Jericho, offered a nod, the look between them cold—a story for another time perhaps. "And one Detective Steve Sholes."

"Sunny, are you volunteering me for something?" he asked and forced a smile. He cocked his head, smile gone, his hand on mine. "Hope you don't mind my saying, but you've looked better."

"Did you drive down from Philly just for me?" I asked, wondering how long he'd been here.

"He's been working the case with us," Tracy said, eyes beaming. She clutched Nichelle's arm, adding, "The FBI too."

"Good," I said, sitting up to cross my legs and tap the bed. Nichelle followed my lead, putting the laptop in front of me. "Steve, it was the Midnight Killer. He's got two other women."

His eyes were fixed on my cheek where I'd been given a teardrop. "I see his handiwork. No doubting that you're sure," he said, scanning the team. "We can take it from here. Just point the way."

"I'll do more than that—" I began, but stopped when they traded looks, their words unspoken. "What!?"

"Maybe..." Steve began, blinking fast. I opened my eyelids wide, urging him. "Maybe it'd be good if you sit this one out?"

"Yes," Jericho agreed.

"Uh-uh," I answered, opening the laptop. "That's not going to happen."

"Casey?" Steve rebutted, hands raised, asking why.

"Fuck that!" I exclaimed, dismissing the discussion, my neck and face getting hot. "I have to go back!"

The arguing stopped when my face appeared in the screen's reflection, the black mirror showing wrinkles creased across my forehead and newer ones at the corner of my eyes. Each of them a worry, a disappointment that I'd only been able to save myself. "He cut me," I said sadly, seeing the truth, a chill sweeping across my body as I touched what he'd done. Nichelle leaned over the laptop and thumped the spacebar, my reflection disappearing into a map of bright pixels.

Jericho rubbed my shoulder, assuring me, "The doctor's said it'll heal without any scarring." He moved the cursor, the map zooming in on an area across from Wright Memorial Bridge. "You appeared here... presumably from the woods," he said, pointing to a section of road with four lanes, a median strip, the road bordering woods on both sides. "But we've been wondering if you might have been dropped off by a car."

"No car. I ran through the woods," I answered, and thought of the hand that appeared when I'd been drugged in the alleyway. There were the extra steps I was certain I'd heard too. I touched the teardrop cut into my face which had scabbed over. The touch wasn't like his. It was tender. "Steve, I think he is working with someone."

"An accomplice?" His brow rose. We'd had years of investigating the Midnight Killer, but we'd never suspected a second person involved. He tapped his phone and began to text. "You're sure?"

I motioned to my legs, saying, "This is what he does." I ran my finger over the cut on my face, the same way as the killer's accomplice, adding, "This is what she does."

"She?" Tracy asked. "His accomplice is a woman?"

"I think so," I said, but couldn't be sure. "It was the way she touched me."

"We'll know when we get to where they took you," Nichelle said, nudging the laptop.

"I came through a thick patch of woods," I explained, moving the map, the tiles rendering slowly in the poor network connection. "But I don't know which direction."

"The road is east to west," Tracy said as I dropped a thumbtack on the location where I was saved by the man and woman. "You were in the eastbound lanes."

"That's what I needed to know," I said and moved the map. "I came from the woods on the southern side of the road."

"What's there?" Jericho asked, the team circling around my bed to see the screen. When nothing showed except more trees, I moved deeper into the woods, realizing I must have been running longer than I could recall. I wiggled my toes, stiffness in the joints as painful as the raw skin. I really had no idea how long I was running, but the damage said it must have been a while. "There!"

I stopped on a blank space. A large block of lime green that had no title. It had no name or any indication of what it was. "Strange that it's blocked out."

"Some government facilities don't show on public maps," Tracy offered. "Ya know. For security reasons."

"A government facility?" I questioned and thought of the pipes and the chlorine.

Jericho pointed to a thin path, saying, "That looks like an access road back to the highway."

"Open the street view, the satellite images. That'll show us what is there." I used a wad of tissue and medical tape to make a bandage where the IV tube had been. There were cuts and bruises across my hands and forearms, my fingertips blackened like my toes. I wanted a deep, hot tub to soak for hours, and to wish the last days down the drain. But I couldn't fight the urgency and traced the map, panning to the west, returning to the highway, zooming in far enough to read the name of the access road. When the pixelation cleared and the name of it appeared, I mouthed, Slip and Slide Court. And I knew it was where the killer had taken me. "There. Slip and Slide Court."

"I know that place," Jericho said, slipping a radio from his hip, turning it on with a squelch.

"I know exactly where it is," I said, having passed it on every trek back to Philadelphia. When the street view rendered, the abandoned water slide park came into focus. "The girls are in there."

I had my clothes. And I had my gun. To my surprise, I also had my phone, which was recovered from the alley. Nichelle had used the cell towers to identify my last pings the night of my abduction. That's how they narrowed my last known location. While my phone's screen was cracked and brittle in parts, Tracy mended it with clear tape, and had kept the battery charged for me. As we drove over the bridge, I had Jericho next to me, his hand in mine and sitting close as we gathered a broad team to search the abandoned water park. Steve Sholes drove the car while Tracy provided him with directions.

Out of habit, I reached for my badge, only to find it was missing. Taken by my abductor. What else had he taken? Did he keep mementos other than my injuries and scars? I was itching to find out and dipped my head to see the sun and let the heat of it warm my skin. The days in captivity had chilled me to the bone. Even with the muggiest of the days coming with my escape, the outside turning our room into a hot box, I still couldn't shake the cold. It was more than physical. It was emotional. A damage he'd inflicted that might take years for me to understand and mend.

Six cars had lined up along the single road outside the abandoned water park. Water slides stood leaning and derelict high above the ground, their carnival colors faded by the weather and years of neglect. The medicine in my eyes helped clear my vision as I stared at their silhouettes and found the towering monsters I'd seen when I ran from the killer. Though they were lifeless, they had appeared ominous in the absence of definition. Even now, the sight of them gave me a fright. I stumbled back. A reaction to their presence in the daylight.

"You okay?" Jericho asked, his hand on the small of my back as he cared for me. I gave him a nod; my eyes were clear and my strength gaining. There was an echo of nerves, knowing my abductor could be nearby. My legs were wobbly, but I wouldn't dare show it.

"That way," I said, my gun drawn, my knuckles aching with it in my grip. I lined up alongside Steve Sholes, Jericho taking to the other side of me. Nichelle and a half dozen FBI agents appeared with us, their badges slung from their chests, sunlight glinting sharply from the metal. "Bolt cutters?" I asked.

"Got it," one of the agents answered, cutting through the chain-link fence, giving us the room needed to file through. We spread out, putting an arm's distance between us, and began the task of searching.

"Where do we start?" Steve asked, leaning back to take in the view of the entire park. In the daylight, it was massive, two, maybe three football fields of pools and water slides, along with rides for children and buildings with showers and lockers.

There were bamboo huts with old signs for snacks, the front of them boarded and graffitied with neon colors. The slides were many, dilapidated, a few having fallen to the ground and sitting on their sides. "We could be here all day."

"The pipes," I answered, taking the lead. The team followed me, the pale green pipe next to my feet. There'd once been concrete beneath it, but that had crumbled and broken over the years of abandonment, replaced by crabgrass and sprouting grass along the sides. "There's a building where the pumps are located. It's where the chlorine is stored, which I smelled and felt in my eyes. That's where he kept us."

A rabbit scurried into a shallow pool, an agent raising his gun, jacket swishing at the sudden motion. "Sorry," the agent said. The lining in the pool was torn, a leafy meal hanging from the soil bed behind it, the rabbit's interest in taking a bite. "Didn't know what that was."

"Take it easy," Steve warned gruffly. "We don't need anyone getting shot today."

I raised my hand to quiet the team as I carefully stepped up to the building. It was just as I'd imagined it: a red-brick building above ground, the foundation made of cinder block, and the failing mortar that helped me escape. There were pipes flowing in and out from the sides, a single access door near us, the walls without windows. There were no chains on the ground, which meant that the killer might be inside. "That one," I whispered as agents scurried around me, boots grating the brittle pavement. I sucked in a breath as an agent took hold of the doorknob, his gun poised, his lips moving to a countdown of three, two and one. The door swung open, our guns aimed, the sun beaming into an empty space with dust shimmering in the light.

"Clear," I said, taking a position to step into the small room, the door with the chains opposite of the entrance. Unlike my time in captivity, the chains were on the floor and the door was wide open. I held up my hand again, moving swiftly to the top of the wooden staircase, taking care as I aimed down, knowing that Samantha would be there. Footsteps followed behind me, the basement space too dark for us to see. It was too quiet, the silence unbearable. My heart was crushed with the understanding of why. "Flashlights!"

"I got it," Steve said, his hand over my shoulder, his light showing the restraints where Samantha had been. "It's empty."

"No!" I screamed, taking the light and flying down the stairs into the empty room. Steve and Jericho followed, footsteps striking wood, leather creaking as guns were holstered. The walls were bare. The lock-loop and backplate in place, but without Samantha and Jenni. "They're gone!"

"Careful where you step," Tracy said, shining a light on the floor. There was dried blood where Jenni had been. Not a lot, but enough to show he'd been at her. My skin crawled with the thought of what took place, hair rising on my neck about the possible outcome. Tracy knelt closer to it, saying, "Uhm, I think it's fresh—"

The team's words faded as my knees thumped painfully against the concrete floor. My last strength had gone as failure devoured me like a sickness. "I promised them."

SIXTEEN

My time with the team was going to be short. Jericho tugged my arm, urging us to leave and let them work. As he suggested, I was no good to anyone if I didn't take care of myself first. Maybe I was feeding on the broken promise, Jenni and Samantha still missing. Maybe guilt was all I needed to continue forward. I shook my head, holding back, ignoring Jericho's disappointment. Even if we left the scene, how could I eat? How could I rest knowing they were out there? It wasn't possible. He held up his hands, fingers spread to indicate ten more minutes. I negotiated, mouthing thirty with a promise.

We turned back to face the team—the abandoned water park had become a crime scene. The concentration of our investigation was on the pump house. There was already a team from the FBI on site with us, their arriving soon after my abduction, coming to the Outer Banks from the offices on Arch Street. With the Philadelphia cold case awakening in the Outer Banks and my reaching out to Nichelle for help, the FBI had an interest in the multi-state murders. They were investigating what happened during the killer's ten-year hiatus. Were there more unsolved murder cases elsewhere, his teardrop signature perhaps overlooked?

We were one team working shoulder to shoulder, scouring the footpaths across the park's untamed weedy overgrowth. With the sun beating down in the mid-morning hours, we saw a path, the tall grass trampled, the killer walking heel to toe, single file steps. The path was well worn, hiding any shoe impressions that could be measured and lifted. It also hid the count, my wrestling with the idea of there being an accomplice, a second person involved. I thought of my abduction again, trying to understand how he'd got me into his car. There were blurred images of the car door and a ghostly hand waving me inside, but a drugged mind is an unreliable witness.

"Tracy," I said, coming upon a faint impression of a tire track. The wind began blowing, scattering loose sand, and bending the tall grass. I raised my arms as though protecting my find but saw that it was safe. In the years since the park had closed, the rains added a thin batter of silt and sand, producing a sheet of caked mud that had perfectly preserved the tire's tread and the distance between them.

"Find something?" Tracy asked, her hair whipping around her face. Her brow rose when seeing the treads.

"We knew he was coming when we heard the car." I searched for a footstep, thinking the mud might have more secrets to share. There was one print, the tip of a shoe maybe, but not distinguishable enough to lend help. "No shoe prints, but we might get a vehicle make and model from the tires."

"I've got an app for that," Nichelle said, her hair leaning to one side. An FBI agent joined us and carefully placed orange cones around the tread while Tracy photographed them.

"An app?" I asked, glad to have an arm of the FBI working with us. "How long will—"

"It's a Jeep Latitude," Nichelle answered before I could finish asking. She held up her phone, showing me a picture of the vehicle type, adding, "And this tread is a Goodyear brand, Integrity type, the size 225—"

"Okay, got it," I said, impressed by the efficiency, and began relaying the information, but stopped. "When I was taken, there was an SUV that had followed me into the parking lot of the club."

"A Jeep Latitude?" Jericho asked, eyes wide. He'd been texting and stopped. "I can get patrols moving to search all of the Outer Banks."

"I don't remember a color," I said with a frown. "Just the windows. There was something about them..."

"Were they cracked?" Nichelle asked, cocking her head. "If so, that'd be easy for a patrol to spot."

"Not broken," I answered, tapping my chin, the memory of what was unique about them sitting just out of reach. I gripped my hair, as if to squeeze out a memory. "I can't remember."

"You will," Jericho assured me, the sunlight glinting in his blue-green eyes as he coaxed my arm away from my head. "We've got a make and model. It's something."

"We need more," I argued, too frustrated to stay still. I moved to go inside, see if there was progress, my voice trailing as I said, "There's too many SUVs in the Outer Banks."

I stood at the center of the room where he'd held us, the tip of my toe nudging the padlock and steel plate that had held me captive.

"Ma'am?" an officer asked, tucking wispy hair behind an ear as he eyed my foot. He knelt to place an evidence marker next to it, asking, "Do you mind?"

"Sorry," I muttered and went to where Samantha had been. On the concrete floor, I could have sworn there was an outline of her body from the endless hours of sitting in one place. But it was bare. She was gone. Tracy stood at the top of the stairs, photographing the door and walls. The hardware had been bolted into the walls so when the chains were in place, the room was inescapable from our side. I motioned to the wall as she took to the stairs, and said, "Samantha."

"We'll find her," Tracy said, trying to assure me. She tried to sound encouraging, but I heard her hope waning. It wasn't that she was pessimistic. Instead, it was because she'd experienced the gut-wrenching statistics in this field. She began taking pictures of the wall, her flash striking the backplate. It had remained intact, the lock-loop empty, the padlock gone, the thick metal binding Samantha's wrists.

"Continue down here?" I asked and flinched when the water dripped into the bucket. The hollowness of the sound rang in my head, each plop a suffocating reminder.

When I began pawing at my skin as though an army of ants had found me, Tracy asked, "Are you okay?"

"I think I need to get out of here," I answered shamelessly. I felt I was nearing the thirty minutes I'd negotiated with Jericho, my body telling me to go, my mind demanding it. "You'll continue?"

"I got this," she said, eyeing the shadows moving at the top of the steps. "Go. I'll be out in a few."

Two steps at a time, my legs weak, the sunlight my savior. I ran from the building, inhaling sharp and fast, filling my lungs. I turned around and decided that I'd never step foot in that building again.

* * *

The two rooms were swept, the surfaces powdered with a hope of finding a strand of hair or a fingerprint to lift. That's when the call came in. I was standing on the side of the pipe room forcing myself to eat a protein bar Jericho brought me and answering agent questions between mouthfuls. As if on cue, the phones rang, and everyone stopped what they were doing. We always knew it was bad when the calls came in at the same time. Only, I didn't know just how bad until seeing the grimness on Jericho's face as he walked over to me. And though I'd given up my phone for the day to get the screen fixed, I reached for it anyway, gripping my leg instead as the angst rose in me like acid.

"What is it?" I asked.

"Route 12," he began to say. He put a hand on my arm, bracing me.

"What... What happened?" But I already knew.

"Another body," he answered. I shut my eyelids and wished I could turn off the world. "The description matches the one you gave for Jenni Levor."

Every muscle came alive with electricity, the strain of it powerful enough that it might break my bones. Jericho led me around the vacant side of the building where the weeds stood knee high, and grasshoppers and crickets trilled peacefully. But peace was the furthest from what I could feel. We were alone and I grabbed him tight, fingers clutching his shirt as I pressed my face into his chest, yelling, "I promised her—"

"This isn't your fault," he tried to console, his empathy for me putting a shake in his voice. "You were a victim here."

A victim! I reared back, shaking my head like it was an offense, squinting against the sunlight. "It was my responsibility to save them."

"You had to save yourself first," he said, his face shaded, his eyes weepy. He sighed deeply, chest rising against mine as he brushed the tears from beneath my eyes. "You did everything you could—"

"Did I?" I asked, voice abrupt, a hundred questions spawning in cue behind the first.

"Oh Casey, don't do that," Jericho warned, lips pressed tight. "Babe. You can't second guess any of this."

"Jericho, it's my fault," I said, objecting as I put my finger to his lips. He didn't rebut or counter what I said and held me instead.

Second guessing was all I had at this point. I could feel it burning in my heart. I would forever question my moves. I had to question them. It was my job to protect and serve, and I ran. What if I'd stayed behind instead of tunneling along the pipes to the outside? What if I'd stayed and attacked our abductor, killing him in his own lair like the boy who'd slayed the dragon? Isn't that how you strike a monster, catch them off guard, attack them when they least expected it? I might have been weak and injured, but I could have tried. I had the weight of Jenni's murder—and Samantha still missing—on my shoulders.

SEVENTEEN

We arrived on site within the hour. The sun was perched at its peak for the day, the heat shimmering above the sands and the road, the sky cloudless, a dusky blue, a summer haze settling over the Outer Banks. We parked near the patrol officer who'd helped manage the traffic with the previous victim. He dipped his hat, seeing me, doing a double take when he saw my face, the swollen eyes, the cut on my cheek. Thankfully, he didn't ask, and continued waving the traffic to turn west toward Currituck Sound, and away from the beach and crime scene.

"Get him," I heard a mother yell, the crime scene bordering an intersection bustling with tourists. While the road had the same towering hedges, hiding what the killer was doing, the intersection was open. On one corner, a row of single-story buildings, cedar shingle roofs, pressure-treated lumber, weathered by the nearby ocean. Locals and tourists were wrapped around the building, half in line for a bait shop, anticipations of a night fishing bite with the forecasts of a clear evening and full moon. The other half waited for their turns at an ice-cream parlor.

"I got him," the father answered, grabbing the child. The

family of four gave me no mind and gawked at the crime-scene tape, the patrol cars, and the muted red and blue flashing lights. I could smell vanilla and chocolate and sunblock, the father giving me a nod, her gaze falling to my chest and badge. "Ma'am."

"Afternoon," I answered as they continued east, the beach a block from us. Breaking waves rode on the breeze, but the ocean stayed hidden by the hills of grassy sand dunes in this part of the Outer Banks. "Have a good time."

"Thank you," the wife answered, her sunhat bending with a gust. She licked her ice cream, asking, "Car accident?"

"Something like that," I answered. There was no need to get into specifics and I gave them a wave and approached the patrol officer.

"Ma'am, it's good to have you back safe," he said, motioning toward his face. He asked, "From the abduct—"

"Indirectly," I interrupted, not wanting to go into the details. As more of the tourists walked around us, I asked, "Listen, about the foot traffic?"

"I'm in position," he answered, already regarding my concern. He pointed to the crime scene where the medical van had parked. It was perpendicular to the side of the road, which helped to block the view. "I'm to block anyone who tries to walk south."

"Good, thank you," I said, eagerly moving on, Tracy shutting the trunk of the car, gear in hand. She handed me a pair of latex gloves. When we circled around the medical examiner's van, the anticipation of seeing Jenni gripped my heart again, the clutch icy. I shouldered the side of the van, a lightheaded spin stopping me. "Gimme a second."

"Casey, your color is bad," Tracy said flatly. She put the kit and camera down and came and took my free hand. "How about you wait in the car."

"I have to do this," I said and gulped a mouthful of warm water. "I think it's the dehydration."

"To say the least," she said with concern and shook her head. "You're really pushing it."

"I have to!" I snapped with immediate regret. Her lips tightened as she eased back a step. "Ignore me."

She stood on her toes, looking at the crime scene, saying, "Whatever you need me to do."

Tracy helped me get steady as we entered the crime scene, Jenni's hair showing first, the look of it dramatically different in the sunlight. Her skin was fairer too, almost an alabaster, but had turned gray with murder. "Doc," I said, the medical examiner's wispy comb-over flopping. His assistant's green eyes followed me as I knelt next to the body. "Carla."

"Detective," she began, and continued, "it's really good to have you back safe."

"Thank you," I answered while sleeving the gloves around my fingers. Jenni's body had been dumped like the previous victims. The killer stopping, opening the car door long enough to shove the body onto the road. I reached for Jenni's face, wanting to move her hair. I needed to see what was done. "Doctor, may I?"

"Certainly," he answered, his wiry mustache bouncing. "It's your scene until released."

A camera's flash snapped sharply and then whined with its electrical release and recharge. The process repeated as Tracy followed my motions to reveal Jenni's face and the deep cut running down her cheek. The air was electric like a lightning bolt had struck, the flash used to freeze the moment in a still image we'd use to record the evidence. "I'm going to move her head if that's okay."

"Let me help," Carla said and knelt next to me. I recognized the body wash she used, the fragrance the same eucalyptus I'd sometimes use. Jenni's skin was beyond pale. It was almost translucent. Enough that we could see the veins and arteries on her neck and face. Carla cradled Jenni's head, carefully rotating, rigor mortis already setting, the skin on her neck dry and without elasticity. "Tell me when?"

"There," I said, holding up a hand when sunlight struck Jenni's eyes. They were dulled and already clouded and without reaction, any pupillary constriction. In death, Jenni didn't flinch. She didn't wince. She didn't try to shade herself from the brightness. The extent of color changes did give us a timeline. "He didn't wait very long."

"How's that?" Carla asked, Tracy appearing over her shoulder and taking a close-up picture of Jenni's eyes, her second camera outfitted with a macro lens and ring flash.

"I'd say within a couple hours of your escape," Tracy suggested. She turned to Carla, explaining, "The rigor mortis starts around the head and neck, traveling down to the feet after. The eyelids are stiff and remain open. The corneas progressively cloud, their opacity diminishing."

"Excellent," Doc Bob said, his listening as we worked. "I like it when investigators have some background."

"Thank you." Tracy's brow jumped with the compliment, but she did well to mask it and moved to take pictures of the second teardrop cut. She stopped and asked, "Post-mortem?"

"Carla?" Doc Bob asked, nudging his chin, wanting her to field the question.

"Umm—" she began, a startled look on her face.

A motion in the crowd caught my eye. I stood up abruptly, the doctor and his assistant veering back as Tracy joined, asking, "What is it?"

"In the crowd over there," I answered breathlessly, and pointed to the crime-scene tape on the south side of Route 12. "Tall guy. Very tall. Hands in his pockets."

"Yeah," Tracy said, following me to the patrol car. I jumped onto the hood when I lost sight of the guy, Tracy raising her voice, asking, "Casey!? What are you doing?"

"He was big like the guy who abducted me," I answered, shielding my eyes as I searched the crowd.

"You think he's here?" Tracy asked, instinctively guarding her front.

"He's a serial killer," I told her. "They like to admire what they've done." I shaded my eyes to study another group standing on a balcony. Smoke rose from a grill, thinning at the roofline and then tapering to nothing.

"Do you think he's looking for you?" Tracy asked.

"Let's get down," I said, not responding, taking her hand and dropping back to the road.

"I might just be paranoid," I said, feeling foolish as we returned to Jenni's body, the heat rising from the road along with concern for the time we had. "It could be he's watching in other ways. More passive ways, like the news reports."

"Quite the gathering," Doc Bob said, our turning to the pool of them gathering behind the crime-scene tape.

"This guy is getting a lot of attention," Carla said with an odd look of amusement on her face.

"How's that?" I asked, voice terse.

"The reporters," Carla answered, sitting up, sensing the tension. "I was only mentioning them—"

"Got it," I said, shaking it off, the paranoia continuing and making me hear things too. I glanced over at the news vans that were some distance from the scene, and thankfully blocked from viewing the body. They'd picked up on the radio dispatch about a body and had been steadily arriving since. There were television and radio stations whose call letters I recognized from Philadelphia, the unsolved mystery of the Midnight Killer resurfacing in the news. There were the local reporters too. The ones I'd known from previous cases. They wore sandals and shorts, dressed for the weather from the waist down while maintaining a professional look for the cameras with suit jackets or a blouse, preparing to deliver news about a serial killer striking again. Having been a victim myself and almost murdered, I was beyond tense. But that was no excuse. "Everyone, you'll have to excuse me if I'm short."

"Understandable," Doc Bob said, taking Jenni's shoulder to unfold her body on the ground. "I commend you on being here. That's quite the dedication."

"Dedication," I scoffed beneath my breath as joints creaked and muscles popped, the rigor mortis speaking for Jenni's death. "I owe it to her."

Doc Bob held up his personal recorder, the black case turning white with the light shining on it. He pressed a button, raising a hand to hush us. "Note a distal fracture in the left arm, ulna bone below the wrist area."

I raised my hand as though I were in class, his turning off the recorder. "That occurred while we were trying to escape."

"That's a tough bone to fracture," he said, looking perplexed. "It takes a high force. What happened?"

"The restraints," I answered, and hated that I had to see it again, to relive it. "She was twisting the restraints to loosen the hardware mounted to the wall."

"I see," he said. He gave us a slow nod, saying, "Twisting would certainly apply an unusual amount of force."

I motioned to the bruising around the fracture, and added, "It's an older injury, like the torture on her legs." I went to Jenni's chest, to the single insertion of a pick or stake, the instrument touching her heart and killing her. My breath shuddering as I continued, "This one occurred while I was escaping. I think I heard when it happened."

"Oh, Casey," Tracy said, covering her mouth. "I didn't know that."

"He went to Samantha first, but then he was on Jenni. She was screaming." The single hole in her skin was black and perfectly round, a powerful site that had me shrinking with fear. "The site had blood where she'd been held. Not a lot though."

"There wouldn't be," Doc Bob said. He held up his recorder, adding, "Victim has a single puncture wound. Appears to be same as previous victim. Made by a round instrument through the victim's sternum."

Tracy held her camera up while searching Jenni's skin. "You won't find it," I said, knowing what she was looking for. I held up a finger, indicating one. "Only with Pauline Rydel."

"No Braille? Why not?"

"Pauline Rydel was his first when he arrived to the Outer Banks," I answered and shook my head, sickened that he'd followed me here and stained our home with his touch. "The Braille was a message telling me he was back."

A radio blared in the distance, the beat thumping loud enough to turn our heads. On the southern side of the crime scene, the traffic was backing into the next intersection, further than I could see. Annoyed by the raucous beat, Doc Bob turned off the recorder as I stood and told him, "It'll pass, they'll be turning west in a sec—" I stopped and stared at the car, the color of it a custom bright green neon and orange, the loudness of them clashing, but also working together somehow. It was the windows that had me staring. They were black like the screen on my phone.

"Casey?" Tracy asked, standing next to me. She got on her toes, her gaze following the music. "Do you recognize the car?"

"Not the car." Tracy had an inch or two on me and I had to crane my neck to see. "It's the windows. When I was taken, the car had windows like that."

"The tinting," she said, showing examples on her phone. "It's popular, especially on the coast."

"Yeah, but this was more than just a tint." I texted in our group chat, Nichelle and Jericho included. They'd remained at the water park, continuing the efforts there. As I texted, I asked

Tracy, "I know there are laws when it comes to custom window tinting. We had them up in Philly."

"Already researching..." Tracy said, holding her phone close to her face. "I found it. The window tinting cannot be any darker than thirty-two percent when measured by a window tint meter."

I wrinkled my nose. "Too subjective. It'd need an officer to judge it by the look," I said, wanting a clear reason a patrol would pull over a vehicle and issue a ticket. "What else?"

Tracy held up a finger, saying, "Wait. There's one more. The tint on a windshield cannot extend more than five inches below the top of the windshield or below the AS1 line of the windshield, whichever is longer."

"That one," I exclaimed. "If the entire windshield is tinted, it could warrant a ticket."

Tracy added the laws to the group text, three dots bouncing with replies already starting from Nichelle and Jericho. "Do you remember the windshield?"

"It was after sunset, so the sun wouldn't have caused any glare," I said, straining to remember every detail. "With no sun glare, I should have been able to see clear through the windshield. I couldn't!"

Tracy's eyes bulged and she texted the idea we were working. "That'd be a full windshield, enough to get pulled over."

"A Jeep Latitude, Goodyear brand tires, size 225, and custom tinted windows. Add, the windshield could be in violation with the possibility of outstanding tickets. Have Nichelle search for any issued in the last week." I had to sit, my legs turning to rubber again.

"Detective White!" My name carried on the fading bass beat, a salty breeze washing over my face. It was the reporters calling for a statement. I had ignored them until now, but it was hard to do so with the vileness gnawing inside me. I wanted to face the killer, challenge him, dare him to come after me again.

That'd get him out in the open so we could save Samantha. But I remained still, Jenni's bare feet next to me, the rigor mortis turning them an ugly dark purple where the blood had started to pool. My heart ached for her, and I wanted to mourn her loss. We'd made a connection in that basement, me and her and Samantha. If not for the luck of poorly cured mortar between the cinder blocks, then that could be me on the ground. Seagulls flew over us, the hot sun baking Jenni's dead skin. I was tempted to touch her feet, to console. But there was no consoling the dead. Jenni was gone, and I was a cop with a job to do. The reporter's voices came again, two more joining in the call to me, the first asking, "Do you have anything to say?"

"Yeah!" I answered, standing, and ripping the latex gloves from my hands. Powder scattered in a puffy snap as I turned away from them briefly, instructing Tracy, "You continue here and have Nichelle work the tinting into the vehicle description. There can't be many cars like that one in the Outer Banks."

"You sure about this?" she asked with concern regarding the reporters.

"I'm sure," I told her. To the patrol officer working traffic, I instructed him, "Let's tent the crime scene. We'll be here a while."

"Casey," a reporter shouted, their waving and trying to get my attention.

I faced the microphones rising on boom arms, sponge covered and swaying. Cameras were poised steady, hooded lenses nosing through the crowd of gawkers. The broadcast antennas craned above the trees. I pointed up at the sky and told Tracy, "He's watching. And I've got something to say."

EIGHTEEN

A bathtub. Porcelain coated steel. Samantha's thinning skin was unable to offer any comfort against the hard surface. She tempted a move. A small one to shift the weight from her hip. Perspiration rose on her skin, turning it cold as she tried the move without his hearing her. He heard everything though. Like a bat. Her breathing. Her moans. Even her heartbeat. She was sure of it. There was a radio or a television he'd blare whenever she spoke too, the volume snuffing her voice and leading her to think the walls must be thin. He was hiding. He was hiding her. That meant they had to be close to people.

"No moving!" he said from the other room, his voice guttural. An ache rose from her legs. He'd been at her when they had arrived. He'd taken a chunk of skin and muscle, pinching, and huffing a gratified moan as her eyes rolled into her skull when she passed out. Movement! The bed springs squeaking. Her heart thumped and she braced for the punishment. Fingers glided over the walls as his footsteps approached, the tips of them scraping like nails on a chalkboard, a chilling sound that made her shudder. She smelled him then, her muscles straining tense. But it was too late, his fingers driving through her hair, his hands large enough to grip her head like it was a small ball. "What did I say!"

"I'm sorry," she peeped dryly. With his presence, his squeezing enough to raise tears behind her taped eyelids, she had an opportunity to squirm, to reposition herself. It wasn't a lot. But just enough to bring relief to the arm that had turned numb. "I... I won't do it again. I promise I'll be good."

"Hmm," he answered her with a grunt. They remained still like that for a breath, Samantha sipping the air quietly. He let go abruptly, her head falling to the side. She stayed motionless, heart seizing, fearing what he'd do more.

Her lungs burned as she held in the air and waited for him to leave. He stood, his interest waning. She counted his steps. Counted the ones she could hear. She'd been made blind, but if the chance to escape came, she'd need to know the layout.

A hotel room? she wondered, the bed springs squeaking again. *Or maybe it was a motel room?* she questioned. In her head, she saw cheap motel buildings, the room entrances on the outside facing the parking lots. Wasn't there traffic rumbling in the background whenever the door opened. *A motel,* she concluded. *But which one?*

There were dozens of *no-tell motels* as her aunt Terri used to call them. She'd talk of them as a kind of place where middle-aged men who'd grown exhausted by life went to die alone. Or where people chased a high too far. *Lots of death in those rooms,* Aunt Terri would say. Samantha shook with the thought of being on one of those calls to the medical examiner's office. She would be a body in a bathtub, wrists and ankles bound, eyes taped, tortured and found murdered at twenty-nine.

Tinny voices broke the air, stealing her attention. It was a pair of news broadcasters, she'd heard earlier when he'd watched television last. The speaker rattled with static, which told her there was no cable feed, only television antennas, rabbit ears for signals over the air. The voices grew louder as he turned up the volume, giving her time again to feel out her situation.

Her wrists were bound to what felt like bathroom plumbing, or maybe an iron radiator mounted next to the tub. The metal was thick and cold, offering no movement either, fixed solidly to the floor or wall. The shackles on her wrists had begun to cut deep, the weight of her arms resting on them. She did her best to drape them across her chest, but her motion was limited, the shackle lifting and falling a couple of inches.

Samantha sniffed the air, an ever-present scent of commercial cleaners and soaps filling her nostrils. It had become muted though, her senses fading. She'd be dead soon. She could feel it. And for the first time since he took her, she thought maybe that was okay. Maybe it would be better that this was over. Her heart leapt then when she heard Casey's voice in the other room.

"Hmm!" her abductor snorted. "Detective Casey White."

"Can you tell us if that is another victim?" a reporter asked on the television.

"I am standing here today, not as an Outer Banks detective —" she began to say. A thud shook the floor. Samantha flinched. She couldn't see it but imagined her abductor had left the edge of the bed to kneel in front of the television. *"I am standing here today to deliver a message!"*

"Is it to the Midnight Killer?" a reporter asked, a car horn blaring in the distance. When Casey didn't reply, the reporter rephrased her question, *"What is it you want to say?"*

"Outside," Samantha whispered, hearing the horn, and thinking of reasons why they wouldn't be holding the press conference inside the station. It was the screams. Jenni's screams that bounced in her head, the memory of them fresh, the sound of her wailing still raw. It was in the seconds and minutes that followed Casey's escape, as the killer searched frantically, his knees and hands scraping across the floor, and then scratching and clawing the walls where Casey had been.

His voice had turned maniacal before he took to the wood stair-case in a chase. Jenni's had turned manic too, yelling after Casey, screaming for her. On his return, he'd smelled like a forest, like the sap of trees and discarded leaves. *A star burns its brightest in its dying moments.* Samantha had never known such a truth until then. Her abductor had come back empty-handed, Casey's escape filling her with a hope and energy made of a thousand wishes. But then Jenni had gasped sharply, her voice deadened by a lack of breath. The heat of Casey's escape, the anticipation of being saved, had fizzled extinct as Samantha listened to their abductor murder Jenni Levor. *You found Jenni's body. That's why you're outside.*

"*I'm here to tell you, that you will* not *get me,*" she heard Casey's cold voice through the television. Furniture crashed. A nightstand toppled with a bedside lamp shattering, pieces raining into a pile. "*You wanted me before and couldn't have me then. You want me now, and still can't have me.*"

"Casey White!" he grunted, plastic crunching in what Samantha guessed was his squeezing the sides of the television. "In time."

Please stop, Samantha begged. She pleaded to her aunt Terri's ghost, hoping there was such a thing. With every word, he was getting angrier, and he'd come at her again. *Please make Casey stop.*

"*To the man who took me, I need you to know that you did not hurt me!*"

"Casey—" he began to yell, shutting up when traffic blared from the outside. A windy gust pushed through the open door, the smell of life beyond the motel room washing over Samantha. But who was it? She sat still like prey hiding in the shade of a bush.

"What are you doing?" A woman's voice now, not through the television. Samantha tried to make sense of the new voice in the room. It confirmed what she'd suspected since the night of her abduction. There was a second person. "Look at this place! Don't you understand the circumstance?"

An accomplice. Have there always been two? Samantha thought back to the night of her abduction, to the rat that had run from behind the dumpster. There was Peter Pan's shadow dancing along the walls too. *It wasn't my imagination. He must have been waiting for me at the end of the alley.* Samantha's body went cold as she shook. *It was a trap. Someone drove me into his arms.*

"Casey White," he groveled, bed springs creaking. "She won't get away again. Not again."

"Casey White," the woman answered and began cleaning debris, the lamp's ceramic pieces stirring. "I don't think there's going to be a third opportunity. We should never have gone after her again."

"We have to—" he tried arguing.

Bed springs interrupted, her joining him as she spoke calmly, "We can't risk a third strike."

"It's Casey White," he said. "You know what she took from me."

"Well, it's not like you didn't start it," the woman scoffed.

"Get off," he snapped. There was a thump.

Samantha listened. It sounded like the woman was pulling herself back up from the floor, recomposing herself, brushing her arms and legs, before attempting to console him, appease his disappointment. "We'll get you another one. I can find you someone who looks like Casey White."

"Are you trying to make a joke about this?" he yelled.

"No! I didn't mean it like that." Footsteps approached the bathroom. There was fear in her voice, which struck fear in Samantha. "I meant that I'll find someone the same height and build, everything as your precious Detective Casey White."

"Needs to be soon," he said, turning the television up, the reporters continuing to ask questions. While they didn't state a name, Samantha knew it was Jenni they were talking about. The killer's mood shifted with the change in the questioning. "We did that."

Again, Samantha thought as shoes clopped against the thin carpet and then stopped at the bathroom doorway. The reporter had called her abductor the *Midnight Killer*. Was it an old case? Unsolved murders? The killer knew Casey. But how?

"Water?" Samantha asked, sensing the woman standing next to the tub, staring at her.

"Does it matter?" the woman answered coldly. She let out a sigh then and cranked the handle, the faucet running. Samantha could only see the faint light bleed through her blindfold and listened to a finger beating the stream to check its temperature. Did the killer's accomplice care? Or was it simply out of habit? When the water stopped running, a knee popped as the woman knelt next to the tub. "Couple sips of water."

"Thank you," Samantha said, her mind stuck on the word water. Only, what she heard was *wooder*. This woman kneeling next to her sounded like Casey. It was a Philadelphia accent she'd picked up on when working with the detective. There were other words like dollar, which sounded like *dolluh*. And whenever she saw the team, she'd say yo, its sounding like *ye-oh*. But water was the one that stood out. There was no mistaking the pronunciation of *wooder*. The Midnight Killer must be an old case from Casey's hometown. But now he was here in the Outer Banks.

"Mm," his accomplice said as she ran her finger down Samantha's cheek. The woman breathed softly and touched Samantha's other cheek, running the tip of her finger along her skin where there was no cut. "I think we'll finish this tonight."

NINETEEN

I never thought I'd be so happy to see the station again. To see my desk and my computer with its dusty monitor and keyboard. I was even happy to see our empty conference room, the monitors displaying maps of cell towers, the long table littered with the remnants of activity. There was computer gear and case files, empty coffee cups and water bottles, the whiteboard had been scribbled on and erased a dozen times over, the room used to coordinate the search for me. It wouldn't be empty for long, activity resuming, a team of FBI agents arriving behind us to help with Samantha's search. I stepped into my cubicle, clearing the path as they made a beeline toward the conference room.

On the far wall there was a new display, a projector hanging from the ceiling to show a blue and green map with a string of cell towers across the Outer Banks and along the western shores of North Carolina. On each of the towers there was a red beacon, its color flickering like a flame. It was Nichelle's work, a map of the cell tower pings, the marks like breadcrumbs left by my cell phone and its last positions before my abduction.

"Philadelphia," I said to her as she entered the room. She stood next to me as I stared at the cell towers. We hadn't been alone since the car ride to Arch Street, and I wanted to hear how she felt about the move. "It's a huge move."

Nichelle said nothing, a backpack slipping from her shoulder to drop onto a chair. Her arms were around me with a squeeze that took my breath. Her hair was big today, curly and tall instead of the usual braids she wore. It tickled my face with the scent of her shampoo as she spoke into my ear, "I'm so sorry this happened to you. How are you?"

"I'll be fine," I said, leaning back. I nudged my chin toward the display with the cell tower pings. "I think I've got you to thank for that."

She dipped her head, speaking with disappointment, "It didn't exactly save you."

"I got my cell phone back," I said, holding it up, the projector's light glinting on the new screen. "Hasn't looked this clean since I first took it out of the box."

She frowned, asking, "Ever wonder why he didn't take it?"

"I did," I answered, tucking it safely into my back pocket. "I remember dropping it when he grabbed me. The alley was dark."

"He might not have seen it?" she guessed. Her gaze changed, focus shifting as she bit her upper lip. It was about Philadelphia, the discussion making me nervous with butterflies in my belly. Nichelle watched Tracy through the conference room windows, saying, "She's torn about the move, but she won't admit it."

"Not going to lie, but I'm torn too." A part of me was happy to hear about the struggle. I'd just gotten Tracy back in my life. I was eager to get to the case, Jericho entering as I tried to assure her, "It'll work out. Promise."

Jericho reviewed the map, the cell towers, asking, "Nichelle, can you show the cell tower pings for Samantha's phone?"

"It's the first map," she replied as new FBI agents filed into the conference room and took to seats as though they were assigned. She flicked a keyboard, answering, "Not very helpful. The last cell tower ping was the night she was abducted."

"It was a long shot. How about the vehicle make and model and the window tinting?" I asked, feeling the strain of the case and needing to sit.

"I stopped by the DMV office in Nags Head," he said, shaking his head. "It's basically a satellite office for North Carolina DMV—"

"We've got access to the systems," an agent interrupted. Early twenties, his glasses with a thick black frame. He pushed them against his nose, adding, "With Nichelle's help, we'll have a list compiled any minute now."

"Better than I could do," Jericho said, turning his attention back to me. "While we wait for the results, what else can you tell us?"

I closed my eyelids to concentrate, to try and think beyond the punishments he'd inflicted. But torture can have a powerful hold. I raised my arms, recalling some details from the night he took me. "A big man. Must be over six foot five, possibly taller." Keyboards rattled and mouse buttons clicked. I splayed my fingers, turning my wrist sideways, the bone and skin yelling back. "His hand covered most of my face."

"Mouth and nose?" an agent asked. I opened my eyelids and followed the voice. "Any particulars?"

"Skin wasn't rough. There were no callouses on his hands," I answered, the idea of callouses leading to someone working a trade, their livelihood made with their hands. I lowered my arms to my sides, recalling how my body felt pressed against his, the feel of a dress shirt and slacks. "He would be someone that works in an office. He dressed more formal than casual."

"White collar," someone commented. "Business attire?"

"Perhaps. And knowledgeable of chemistry, application of sedatives." Questions formed on the faces of the agents. I touched my lips. "It's how he subdues his victims. It's in his palm and he covers your mouth and nose."

"Do you recall there being gauze?" The agent running the DMV query asked. He pushed the frame of his glasses, only to have them slide down his nose again. "Could be ether?"

I shook my head. "I don't recall a sweet smell, the kind with ether." I shrugged, hating that the memories were broken. "I wish I could think of more."

"We've got a car!" one of the agents shouted. "Description is the same. Cited for window tinting on the windshield."

"Tags?" I asked in near yell. "Pennsylvania?"

She nodded, answering, "Pennsylvania."

"Who was the ticket issued to?" I asked, wanting to see a driver's license photograph.

Nichelle frowned, answering, "It wasn't a moving violation."

"You mean it was a ticket tucked beneath the windshield?" I asked, rethinking what we had, what we could use. "Like a parking ticket? Nobody in the car?"

Nichelle sensed the disappointment but gave me a nod. "But we do have a license plate number."

"How about a VIN number?" I asked, knowing it might not have been included. Nichelle shook her head, hair swaying. "Plate number. What can we get from it?"

"What I miss?" Steve Sholes asked, carrying three large pizza boxes. He stopped in front of me and placed the food onto the conference table, the smell reminding me I hadn't eaten. He wrinkled his face then and rocked his head. "Not quite the level of a Philly pie, but it'll do."

I held up my hand to hush him, defending the Outer Banks. "Trust me, it's really good pizza," I said, taking a slice as I regarded the license plate number. "To catch you up. There's the make and model of the vehicle, and the heavily tinted windshield."

"We've got one ticket, but it's not a moving violation," Tracy continued, the team crowding around the boxes as I moved to the window. "No vehicle identification number, just the license plate."

"PA tags," Nichelle added, and read the numbers, plugging them into her laptop.

"From Pennsylvania," Steve commented, swiping his mouth as he watched the screen, the hourglass standing at the center of it and doing somersaults. "You have access to the PA DMV?"

"Would you pass me that water bottle?" someone asked.

A chill ran through me. "Wooder!" I exclaimed, the bustle around the pizza ceased. One by one, questionable looks came in my direction. I motioned to the water bottles. "He pronounced water, like I do."

"Like me too. Wooder," Steve said. With a slow nod, he added, "Pennsylvania plates. That's a good sign that we're onto him."

"There he is," Nichelle said, standing and joining me. Jericho and Tracy stood as well, a row of us in front of the screen, a picture flickering with an expired driver's license for a man named, Dan Viken. I could feel the return of the team's stare, their wanting to see recognition on my face. "Is that him?"

"I was blindfolded," I answered, pawing at my swollen eyelids. "The license says he's six feet nine inches and 300 pounds."

"Whoa," Tracy said, her mouth open, fright on her face. "That's a big guy."

"Turn it off," someone said. The pizza was gone from my hands, its slipping through my fingers and landing on my plate with a slap. The room had suddenly become suffocatingly small and hot like the pump room's basement when the day had nearly baked us alive. I clutched the edge of the table and found a chair, Jericho's hands taking hold as I collapsed into the seat.

"I just need a minute," I said, waving to a bottle of water.

The plastic cap ticked as it was spun free from the top. I guzzled half, cooling my throat, and clearing my head.

"Let us take it from here," Steve insisted, a frown on his face. He lifted his chin in Nichelle's direction and her team, their sitting unmoving like statues, each with the exact same FBI garb, bright yellow embroidered letters on dark blue polo shirts. "We've got this, Sunny."

"I have to," I told Steve.

"Maybe he's right," Jericho said. "We can take it from here."

"It's Samantha," I said, patting Jericho's hand as he gave my shoulder a gentle squeeze. I peered into his blue-green eyes, explaining, "I have to see this through."

Jericho knelt until his face was level with mine. "Then we'll see this through," he said and smiled reassuringly. Steve thumped the desk, his muffled breath sharp as he raised his hands defeated and moved behind Nichelle and her team. He crossed his arms and shifted his attention to their computers.

A name had appeared on the screen. "Viken," I read aloud as I recalled the name from the *Philadelphia Inquirer's* society section, remembering the family's interludes with everything from politics to CEOs and even the city churches. "There's a lot of money and power there."

"Dan Viken, University of Pennsylvania graduate. A top surgeon for most of his career," Nichelle read from her screen. "He retired abruptly ten years ago and became a recluse."

"A surgeon, and a serial killer?" I commented, asking aloud. "He went into seclusion after our rooftop chase?"

"Yeah, I bet he did!" Steve scoffed. He fixed a hard look at me, his thumb pointed at the screen. "Is that our guy?"

"A surgeon, like Jack the Ripper," Tracy said, adding a reference to the notorious serial killer.

"Our Midnight Killer had five murders. Like the ripper's five," I said, seeing the connection. "But add Jenni Levor and Pauline Rydel, we're at seven."

"Samantha would be eight," Tracy added, her stare telling me what I already knew. That I could have been number nine. I'd have been one of them too. "Ripper was just a thought."

"Keep at it," I said, not wanting to see her discouraged. "It's those thoughts that sometimes find us the most helpful insight."

"Not much family," Nichelle continued as she scanned the web pages.

"What else?" I was concerned about why he'd disappeared. "Does it say anything about his retirement?"

Nichelle read on silently, lips moving. "Uh-uh. Some press about possible medical issues."

"Medical issues?" I asked, recalling his grip around my body, the strength in it. "Whatever it might have been, that was ten years ago."

"Not relevant?" Steve asked, sounding skeptical. "But you think this is him?"

I glanced around the room, knowing I was the closest thing to a witness we had. "Viken has the height and build which matches the man who attacked me."

"Was there anything else distinguishing you recall?" an agent asked me.

"Nichelle, you said not much family. Wasn't there a sister?" I asked, unable to break my stare on the screen. Viken was a handsome man. Chiseled features. A high-class debutant look to him with straight teeth and perfect nose. His brow was without blemish, his hair black and combed back. There wasn't a crazed look in his eyes. Not the maniacal glare I'd seen in some killers. To look at his driver's license picture, he was entirely facile and without distinction. That is, except for his size which gave me pause if we were to come toe to toe with him.

"Good memory," Nichelle said, posting a grainy picture of Viken and his sister. The picture took me back to a time when tall hair was sprayed out of a can, and when clothes were made of polyester instead of cotton. Their faces were pitted in shade, both wearing hats, his a derby, and hers a fashionable top that I thought looked gaudy. "She was killed in a car fire."

"Twelve years ago," Steve said. "I remember the parents insisted we open an investigation. They died shortly afterward."

"What did the investigation turn up?" Jericho stood up, his question focusing on a possible homicide. A brother killing his sister. "Murder?"

"The fire was found suspicious," he answered. "I think it's still an unsolved case."

Tracy began typing. "Could be something there."

I lifted my chin, approving the work. I faced the screen again, asking, "Is that the only picture we have?" It was impossible to shake the notion of a woman having been involved in my abduction. Nichelle shook her head. "Send me the one you've got."

"What are you thinking?" Steve asked, a frown forming.

"There was someone else in the pump house with us. I'm sure of it." I gazed at the table and my slice of uneaten pizza. "Nichelle, also search old society page articles on budding romances. Was he always a bachelor, ever engaged?"

"I gotcha," she answered. "Searching."

"The accomplice?" Jericho asked. "You think a couple is working here?"

"I only know he's not working alone," I answered, the room stirring with my comment. "But I've got no hard evidence to support that either."

"Sunny, I can't buy into there being two," Steve said, his brow furrowed. "We've never suspected there was anyone else involved."

I could feel the agitation. Jericho did as well, his body tensing. "Playing it safe. If we get a location, then we have to go in knowing there could be more than one person!"

Steve lifted his head and regarded the risks. "That's fair," he agreed.

"Looks like we'll have a chance to find out," Jericho said, holding out his phone so we could see the screen. "We've got a sighting for the car with those PA plates. It's a motel across Wrights Bridge. The car is parked in front of room 12b."

"Let's roll!" Steve shouted, the room bursting with activity.

"Badges, vests and firearms," I yelled over the noise. Hoping positively, thinking about Samantha, I said, "Have an ambulance there as well!"

TWENTY

A steady rain began as we crossed the bridge, Currituck Sound beneath us, windshield wipers swiping the glass with a whomp whomp in every pass. I couldn't break my stare, the patrol vehicles in front of us blurred by the downpour, raindrops the size of grapes exploding on the glass. Steve's car smelled of the dampness too. A scatter of crumped food wrappers on the floor, along with empty soda bottles.

"I see your diet hasn't improved much since we worked together," I commented while he slouched close to the steering wheel, concentration locked on his face.

"Yeah," he answered, half listening. When he looked down at my shoes, he added, "Oh, yeah. You know. Cop to cop, on the road."

"Yep, eat whenever and whatever we can." I tipped a fast-food burger bag, recalling the number of times my car had looked the same. We were still three miles from the motel, Jericho driving with Tracy and Nichelle. "Listen, I wanted to say thank you."

Steve glanced over his arm, the look brief but warm before returning to the drive in front of us. "Are you kidding? I had to come down here. I couldn't see you take all the glory for catching this guy."

"You know what I mean," I said, wanting to smack his arm.

He looked over at me again. Longer this time, and with sincerity in his eyes. "I'll always think of you as a partner. You know that. Anything you need. Anything ever."

"I appreciate that," I said. "It's been good here."

"I know. I see it." He spun the wheel, turning it left, the motel's parking lot filling with patrol vehicles and unmarked FBI vehicles. "I'm glad you're okay. You've got one heck of a fan club down here."

"Yeah I do." I smiled at the thought of the team. My family. I pulled my badge from beneath my vest, the metal untarnished and without a single scratch. It was newly issued, replacing the one I'd lost. "Ready?"

"Ready!" Steve answered, his voice filling with excitement. "Ten years I've been waiting for this guy."

My blood felt hot as it ran fast through my veins. I was ready and feeding off the vibes. "Let's do it!"

We exited his car, shoes clopping against pavement, sloshing in puddles, the FBI taking the lead with a battering ram. I ducked next to Steve, our bodies behind an agent carrying a ballistic shield, the momentum racing with my heartbeat. An agent held up his fist, three fingers splayed. I swallow the spit in my mouth, clenching my jaw when he counted down silently, leaving his middle finger perched to tell us it was a go on the next count. "Here we go," Steve whispered and licked his lips, his eyelids peeled back. He glanced over at me, brow bouncing, and mouthed, "And one!"

The agents swung the battering ram with a collective heave, the butt of it smashing the motel room building with unforgiving force. The door splintered easily, wood shrapnel and paint scattering in an explosion, metal ringing through the air, the door's lock and handle flying freely. "Freeze! Freeze!

Freeze!" the team yelled, their guns drawn as we poured into the room.

I kept to the single file, staying safely behind the agent with the shield. The walls were a dingy eggshell color, the corners chipped and worn, the carpet threadbare. I slowed when seeing the man who must have abducted me.

His head was turned away from my eyes and then disappeared completely when agents dove on top of him, the motel bed frame crashing from the weight of them all. "Samantha," I told Steve, racing past the agents to the only other room.

"Go!" he said while working his way around the bed.

I passed the television, which was showing a news broadcast, the motel showing in a live feed, the reporters already on location and broadcasting. On the screen, there was the parked car, the windows tinted dark, almost black. It was the car from the parking lot of the K-Beatz night club, the sight of it validating my memory of that day. When I got to the other room, I brushed my hand over the wall, searching for a light switch, tripping it when my fingers struck the wall plate.

The bathroom was tiny with rose-colored tiles on the walls. A lime-green toilet and sink were an arm's length apart. The tub was the same color, narrow and short, the faucet dripping onto Samantha's feet. Her body was curled in a fetal position, her knees locked against the porcelain, frozen in place and without movement. She wore only a bra and panties, her skin a grim color, the bruising from the killer's torture covering her thighs. He'd moved toward her feet, snacking on her calves and around her knees, the skin broken recently, leaving bloody welts that showed his behavior was escalating.

The floor was tiled black and white where I spotted dried blood, the injury coming from an open wound on Samantha's wrists. Her arms were pinned above her head, hands chained to the plumbing. My heart lifted as she stirred to the sounds outside, her face covered in duct tape, eyes and mouth hidden, her nostrils flaring as her breathing deepened. She scurried back like a caged animal, fear driving her movements. "Samantha!"

"Mm!" she replied, recognizing my voice, her body shaking uncontrollably.

"Keys!" I yelled over my shoulders, the locks on her shackles triple what he'd used on us in the pump room. "And send in the paramedics."

"Mmmmaaaccy," Samantha cried behind the duct tape as she tried to say my name.

"Let's get this shit off of you," I said and carefully removed the blindfold, thankful to find that the duct tape wasn't directly on her skin. The cloth he'd used before was beneath it, saving her eyelids. "Try opening your eyes."

"Mm mm," she answered, squinting fiercely, cringing at the brightness. There was enough light coming from the other room and I flipped the switch on the wall. She focused on me with a lazy gaze but smiled when my face became clear to her. "Mmmk meddder."

"Much better?" I said, interpreting her words. She opened her eyelids, pupils expanding as she studied my face. Tears fell when I touched my forehead to hers and kissed her face. "We've got you. You're safe now."

"Mmm!" Samantha cried, cheeks wet, chain rattling. Her focus shifted to her wrists.

"Mouth first?" I felt choked up but kept at the work. "This is going to hurt." The tape on her mouth was in direct contact with her skin, pulling and stretching it wildly as I pinched and lifted the edges. I stopped, not wanting to hurt her. "Samantha, don't hate me. But I think the paramedics might know a better way to do this."

"Mmm Kaayyy," she said with a nod, her words unintelligible.

"Casey!" Steve yelled. "I think you're gonna want to take a look at this!"

"Send the paramedics in here," I yelled back, adding, "And give them the keys. He has them. He always has them."

"Casey!" he replied, raising his voice. "You need to see this!"

"When you need something, I guess it is best to do it yourself." I put on a sad smile, telling Samantha, "I promise that I'll be right back."

"Mmm hmm," she said, which I interpreted as an okay. I kissed her again, touching the teardrop cut on one cheek. I was elated to see her alive, to have gotten to her in time. "Be right back."

"Casey," Steve said as a pair of paramedics entered the motel room. They stopped and gave the activity on the floor a cursory look, an agent shooing them along into the bathroom.

"In here guys," I told the lead paramedic. "There's duct tape I can't get off her face."

"We'll get it," the paramedic said, her gaze fixed on the floor, on a pair of legs and stocking feet.

"Did you find the keys on him?" I asked Steve. He grunted and strained as he knelt on the suspect. The man was a giant and needed three agents to hold him in place. Even then, the men bounced whenever the suspect bucked. Lying on his belly, his face shoved into the floor, his legs were nearly a yard beyond the end of the bed and as big as scuba fins. It wasn't just his height that struck me. It was the width of his shoulders, they were broad and muscular, his waist was thin, his build like a body builder. "Keys!"

"Here," Steve said, handing them to me. Nerves grated through me like a razor, turning my skin electric as though conducting a voltage. I shuffled my feet, not wanting to be anywhere close to the man who'd tortured me. I inhaled sharply at the sight of the pliers on the nightstand, the tip of them an inch thick, the size of them large like he was. The suspect stirred from beneath Steve's knees, his head turning toward me.

If I didn't know any better I thought he was enjoying how uncomfortable I'd become. "Big boy."

"What did you want to show me?" We already knew the suspect was a big man. There had to be something else. I jangled the keys, adding, "I want to get back in there."

"I think I know what happened to him ten years ago," Steve said, whistling a deep breath as he and another officer worked to move the suspect up. "Take a look at this!"

Steve's face turned a brilliant red, the suspect's weight making him strain as he manhandled his position. My concern for the officers and Steve's welfare disappeared when the abductor peered up at me. I did all that I could to remain standing. "What the—" I began to say.

"Detective Casey White," Viken exclaimed and sniffed at the air. "I can still smell the antiseptic from your layover at the hospital."

"Quiet!" Steve snapped while I stared with disbelief. There was only a faint resemblance to the picture we'd found on the DMV records. His black hair hung limp across his forehead, strands of salty gray strewn throughout. The same grays were around his mouth and beneath his nose, a week's worth of stubble growing thick. It was his eyes I couldn't stop looking at. The skin around them was marred with deep scars, some gnarled like the bark of an old oak tree while others were pencil-thin in crisscrossed slashes. A few were the length of my index finger, dividing his left brow with a cleft the width of my pinky. The other brow was mostly gone, as if the skin had been torn away from his face and replaced with a graft. The remains of his eyelids were open, flickering with a tremor that seemed unintentional, the nerves and muscles beneath damaged beyond repair.

Viken's eyes were fixed on me. I couldn't break free of them. They were milky gray and white, one of them puckered with a dimple. His eyes shifted whenever I moved as though he were watching me. But of course, he couldn't be. Did he know I was staring at him? He winked as if he'd heard me, the suddenness making me jump. He heard me move and laughed, Steve wrestling him quiet. The Braille message on Pauline Rydel's body suddenly made sense. The Midnight Killer was blind.

He blew me a kiss, laughing, "Ain't I a sight!"

TWENTY-ONE

The rains never let up, fat drops drumming the motel roof. The downpours relaxed now and again, taking a breath before the next wave, but the forecast warned we wouldn't see sunshine until Monday. Viken was taken into custody, the jurisdiction coming into question. For now, amidst the activity of a crime, namely Samantha, North Carolina presided over Pennsylvania given the arrest took place here. There was also my abduction and torture, while Philadelphia's cases were cold cases. In time, Viken would see the inside of the courtrooms in both states.

I was surrounded by my team, all of us working to investigate the hotel room. It was a crime scene, but thankfully there was no body, no need to call Doc Bob and his assistant, Carla. Light flashed from Tracy's direction as she took pictures of Viken's belongings. Nichelle and her FBI team scoured through them, which wasn't more than a duffel bag with a day's worth of clothes. An agent spread the clothes on the bed, using the end of his pen to fan the arms of a shirt. Why would he have just one day's worth? Where was he coming from? A better question was, where was he going?

"You believe me now?" I asked Steve. He stood with Jericho

to watch the mayor give a news conference. A shadow of her tall figure was cast by the news conference lights. "Viken has an accomplice."

"I suppose he must have," Steve said, pinching his chin and making tsk-tsk kisses. It was a tell of his. Whenever he was wrong about something. "If he was working alone then he is the only blind man I know that can drive."

"Exactly," I said coldly. "So who did the driving?"

The rattle of a gurney interrupted us. "Guys," Samantha said faintly, her fingers clutching Nichelle's hand as the paramedics rolled the gurney.

"You'll be back on your feet in no time," Nichelle said, her voice choppy. "I'm so sorry we didn't walk home with—"

"Stop a minute," Samantha demanded, wrists limp, her strength weak. "Uh-uh. This isn't anyone's fault."

"We should have walked with you," Tracy said, her arm around Nichelle as the two huddled closer to Samantha.

"Nobody's fault," Samantha continued to say, the paramedics insisting they keep moving.

"I'll stop by the hospital," I told Samantha, brushing her arm with my hand, the touch of her cold. I hoped she'd bounce back from this. But truthfully, I wasn't sure. An attack like Viken's could cripple even the strongest of wills. "We love you."

The paramedics exited the motel room, Samantha raising her hand in a wave, the scene of them flooded by flashing lights. With the light, it was in the darkest corners of the motel room that I began my search. Wood scraped wood with drawers opening and closing, the odor of mothballs and mildew filling the room. Jericho joined in the help as we searched every available space.

"There's only those," Jericho said, eyeing Viken's clothes on the bed.

I picked up the keys from the nightstand, a key fob on the biggest of the keyrings. "We can check the car next," I said,

peering through a curtain to see the reporters disband. Two officers wrapped yellow and black crime-scene tape around posts to
guard the room. The door would be blocked after we left,
marking the room as evidence in an ongoing investigation.

"Viken is blind," Jericho said as he faced me and Steve.
"Someone checked into this room and drove that car."

"It was Viken," Tracy answered. "I checked with the front
desk. They remembered him. Said it was impossible to forget
him."

"Viken checked into the room?" I asked, sharing in the
confusion. "There's got to be a second car."

"That, or is it possible his accomplice got an Uber or a
Lyft?" Steve asked.

I raised my hand, Nichelle nodding with a reply, "I'm on it.
Just warning you, they're stingy about customer privacy."

"They won't be when we have our warrant. And we're still
trying to figure out the questions," I said, feeling as though we'd
hit a wall when it came to finding Viken's accomplice. "There's
not a damn thing here to show he'd had anyone but Samantha."

Steve scratched his chin, fingernails rubbing whiskers while
he scanned the room again. "We're done here?"

"I think we are," I told him, handing the key fob to an agent.
"You'll report your findings?"

"Yeah, sure," he said, looking to Nichelle for confirmation.
She gave him a nod to include me.

"Viken?" Nichelle asked. "He's next?"

"He's the only place we'll get answers," I said and tried to
muster the courage to do the interview.

"Do you think he'll tell you who he's working with?" the
agent asked.

"We'll see. But that's not the only thing we need from him."
I went to the motel room door, the parking lot bare and the
reporters gone. Streetlights bounced off the puddles, the air
misty and warm, patrol officers guarding the door and Viken's

vehicle for fingerprinting. I looked over my shoulder, adding, "We want to know what happened ten years ago."

We added to our team. Nichelle calling in additional FBI support to cover the motel room and Viken's vehicle. We'd extended our team already with a few still working the abandoned water park, the pump room and investigating the path Viken had taken from Philadelphia. Nichelle sent pictures of the new members, their wearing forensic body suits and arriving with a van filled with equipment. The walls, the furniture, the bathroom sink and toilet were all candidates to dust for fingerprints. They'd shine UV black lights against the walls to detect bodily fluids. They'd work on their hands and knees to tease the carpet fibers, seeking out a strand of hair or a fingernail, a piece of skin perhaps. We'd take anything that could support DNA, hoping to link Viken to Pauline's murder and the scenes from years ago.

While half the team worked the motel room, the other half would devour the vehicle. Nichelle sent pictures of that too, the level of resources and expediency something to be in awe of. They didn't risk moving Viken's car to a garage. Instead, they cordoned off the motel's parking lot and erected a tent around it. Pumps with electrostatic filters controlled the airflow, puffing the walls of the tent when producing a negative pressure. The car remained closed until the lower air pressure was established inside the tent. That way, when they opened a door, anything that we could use, from the smallest fiber of dust to the tiniest hair follicle, would remain contained. They left nothing to chance.

With a primordial soup of hairs and fingerprints and skin, we were certain to find Viken's DNA. And we'd also recover DNA from Samantha and Jenni Levor. Even my prints and hair and my DNA would be recovered. But once all the victims and

Viken had been reconciled, if there was any finding left unaccounted, then it was a clue for us to use in finding the killer's accomplice.

I was weak, my body and mind feeding on adrenaline, sipping at it like it was a firecracker cocktail. It kept my heart pumping and my thoughts churning. I'd collapse soon enough though. But if I could help it, I'd keep pace and work non-stop until Viken's accomplice was in custody. The cut beneath my eye had started to scab. I knew I was awake, knew I was alive whenever the healing stitched a new thread of skin, making it itch. I had to be thankful it wasn't worse. That it wasn't like what I'd seen on the other victims.

Coffee. It tasted different today. Then again, the station smelled different too and had begun to empty. It was Saturday and the wall clock passed the five o'clock hour as the station played a medley of laptop bags being packed, the rustle of rain jackets, zippers in motion, chair wheels crawling beneath desks, and the steady murmur of *goodbyes* and *see ya tomorrow.* To me, the sounds were off, but I couldn't place why. I closed my eyelids and listened, sipping the coffee again, the blandness of it. What was different was in my head. It was me. It wasn't the station. I'd been a victim, and maybe that had changed me.

"Uh-uh," I scoffed. Convinced it was exhaustion from the days and nights running together. This had been a long, sleepless nightmare, but it'd be over soon. "Then I'll sleep."

The air was humid, the late hour at the station without the hum of air conditioning, the municipality working an energy saving campaign. That included turning off most of the office lights, and some of the television monitors to help lower electricity costs. The results were eerie, putting the station's office space in shade, the cubicle walls invisible, the glass separating the rooms turning into ghostly reflections. There was just the one television that remained on, the screen throwing light onto the ceiling with the broadcast of the mayor's announcement about Samantha's rescue, and the capture of a suspect.

While she wouldn't call him the Midnight Killer, the reporters from Philadelphia weren't shy about making the connection. They knew who we had. But they had no idea who he really was. How long would it be before they ran the license plate number? The owner of the car would be public knowledge. By daybreak, I'd expect national-level news about the once famous and rich Philadelphia bachelor being named a serial killer.

The coffee was too hot to hold, the tips of my fingers burning. Maybe I held it a moment too long, disregarding the pain while I watched our suspect. The glass between me and the suspect was a one-way mirror. And though he was blind, I'm sure he knew I was watching. I could tell by the way he tilted his head, turning it subtly to the side like a wolf catching the scent of its next kill. I'd almost been that for him. I'd almost become his next kill, but I'd escaped. Jenni Levor didn't though. Neither did the six other women he'd tortured and killed.

What was it that drove his desires? His compulsions? What was his motive? An ache thrummed in my legs, the grip of the pliers squeezing until I screamed. There was no motive here other than seeing others in pain. In some sick way, I think Viken was a vampire. He fed on us, fed on the agony raged from his punishment.

I raised my hand and touched the glass. One finger only, careful and gentle, softer than picking the petal of a flower. Viken moved, one half of a brow lifting as he turned an ear in my direction.

"No more," I said with a smack against the glass. Viken didn't jump. The sharp strike didn't startle him. He'd tuned his hearing efficiencies in the years of blindness. I opened the door, my gaze fixed on the threshold as I dared to step inside. Chains scraped across the metal seat and table. The shackles on his wrists hung loose, draped but not so loose that he was a threat. He saw that I was standing in the door. Saw me the way the blind can see. He lifted his chin, acknowledging my presence and then politely motioned to the chair across from him. "Where did you go ten years ago?"

"You waste no time," he answered with a pout. "Tsk-tsk. I'm disappointed."

"I don't care that you're disappointed. That's not how this is going to go—"

"Your boyfriend is here?" Viken interrupted, running his fingers across his head, chains clanking. "He's watching us."

Jericho? But he'd gone home. Viken was referring to Steve. "The detective has an interest in the murders you committed in Philadelphia."

"Home," he said smugly. He smiled broadly, showing his perfectly straight teeth, without stain or age. "Will I be extradited soon?"

"In time, I'm sure." I couldn't help but wince when I crossed my legs. Viken shifted as if feeding on it. "I understand your lawyer is on the way."

"Lawyers," he corrected me. He made a tut-tut sound and licked his lips, expecting me to offer him a drink. I sipped my coffee instead while he pinched the sides of his mouth and ran the tips of his fingers across his lips. "But don't you worry yourself. We can still chat."

"Are you sure?" I questioned, wanting to challenge him. "I wouldn't want you to incriminate yourself."

"A damp towel in the refrigerator," he answered, ignoring my question. His gnarled eyebrows bounced subtly while motioning to my legs. "Compression for ten to twenty minutes. Repeat every few hours. They'll go away sooner."

"I already have a doctor," I said, tone sharp with annoyance. "Tell me what happened to you ten years ago."

"To what are you referring?" He flashed another smile,

finding fun in the conversation. But I wasn't in the mood to play games. It could be he was just buying time while his lawyers traveled from Philadelphia. "I live a full life. You'll have to narrow it down for me, Casey."

"Detective White." I shifted again, the chair's seat proving too hard as sweat beaded across my brow. I took my mind off it by staring at the injuries to his eyes. I focused on the dimpled one, saw how the puckered scar moved as though he could see. "Who did that to you? Did you cross a woman who fought back?"

He slammed the metal table with a laugh. Raucous and violent as he threw his head back and stretched his arms as wide as the chains allowed. Instinctively, I reared away from him. There was motion behind the mirror, Steve shuffling to inter-vene. I held up my hand to show I was okay. When Viken recomposed himself, he cleared his throat and said, "You really have no idea. Do you?" He dragged his finger beneath one eye, pulling open the ripped skin to show the depth of the scarring. I gasped, the sound of it nearly silent. But with his hearing, he heard my reaction. He began to chuckle and said, "Isn't it a sight! Of course, I'll never know just how gruesome."

"You know what I think? I think you attacked the wrong woman, and she made you pay."

He nodded, agreeing. "Yes. In so many words," he said, and turned serious. "Only, I never got her like I had planned. I was close though."

His accomplice, I thought, and wondered if in some crazy way, the woman who'd done this to him, enjoyed it. He might have crossed paths with a woman just like him, the two nurturing their sadistic needs. "Is she the one who's helping you now?" I asked, moving to gage his reaction, searching for a tell, a twitch or a change in his breathing, anything that indicated when he was telling the truth and when he was lying. "Was she the one in the car when you took me?"

"Oh she was there," he answered, leaning closer, gesturing to me. Steve tapped on the glass, warning me to stay clear. "You really have no idea?"

"Who!?" I demanded, becoming frustrated. "Who did that to you?"

"You did!"

TWENTY-TWO

My questioning Viken ended abruptly. He was educated and smart and had been playing a game. I wouldn't have another opportunity to speak with him. Not without his lawyers and the DA in the room. I made a beeline toward the conference room, the scent of pizza still lingering, most of the seats empty. There were only a few of us remaining. I'd given the okay to stand down, to pick up in the morning. Samantha was in the hospital and safe with a patrol officer guarding her room. We had Viken in a holding cell and without knowing it, he'd given me a significant clue.

"Want me to call anyone back?" Nichelle asked. She pressed the side of her head, frizzy hair leaning as she rested against Tracy's shoulder. They looked exhausted, but I wanted more before I rested my head on a pillow. Jericho had joined the impromptu meeting, his arriving to take me home. I figured Steve had sent him a text, telling him we were done with Viken and suggesting Jericho take me out of the station before I collapsed. "Casey? I can get a couple of them?"

"A few queries," I answered and rolled a chair from beneath

the table, inviting her to sit. She rubbed her eyes as I opened her laptop. "I promise this will be quick."

"Sunny? You got something out of that?" Steve asked, his mouth full as he chewed on a rind of dry pizza crust. Jericho frowned, not knowing the outcome. Steve slowly shook his head, adding, "Viken lawyered up."

"The DA will have him on charges here," Jericho said, taking a slice of pizza. Since my abduction, he'd been working around the clock too. The fatigue was getting to him, showing with bloodshot eyes saddled by dark bags and his mouth sagging. His face was gaunt too which had me thinking he hadn't eaten.

"Some water?" I offered, moving next to him, my hand on his back. It was after hours, public displays of affection allowed. My guard was down and I wrapped an arm around his middle. "There's plenty of food."

"What queries did you have in mind?" Tracy asked as she teamed up with Nichelle, the glow of laptop screens shining on their faces.

"Philadelphia 911 archives," I said without looking up.

"From the rooftop chase?" Steve asked, coughing on the crust. He waved his hand, telling us he was okay and went to Nichelle. "Doubt the FBI would have access. Allow me?"

Nichelle rolled her seat away from the table, giving Steve room to use her laptop. She used her phone while he worked her laptop. When her brow lifted, she said, "No direct access to any archives. Not from the federal level. That's handled at the local level."

"Yes, it is," Steve said, handing control back to Nichelle. Her eyes were big with appreciation, a fondness for the access. "I worked on the committee to fund archives and come up with a retention policy."

"What's the policy?" Nichelle questioned.

"To keep records for ten years," he answered with a grim look. "At that point they'll be stored on media."

"Let's see if there's anything from the night of the rooftop chase," I said, searching my calendar and old notes. "It'd be ten years ago, the date is July 5th."

Nichelle glanced at Steve, his participating that evening. "Yeah, that sounds right." He shrugged. "I remember it was a stormy night, hot and muggy."

"Where do we start?" she asked, leaning back as she shared her screen on the conference room monitor. "We've got data, just too much of it."

"That's too broad," I said, pitching an elbow on the table and resting my chin on my hand. "His eyes. There's an injury there. How about 911 calls for an ambulance?"

She applied the filter, the list thinning. "That's better. What else can we try?"

"The address?" Jericho asked.

"Right! An ambulance must have a destination," I agreed. I gave them the address of the building.

"Here goes," Nichelle said, plugging in the numbers and street name. She hit enter, a spinner at the center of the screen rallying around our query. When it stopped, the query results appeared with a bug red zero. "Shit. Thought we had something."

"It's getting late," Steve said and planted his hands onto the table, palms flat as he leaned and stretched. He let out a groan, the table replying with the same. "We got Viken in custody. Your DA is gonna do her thing. Philly's DA is going to do his thing—"

"I can stay," I interrupted and gulped my coffee. "I don't want to leave until we've exhausted any possible leads on his accomplice."

Steve looked behind him as the station's front doors opened

and closed. The station had shifted into night mode, the third shift, the graveyard shift. "Come on, Sunny."

"I'll stay. There's a late-night cupcake shop that opened," Tracy said, searching our faces for approval. "It's a new place called Midnight Oil." She counted the fingers on her hand, adding, "There's caffeine infused, protein powder, some vegan alternatives."

"I'm in," Nichelle offered, the support warming me.

I looked to Jericho next. Though he wasn't officially one of the team, he'd earned his place at the table with years of service to the Outer Banks as their sheriff. He also had a place in my heart and would forever be on my team. "Cupcakes?" he asked and licked his lips.

Tracy started texting, and added, "They deliver."

"Fine! Fine!" Steve yelled, standing straight with his arms stretched above his head. He shook his head. "Cupcakes and 911 queries. It's not like I've got anything planned for tomorrow."

My smile faded in an instant. "What did you just say?"

Steve lowered his arms, confused. "What's that?"

"You said tomorrow." I thought back to the night of the rooftop chase. "Guys, the time of our query is wrong. It was past midnight."

"Which means it was already tomorrow!" Nichelle chimed, a bright smile shining as she reworked the query.

"Wait, I'm not tracking. What—" Steve began.

"Watch this," I said and pointed at the monitor. The spinner returned, the room taking a collective breath as we waited.

One result appeared, Steve brushing his hair back as he continued, "—look at that. An ambulance was called to the building that morning."

"What's at that street location?" I asked, rubbing the itch from the cut beneath my eye. Nichelle clicked through to street view on the map and showed us the front of the building. "GlassTek."

"It's a glass manufacturer," Tracy said, typing fast to give us a summary. "In business forty years with fifty employees."

"Can you play the 911 call?" I asked, shifting to sit on the edge of my seat.

"Just under the wire," Nichelle said, highlighting the date to note Steve's comment about the retention policy. "I'll get a backup of it as well. In case we need it."

"Let's hear it," I said and shut my eyelids.

The audio recording began with static, air pops, and a low whine that made my skin crawl. It cleared with the voice of a woman, *"Nine-one-one, what's your emergency?"*

"Send an ambulance!" a man yelled with a Spanish accent. The recording was poor, but we heard the panic in his words.

"I have your address, sir, ambulance dispatched," the operator replied. *"How many people, sir?"*

"We found him here," the caller said with background voices speaking Spanish, all with alarm. *"We got a hole in the roof. He fell through a skylight."*

"Okay, sir, do not try to move him. Is he breathing?" the operator asked, assessing the injuries for the paramedics.

"Sí... yes, ma'am! He's breathing. El rostro!"

"His face? He sustained injuries to his face?" the operator asked.

"Sí. He's cut up bad. Whole body." The caller was on the move, the chatter behind him growing distant. His voice turned quiet as he said, *"Ma'am, his face is the worst. Hurry."*

I held up my hand having heard enough. "He didn't escape from us," I said, facing Steve with fleeting validation. "He fell through the roof."

"That's one way to ditch the cops," Steve said lightheartedly. His expression firmed. "I'm thinking he was unconscious and his face was cut to shreds. But then what?"

"There'd be paramedics, an ambulance, and a ride to the hospital's emergency room," I answered, wondering why there wasn't a police connection to our rooftop chase. When I figured it out, I nodded and continued, "He called someone. He called his accomplice who got him out of there."

"You mentioned he was well known?" Tracy asked. "Would the paramedics have known who he was? Like, before his accomplice got to him at the hospital?"

Steve's face cramped at the question. "Maybe if they followed the society column. My money is they didn't." He waved his hand around his face. "A glass factory. Of all things to fall into."

"That's not something you bounce back from," I said, thinking of the recovery time and the extensive rehabilitation. "His sister was dead. His parents were dead. Who took care of him?"

"We got cupcakes coming," Nichelle said and swapped the screen to show newspaper articles from the *Philadelphia Inquirer*. "Maybe we'll find something in the newspapers?"

"Maybe," I answered as I tapped the bottom of my coffee cup on the table. "Whoever it was, it could be his accomplice."

* * *

A caffeine and sugar buzz coursed through me as the hour neared eleven at night. It was late for me, and for Jericho, but Tracy and Nichelle were catching their second wind. I couldn't leave. Wouldn't leave. Our idea of newspaper articles came up empty. There'd been mention of Viken's sudden retirement from the medical field and his mysterious reclusive behavior. But nothing for us to work with. Just speculation, the cause suspected to be his grieving due to the deaths in his family. We knew the truth. He'd lost his sight. What he had not lost though was his sadistic hunger and his murderous ways.

It was a partial print from the motel room that would fuel our research. The FBI team at the Sleep-*Inn* motel had finished with Viken's vehicle, all fingerprints accounted. Of particular interest was the steering wheel and dashboard controls. They were clean. Not a single print lifted. That told us Viken's accomplice was consciously wiping her presence clean, wearing gloves perhaps. Only, she'd missed one. It was a partial lifted from the bathtub's faucet. I recalled looking at it sprouting out of the lime-green tiles, the mouth crusted with limescale from the hard water. Maybe she'd leaned over to see Samantha, the moment brief, the touch accidental? It didn't matter to me how the partial print got there. We had it and that's what counted.

"Too small to be a pinky finger," Tracy said, voice muffled by half a cupcake covering her mouth. "Could be an index finger though."

"You guys know that the odds are high when it comes to working with a partial," I commented. I stood in front of the room, hands on my hips, blood racing in my ears. I waved at the monitor's screen, the partial distinct, but incomplete. "Alone, it's not going to get us anything. We need a list of suspects."

"Is it okay to submit for broad search?" Nichelle asked, shrugging, and adding, "Off chance we get a hit."

"Of course." I turned to face the partial print, squeezing the ends of my fingers. "We've all been ruled out of a match?"

"Uh-huh," Tracy answered.

"What's your plan, Sunny?" Steve asked. His attention was waning. Like me and Jericho, the hour was late for him too. He leaned back, the chair groaning as he bounced a knee. "We need friends and family. Work a list like we'd do with any suspect."

"Until we have something else, that's all we can do." I leafed through the folder we'd created for Viken, skipping over his parents who'd died and running my finger down the list of associates. "They are all doctors. And none of them are women."

"No female friends?" Tracy asked, looking surprised. I nudged toward a second screen showing a list of his victims both old and new. She realized what she was looking at, saying, "Because he only hunts women."

I started to pace, my head filling with ideas that fizzled as fast as they got hot. "It was a woman that did this," I said, talking to myself, meandering in front of the monitors. Feeling exhausted and edging frustration, I asked, "I'm totally shooting in the dark here, but has anyone from the list of family and Viken's associates been arrested before?"

"Why?" Steve asked, his face resting in his hand. I shook my head, having nothing to add. He opened his hand, his fingers splayed, and then touched his cheek. "You said she was female?"

I had no concrete evidence but sensed that she was. "The hand in the car was a woman. I'm sure of it."

"None of his associates were female—"

"His sister was arrested," Nichelle interrupted. "About two months prior to her death."

"Is that right?" I faced the monitor, Nichelle taking my cue to display what she'd found. The screen flashed to show his sister's mugshot, eyes half-lidded, corner of her mouth drooping. She was a petite woman with shoulder-length dark hair, the same color as her brother's. Her nose was narrow like his, and her eyes the same chocolate brown that had been listed on his old driver's license. "What's the arrest for?"

"It says here, Elizabeth Viken was arrested for being drunk and disorderly." Tracy clicked her mouse, adding, "Assaulting a police officer."

"Ouch, that'll buy her time in jail," I said and tried to recall her face and name. The family was well known, but I didn't recognize her. "Did she have any priors?"

"A few, the same, along with a driving while intoxicated."

"She's dead," Steve said, his voice dry, sounding hoarse. He glanced at the clock. "Let's wrap this up."

"Show me her fingerprint card," I said, choosing to ignore him. Nichelle loaded the image, displaying it on the screen. There were ten clean prints, the impressions clear for using. "And the partial."

Nichelle loaded it, placing the image next to the fingerprint card. "The agents marked top and bottom, I've oriented it upward."

"I don't understand why we're looking at these," Steve said, his tone harsh.

"There's nothing to lose in looking," Jericho said and stood from the table. He cocked his head, working the fingerprints to see if there was a match.

"We won't be able to do it manually," I said and shifted focus to Nichelle. "It's a good thing we have computers."

"Way ahead of you guys," she said. She'd been typing feverishly since Steve's first objection. When her brow jumped and the whites of her eyes bloomed, I knew there was a hit. "No way!"

"What?" I asked as motion around the conference table closed in on the laptop screen. "She's alive?"

"Look at the screen!" Nichelle thumped the return key, the partial print highlighted in bright red, hovering over the print of the right-hand index finger. It rotated one degree at a time, the color staying red. On the seventh degree, the color blinked, turning green, the ridges marrying to the fingerprint beneath. "The partial is a match!"

"Let's not get too excited. We're still working with a partial," Steve warned, and snapped his fingers. "That said, someone please tell me the odds that a partial from one person could match another person?"

"It's a decent size partial," Jericho commented, calculating the numbers. "More than fifty percent coverage from the looks of it."

"It's not possible, is it?" Steve said. He stood up, bumping the table as he approached the monitor. "It's impossible to have matched."

"Unless she is alive," Tracy said, awe in her voice.

We all stood then, footsteps approaching the monitors, and my asking the only question that mattered. "If Viken's sister is alive, then who is buried in her grave?"

TWENTY-THREE

Dan Viken wouldn't sleep. Not yet. He stayed in old moments where he dreamily saw his girls, where he heard their voices whenever he touched them. It was like music, the sounds they made. And the scent of their fear was like a feast. He recalled what their flesh looked like too. Some of them were bronze, and others an alabaster white. All of them were perfect and without a single blemish. That is, until he got to them.

His muscles tensed when the next image entered his mind, the one with Detective Casey White. He saw the memory of her face before his eyes were taken from him. Before they needled like pinpricks and only gave him a splash of cloudy light. She'd done this to him. He stirred with an anger like a cancer that ate him up over and over again. He grimaced at the thought of her escape and bit his upper lip until there was a taste of blood. He imagined his hands on her body. The joy of touching her, of bringing her the pain she deserved.

He rubbed his ankles and wrists where they remained shackled, the skin tender, the metal striking bone. His back was against the holding cell wall, his legs hitched up to his chest as he sat on a metal cot. She must have enjoyed seeing him like this. Seeing him bound and imprisoned, the tables turned. He'd remain that way until the detective returned. Dan Viken squeezed his hands, clutching his fingers as he pretended what he was going to do. When she least expected it, he'd have her again. He wet his lips in anticipation. Dan imagined being back there. Back in that room where there was the faint smell of dust and chlorine. It was her sweat he wanted, especially when it came with her fear. That's what drove him. When she let out a gasp, the pain registering, that's what gave him satisfaction. She was his for a time. But not entirely. None of them were ever really his. She had to have her turn too.

The prisoner in the adjacent cell turned to roll onto their side. The cots were a metal slab, each prisoner given a thin blanket. He could hear every movement. They were his appetizer. A morsel to hold Dan over until the detective returned. While some counted sheep, Dan counted the breaths of his neighboring prisoner instead. It had started with a gentle snore, but as the man's sleep deepened, the rhythm of it changed dangerously. Dan concentrated on the timing as he waited for the apnea to take hold.

The prisoner inhaled with a snort, a soft whistle interrupted. The motion turned them both breathless as the apnea gripped the prisoner's throat like an invisible hand. Dan clutched his fingers and waited for a sudden roar, for the blurting and sloppy voice when the man gasped for air. The moment arrived as if it had been a wish. He listened intently, feeling the struggle, closing his eyelids while drinking in the pleasure of it. For Dan, it was a simple moment, experiencing the pain of another. It was also free. He only had to listen.

"Two to four years," he muttered, his mind working through that part of his life as a medical doctor, as a surgeon and gifted diagnostician. In an instant, he assessed the man's status, the man's health, and made a prognosis simply by the sleep apnea he was suffering. "Give or take."

His eyelids snapped open as he sniffed the air, heard the buttons on a keypad struck in succession. Someone was coming. Was it the detective? The heavy door leading to the holding cells opened, hinges creaking. "Sorry for the late hour," someone murmured, their voice barely registrable. Footsteps approached. One pair was the cheap soles of a patrolman, the other a heavier rubber, the soles squelching when they turned to face his cell. Metal clanked with the cage unlocking. "We need to collect additional DNA. I'll only be a few minutes."

"She's here," Dan mouthed, impressed when he heard her voice. But why should he be impressed? She was a ghost. She could be anywhere. She could do anything.

"I have to get back to the front. It's a shift change," the officer panted, his impatience working for them.

"I'm fine," she said, pausing. He imagined she was flirting to coach him, maybe batting her eyelashes, or placing her hand on his chest. "Look at him. He's locked up safe. Tell you what, go ahead and clock out. I'll be done by the time your replacement is here."

"Uhm," he said uncertain. A sleeve rising up an arm, the patrolman checking his watch. "I'm not sure."

"What's that say?" she asked, her voice demanding.

The patrolman clicked his tongue, answering, "It says FBI."

"Don't you think we're trained for this?" she said as though it were a reprimand. "Consider it an order. Clock out. I've got the prisoner until your replacement arrives."

"Yeah, okay," he said, obliging. The soles of his shoes whooshing against the floor as he spun around to leave.

"Finally," she said with a sigh, the door leading into the station closing. "I thought he'd never leave us alone."

"Yes. Finally." Dan searched the gray light for her figure, but the midnight hour had brought dim overhead lights, giving him nothing to work with. "How did you pull that off?" he asked.

"You know me. I can become anyone. I can be anyplace."
Her touch. Fingers soft and warm and gentle. She was alone
and caressed the bruising around his wrists. She made a tsk-tsk
sound with her tongue, saying, "They've got you locked in here
like a fucking animal."

"You're here to save me?" Dan asked, shifting to stand.

"Shh." She pressed a finger to his mouth, the tip of it
matching perfectly to the cleft on his upper lip. It was called the
philtrum, a question from one of his medical exams that he'd
never forget. "I'm here to *free* you."

He held up his hands, chain rattling with it draped between
his legs. "You didn't happen to have brought a key with you?"

"I did," she answered him, one hand on his shoulder, a
finger on his cheek. He froze when she ran the tip of it down his
face the way his mother used to do.

"What are you doing?" he asked, the truth of her visit
ringing in his head like a bell.

"Shh," she told him, replacing her finger with the tip of a
scalpel. "One for the tears—"

Emotion welled in him, his eyes remaining dry as he joined
in what she was saying, "And one for the pain." She gripped
him tight, a loud pop thudding in his head. He gasped sharply
as she plunged the spike through his sternum, his feeding on the
pain of others becoming ironic as agony gripped his heart.

She leaned in, her cheek to his, and whispered, "Be free."

"Casey—" he tried asking, his heart pierced as she freed him
through mercy. The taste of blood returned to his mouth. Text
and pictures from his medical training flooded his mind like a
wind flipping the pages of the journals he'd studied. He
couldn't speak, but mouthed, "Casey White."

"I will get her for you," she answered, leaving the stake in
his heart. It had been a gift from him to her. It was an antique
medical instrument he'd purchased for the birthday she shared
with him. Cold glided over his cheek. Another present from

him, the sharp blade of a scalpel slicing into his flesh and opening the ragged scar tissue that had stolen his sight.

"Mrr," he choked as blood rushed to his head and called like a siren in his ears. His heart beat wildly, walloping strangely, the chambers broken in halves while attempting to function regardless of being impaired. He saw scattered images of motors ripping themselves apart from a failed bolt or broken shaft and imagined the same was happening inside his chest.

"You're free, Dan," she said, his heart stopping as she added a second teardrop to his face, replacing the ones he could never spill on his own. "Free."

"How did this happen, Sunny!" Steve yelled into his phone. His words were cutting, the speaker sizzling with static. I held it away from my ear, the team hearing his disappointment. *"You guys still there?"*

"Yeah," I answered, unsure of what to say. "We're still here."

"This is a real shit show!" he continued. *"I was just there this afternoon. Standing in his holding cell."*

"Well, he's dead now, Steve," I said as Nichelle and the FBI entered, the door closing behind them. "Listen, I'll have to call you back in a few," I said, hanging up.

"Detective," the lead from Nichelle's team said. He glanced at me briefly before leaning to stare into the holding cell. "Hmm. Like your partner said... a real shit show."

"Yes, sir," I replied and faced the station patrolman who'd been on duty. "Again, what exactly happened!?" I asked, cupping my hand against my forehead. The three a.m. emergency call sounded with an urgency I'd never heard. From the shaky voices of the patrolman, I'd thought the station must have burned down or something. It hadn't. From the look on his face, I am certain he probably wished it had.

"Ma'am—" the patrolman began, his arms crossed tightly against his chest. "We? I, uhm—"

"You were on duty, and he died?"

"I found him like that when I came back," he answered, pinching his mouth when my eyelids sprang open.

"Came back?" I followed up. I looked up and down the narrow corridor, the few holding cells we had empty except for two. We'd put Viken on a death watch as a standard practice. There was no knowing when a prisoner might attempt to take their life, rather than face a trial and life in prison. "You say you left him alone?"

Shoes scraped against the concrete, turning toward the patrolman. He shook his head. "There was an FBI agent here, one of you guys."

I looked to Nichelle and to her team as they exchanged glances, shaking their heads. "None of us," Nichelle answered.

"Nuh-uh!" the patrolman challenged. He pointed in front of him, raising his voice, "Stood here. Right here! Showed me her badge!"

"Okay. Okay, officer," I said when he began to stammer, raising my hand to shush him, thinking it best he say nothing else until the sheriff arrived. With the lead from the FBI present, and everyone having to answer to somebody, it was best to have the right people together at the same time.

"Tracy, let's get this processed. See what we see."

She followed me into the holding cell where Dan Viken's dead body sat upright against the wall. His head was slumped to one side, his shoulders slouched. My throat was thick, my insides quaking. No one had examined the body yet. We didn't know if this was death by natural causes or a murder. Perhaps it was retribution making a house call, the press spreading his name from coast to coast in recent hours. Viken wore the standard issue prison coveralls we had in stock, the color of them a bright yellow. Tracy concentrated on his chest where blood had dried. At first glance, I thought it could have come from a nose-bleed, maybe from his mouth? It wasn't more than the size of my palm. "Yeah, there."

"You say that someone from the FBI requested access?" Nichelle asked the patrolman. Through the bars, his expression twisted as he struggled to answer. Nichelle stood alongside her team, the five of them in full uniform, including hats and shirts and jackets. Even their slacks were the same khaki brown, along with rubber-soled black shoes.

"She was dressed like you are," he finally said.

She tipped her hat, lifting it slightly, bringing attention to the FBI gold letters embroidered on it. "Including the hat?"

"Exactly the same," the patrolman said, pivoting an elbow to point at the FBI agent closest to him. "Only, she was..."

"She was what?" I asked, frowning. My insides were torn up by the idea that Viken had escaped a trial with a jury of his peers. But I was more torn up that I had nobody to deliver to my district attorney, or the one in Philly. There was no one to answer for the murder of these women.

"She was short," the patrolman answered, his mouth twisting. "I didn't really get a good look at her."

"Sir, we'll need a full statement from you," the lead from Nichelle's team said. He crossed his arms and moved to stand in front of the holding cell.

I glanced at my phone's screen, telling them, "The sheriff will be here in a few minutes. Officer, he'll speak with you first."

The patrolman's eyes blazed at the idea of a talk with the sheriff, a possible reprimand in his record. He shook his head, exclaiming again, "I swear! I thought she was one of you guys!"

"That'll be all for now," I said and felt a tug of sympathy. I looked to Nichelle's lead, telling him, "Let's wait until the sheriff arrives before asking more questions."

"I can do that," he answered, turning toward the station door as Nichelle entered the cell. A keypad played a tune that reminded me of a children's song, the heavy door to the station swinging open with Doc Bob and Carla passing through.

"Guys," I said, waving them around the patrolman and the FBI agents.

"Casey?" Tracy said, her voice muted. She was crouched, sitting squat on the floor, the nose of her camera pointed toward Viken's face. "You guys need to see this."

"What is it?" I asked and knelt, the concrete floor cold as I lowered my head. In the shadow of Viken's face, his dead eyes were bulging wide as if he'd been seeking the hereafter during his final breath. My jaw went slack when seeing the fresh cuts beneath them, his old scar tissue opened cleanly by a pair of teardrops etched onto his face. I reared back with a start, my bottom landing on my feet as I sucked in a mouthful of stale air.

"What is it?" Nichelle frowned and knelt between us to see.

"I need gloves!" I said, pressing my hands against my pants to fish out a pair from my pocket. "All of us. Now."

Latex and rubber snapped with an echo, the sound bouncing against the cinder block walls.

"What is it?" Carla asked, bobbing her head to see.

When my gloves were in place, I looked to Tracy for permission. She focused once more, flashing light onto Viken's head and then gave the okay. As I moved him, raising his face for Doc Bob and Carla, they let out a collective gasp. "Teardrops. The same as on the other victims."

Doc Bob moved closer, his eyebrows rising slowly as he studied the blood on the coveralls. "Do you think?"

"I do," I answered as Tracy rapidly fired a dozen photographs on the stain, the crimson pattern shaped like rose petals, the bleeding limited by a life shortened. When she gave me the nod, I shined my phone's flashlight and flattened the coveralls. With the creases removed, we saw what was at the center of the blossom. It was a single hole, void of color and material, its ending somewhere inside Viken's heart. "This is like the others."

Doc Bob inhaled deeply with a slow sigh. "Let's not get ahead just yet. This is only a field assessment," he told us, holding a medical ruler, light glinting from the steel. He clicked his tongue, lips thinning with acknowledgment, and added, "Well, the measurement is the same at approximately four millimeters."

I stood up, hands balled into fists, shoving them against my hips, and walked to the other side of the cage. Someone had come in here and killed our leading suspect. My thoughts went to the accomplice who'd become a ghost in my mind, having had no concrete evidence that they truly existed. Until now that is. When I spun around to face our newest crime scene, the team's eyes were fixed on me. They were feeling it too. Feeling the confusion and misdirection, our path to closure suddenly obliterated. "Shit," I muttered, feeling anxious and frightened.

"What does this mean?" Nichelle asked, her face filling with the same shared confusion.

I held up my phone to call Steve, letting out a ragged sigh, answering, "It means that Dan Viken is not the Midnight Killer."

TWENTY-FOUR

When I got home from processing Dan Viken's murder, I slept straight through the morning. There were no dreams. No nightmares that jarred me awake. I was reeling from the loss of our suspect. And I was in need of healing from the abduction. I'd paid my dues in the hours after my escape, and sleep was for me. It's those moments just before waking when stray thoughts drive the day to come. Elizabeth Viken might be alive. If so, how long had she been working with her brother? Would she have murdered him? Could she have been behind the murders? Where was she now? Who was she going to kill next?

I rolled over and touched the cold part of the bed, wondering where Jericho had gone. I picked at the cut on my face, feeling her presence the way I had the night she sat with me in the pump house. Her touch bordered on tender, almost intimate, as she ran the blade over my skin. The cut was scabbing and itchy and would heal in the next week. Jenni wouldn't heal. Neither would Pauline Rydel or the other women killed. What was Elizabeth Viken about? I understood the sickness that drove her brother, but was it the same thing that drove her?

I cringed at the thought of the Viken family, the sickness of them, the disgust.

"How are you feeling?" Jericho returned to bed, his body curling up to mine. I inched closer so he'd hold me, the thought of the Vikens making me terribly vulnerable.

"I'm good now," I answered, watching the window curtain wave against a sea breeze. The sun was hours past the horizon, nearly above the lip of the window, creating steep shadows that crawled along our bedroom walls. "I can't remember the last time I slept this late."

"You needed it," he said, fingers brushing my side, whiskers touching my neck. "Do you want to talk about the case?"

"I need to take a break for a few," I said, clearing my mind of the Viken family. "Makes me feel sick."

"It would," he said, commenting, "it would make anyone of sound mind feel sick."

I turned to face him, his eyes inches from mine, seeing me the way I believed only he could see me. "Ask me again," I blurted, desperately wishing I'd said yes the first time. I kissed him, saying, "Jericho, ask me."

"Ask?" he said as his face lost all expression, the look making me inch away. Was I too late? Jericho had asked for my hand in marriage once, but I hesitated. I didn't say no. But I didn't say yes either. I told him that I needed time.

I lowered my chin, brow furrowed with sincerity. "If there's one thing I have learned from all this, it's that we can't squander time."

"Squander time?" he said, asking as he tilted his face with caution. "What about Tracy?"

I shook my head as I climbed on top of him, my hands pressing against his chest. I was feeling nervous but wanted to make this right. "So much has changed since the night you proposed." I cursed the tears that stung my eyes.

"It's okay," he said, wiping them dry, and listened.

"Terri is gone. Emanuel is at another station, another town. And now Nichelle and Tracy are moving to Philly..." I planted my lips on his, admitting, "Jericho, I should have said yes."

"I'm sorry they're moving," he said as he pulled me closer. The angst of my mistake ran out of me, my body turning to jelly. "I've been feeling bad because I shouldn't have put you on the spot like that."

I lifted my head, surprised by his comment. "Truth?"

"Truth," he answered, squinting as he braced for my comments.

I shut my eyelids and saw the memory and swooned to the music playing in my head. "I loved it."

"You did?" Brow rising. "I mean, I was so scared—"

I interrupted him with another kiss. A hard kiss that would have been more if not for a knock on the front door that stole our moment. "Yeah. I really did."

"It's just us," Nichelle shouted, her key clicking in the lock clanking.

"We brought you guys some lunch!" I heard Tracy say. She let out a chuckle, adding, "Check that, it's after one. I think it'd be a *linner*, as in lunch and dinner?"

"That's great," I shouted back, fishing with my foot, searching for pajamas abandoned at the bottom of our bed. The smell of food motivated us to rush to put our clothes on.

"Any news about the order for the grave?" Jericho asked. "Did you get it?"

"Certainly did," Nichelle answered. "FBI's Arch Street office worked with your old station and woke up some poor judge at five thirty this morning."

"Elizabeth Viken's body is being exhumed?" The timing left me shocked by the expedience. With the FBI working the case, we could escalate anything. The order was commissioned by them, their giving a solid justification for reasons relating to solving the Midnight Killer's crimes, as well as identification and investigating to determine a cause of death. Still, the quickness of the turnaround was impressive. "That was fast."

A knock came from the bedroom hallway. I gave Jericho a nod while he sleeved his arms through his shirt. "We're good now."

The girls entered, each with tall coffees in hand. A straight coffee for Jericho, his favorite. And an Americano for me, along with two extra shots. "This is a treat," I said and tried to control myself. I could have guzzled half but wanted to savor it. I fixed a look on them, a sentiment returning. "Not going to be the same with you guys up in Philly."

Tracy came around the bed to sit next to me. "Did you give anymore thought to moving back home?"

"With everything that's happened," I began, and handed her my coffee to slip a pair of pants over the bruising. She flashed a look of shock but did well to try and hide it. I looked to Jericho, his giving me a nod. "But I will. We will. After the case. I promise to give it more thought."

"I've got another gift for you," Nichelle said as she handed Jericho a copy of the court order.

He skimmed the page, answering, "Really?"

"What is it?" I climbed across the bed to read the order. "Doc Bob? We can bring the body here for examination?"

"Since the most recent murders have taken place here, and Elizabeth Viken's name is attached to the case, the judge had no reason not to include the Outer Banks medical examiner's office."

"When!?" I asked and imagined bulldozers clawing at the earth. Their toothy shovels cutting into the sodden ground and lifting out the tonnage, piling it next to Viken's grave. "Today?"

Nichelle tapped her phone, texting her point of contact with Philly's FBI branch. "It's done."

"Done?" Jericho asked. He looked at me with a goofy grin, saying, "We could have slept another hour."

"Didn't look like sleeping to me," Tracy joked.

"How soon?" I asked, nudging her arm as Jericho's cheeks turned red. "It's six to eight hours on the road, depending on the traffic."

"There's a relief team coming by helicopter," Nichelle said, her words stammered as she texted a reply. "They're bringing Elizabeth Viken's remains with them."

"Transport by air," I said, rushing to slip a pair of shoes over my toes. "They'll be here later this afternoon."

Tracy held up her hands and gently put them on my shoulders. "Which gives us time to sit and eat and go over the case."

"Right," I said, taking a breath and drinking my coffee as we made our way to the kitchen. Chair legs scraped against the floor as we each took a seat at the table, case files piled between us. I opened one, asking, "Motive? We know her brother was a sick prick, but his sister? Why fake a death?"

Jericho put a breakfast sandwich in front of me, answering, "We can eat while we talk."

Paper crinkled as we unwrapped the food, my finding an appetite and taking a bite. "The brother gets off on inflicting pain." I wagged a finger. "But now he's been killed, I don't think he's actually our killer."

"He just," Tracy began, gaze falling to my injuries, "just did that?"

"Exactly," I answered unapologetically, my mouth full. "*She* was the murderer."

"Death saved his ass," Nichelle stated, picking up a page, a timeline bleeding through it. "I mean, by the time he would have been done here, and then in Philadelphia, he would have never set foot outside a prison cell again."

My stomach growled, pleading for more, the days without food catching up to me. "We might never know more than what the evidence has to show us."

"What do you mean?" Tracy asked, the bottom of her sandwich falling with a thud.

"His motives," I answered. "Beyond the psychological reason, his being a sadist, we may never know if there was a deeper cause to his doing what he did."

"I can live with that," Jericho commented. "It's his sister that raises the questions now. That is, if it *is* his sister."

"That's where I'm going with this." I drank some coffee, finishing the sandwich in a fifth bite. "Her accident occurred before the first murders back in Philly. If she *is* alive, and she was working with him, then why fake her own death? And why kill her brother?"

Tracy gave up on her sandwich, the pile in ruin, her opting to use a fork and knife instead. With my question, she opened her laptop, answering, "I started a profile on her."

"How far back?" There would be years of information given the family's presence in Philadelphia.

"She was a typical bad girl." Tracy turned the laptop around for us to see, her screen showing a small presentation. The first picture showed a young Elizabeth Viken, handcuffed, two beefy patrol officers on each side of her. "That's her first arrest. A drunk and disorderly at some Philadelphia lawyer's campaign."

"What is she, fifteen in that picture?" I asked, wiping my mouth. "What campaign?"

"Jack Brenner," Nichelle answered. "He was the city's district attorney—"

"Jack," I said with a heavy breath. "I butted heads with him on a lot of cases."

"You? Butting heads?" Jericho asked with snark. He turned serious then. "What happened?"

The memory of working with Brenner stirred like a hot coal. "He was always too conservative. If there was the slightest challenge possible by a defense attorney, he'd shy away from placing charges."

"Played it safe," Jericho said. "He wanted to ensure that he had a winning record."

"Viken's parents, they were major contributors to his campaign?" I guessed.

With a slow nod, Tracy answered, "Every one of his campaigns."

"And Elizabeth Viken was arrested multiple times, but the charges always thrown out?" I could see where this was going.

Tracy held up her finger. "All except for the one before she presumably died."

"I bet they had a falling out with the DA," I said and picked at the remains of her sandwich.

Tracy nodded with approval, answering, "There were two arrests that stuck: she got probation for six months on one and a year on another. And then there was an assault on an officer."

"There it is," Jericho said with emphasis. "Were there any injuries?"

"A broken nose and the officer's right arm," she answered, showing pictures on her phone. "I dug these up on the car ride over."

"Viken slams her head into the officer, breaks her nose," I began, going through the motions. "The officer rears back, her arm breaking in the fall."

"Viken's drunk in public looked like a child's timeout compared to the charges the district attorney brought against her," Nichelle said.

"However it had happened, the DA has an assault on an officer with bodily injuries." I finished the remains of Tracy's sandwich, feeling full as the idea of motive came to mind. "If that incident occurred during a campaign year, the DA would have had to press charges. There was no way to hide it."

"It just so happens that it was a campaign year," Tracy answered with a lift in her voice.

Jericho shook his head, "Any campaign donations from the Viken estate to Brenner's campaign?"

"None," Nichelle said.

I got up to walk, to pace around the kitchen. It was a habit I liked to do when thoughts were flowing. "Third offense, assault occurring while she's on probation. She'd be facing fifteen years."

"That's hard time in the penitentiary," Tracy said.

"And that's why she faked her death," I said, pacing some more. "With the help of her brother."

"Assaulting an officer though," Tracy began to say, unconvinced. "Was she out on bail?"

"Overcrowding in the jails, an influential family. Could have been a number of things." I wondered if that was how Elizabeth Viken was introduced into her brother's world, his behaviors, his victims who would then become hers. I shook my head then, thinking it nearly impossible, and asked, "And then what? She hid from the public?"

"Why not?" Jericho answered, hearing the doubt in my voice. "Criminals do it all the time."

"I suppose it's possible. I mean, the Viken estate is massive. It's acres of buildings and grounds behind a fifteen-foot stone wall."

"She could have assumed a new identity?" Tracy suggested. "If they had the money."

"Yeah, that's possible," I said, looking at the time on my phone. "I think that's when they started working together. Killing together."

"Working together?" Tracy asked with a frown. "How's that?"

"Let's try to think like the Vikens," I said, arching my back with a strain, and opened the case files. The pictures of the

victims were still harrowing, no matter how many times I looked
at them. I began to spread them across the kitchen table,
ordering them chronologically, Tracy grimacing. "The brother
is doing well as a surgeon at one of Philadelphia's top hospitals,
while the sister is facing prison time."

"She has motive to disappear," Tracy adds.

"Right," I said, picking up photos of her vehicle, the burned
remains of it. "So what does her brother do? He offers the idea
to fake her death. Maybe he had the means to work it through
the hospital's morgue? Grease a few palms, calling in favors to
help ease the family's suffering."

Nichelle lifted the enlarged photo of the burned vehicle,
the victim hunched over. She looked at us over the photograph,
suggesting, "They murder someone and put the body in place of
Elizabeth's."

"She's got some of that sadistic nature in her too," I said.
"She saved her own skin, but also wanted to do it."

"Are we talking about the birth of the Midnight Killers?"
Tracy asked.

"Her birth," I corrected her. "A killer always has to have a
first."

Jericho tapped a picture of Dan Viken, adding, "He did it to
help keep his sister out of prison, which was a catalyst to who
she'd become."

"Who they'd become. But he only tortured the women."
With a deep pain, my emotions stirring at finding Jenni Levor
and Samantha, I added, "Elizabeth Viken was the one who
killed them."

TWENTY-FIVE

Never had I received a body by helicopter. This was a first. The strength of the FBI's muscle in action. My clothes flattened as gusts batted us, the spinning blades invisible to our eyes. I'd also never been near a helicopter. Not like this. The noise of it was crushing as it beat the air and reverberated through me. The experience of it was frightening and exciting at the same time.

"Thank you," I mouthed to Jericho, taking his arm. I moved closer, guarding us from the helicopter. He knew every inch of the Outer Banks and was familiar with the single airport, First Flight. I had been surprised to learn the islands had an airport, ironic considering the location of the Wright brothers' first flight was near.

"Of course," he said, his words lost to the noise, the helicopter turning around and hovering above the landing pad.

Shamefully, I asked, "Is it bad to admit that this is a little exciting?"

Jericho tried not to show a smile, answering in a yell, "It's a helicopter flying right in front of us. How can you *not* get excited by that?"

"I know, right!" The medical examiner's van pulled up

behind us. I could see Derek and Carla wide-eyed behind the windshield as I waved. They texted, bringing a gurney from the rear, a shine bouncing off the steel legs, their hands raised to shield their faces from the stirred air. "Guys."

"Big bird," Derek said, my reading his lips, his thinning hair a lively tangle above his head. He squinted and looked to Carla, her face filled with fright, eyes huge behind the thick lenses of her glasses. Derek saw her face and told her, "It's okay, they're positioning to land."

"That thing is scary," she shouted, her words barely register-ing. She was dressed for the morgue, the bottom of her lab coat rising in the wind, a pair of her purplish non-latex gloves already on her hands, their color matching her sunlit curly hair.

The helicopter cradled the air beneath it like a cushiony pillow and seemed to stay suspended as if a magician was working a trick. A puff of black smoke bellowed, the machine ascending, touching down. I let out a sigh, relaxing, but remained cautious. "Now?" I asked Jericho, keeping my eyes on the blades, terrified by the idea of one coming loose.

"Wait," he answered, squeezing my arm. "They'll open the doors when it's safe."

"They're getting her," I muttered to myself, watching intently as they worked like a well-oiled machine. The doors opened with two figures appearing, hand and foot placement rehearsed. They wore bright orange jumpsuits with tan belts around their waists, a pair of giant white headphones covering their ears, a microphone with a black radio wire coiled across their shoulders. They stepped down onto the tarry landing pad, heat rising from it, the helicopter blades sounding with a constant whoop whoop. The two were oblivious to the dangers just a couple of feet above their heads, walking freely beneath while they maneuvered to open a larger door. The body came into our view, my heart jumping with anticipation. We knew that since Elizabeth Viken was alive, the identification of the person inside her casket was a mystery. "Who are you?"

"After you," Jericho said, offering me the lead toward the orange figures as they motioned for us. I didn't know what to expect, having never seen a body after it had lain in the ground the last twelve years. I shivered at the thought and ducked when we reached the helicopter's shadow. A young woman with glasses that mirrored my reflection handed me a tablet and pen, her lips moving to the words requesting my signature. I signed where she pointed and then handed it to an agent from Nichelle's team, his bald head gleaming with sweat, his face void of any expression, his manner telling me he wasn't bothered by the surroundings. He signed the tablet and handed it back to the woman.

"Thank you," I told them, putting my hand on the casket, which had aged well when considering the dozen years in the ground. Elizabeth Viken's parents had paid for the best when they buried their daughter. The casket's bright cherry wood color had faded, the metal finishings dingy in the sunlight. But there was no pitting or rot from ground moisture, or from the expansions and contractions that come with the seasons, the soils shifting around the casket. Her parents had also paid to line the burial plot with a concrete vault, extending the preservation. We might be in luck, their money well spent to rob the earth of its prize, to slow their daughter's decomposition. "Guys?"

Derek and Carla came forward, the gurney's front wheel spinning uncontrollably as they rushed to position themselves. The six of us maneuvered to lift and slide it at the same time. "Careful, there's some weight," Jericho grunted.

"Shit! No kidding," Carla belted, her height a disadvantage, showing only the top of her purplish hair, the rims of her thick glasses shoved up against the top of her forehead.

"It's clean too," Jericho said, brushing his hand across the surface, pinching his fingers together. "Like she was buried yesterday."

"That's a good thing. The remains should be well preserved," I commented, catching a breath with the casket lowered onto the gurney. The legs groaned, the wobbly wheel turning before we could apply the straps. I looked to Derek with concern, asking, "This'll hold?"

"Oh yeah," he answered. "This is the good one."

Jericho gave me a look while we cautiously rolled it to the medical van.

I sized up our prize, Nichelle's FBI handiwork winning us the buried remains of Elizabeth Viken. I wondered if her family would have ever guessed where their expensive coffin choice would end up.

* * *

I dressed for the morgue. We shuffled hurriedly, putting our personals in lockers, donning gloves and booties and lab coats. I made it a point to double up on my lab coat, wearing two, knowing the temperatures in that room. We followed a regimen that had been established by Dr. Swales, her voice in my head telling us that she kept a tidy house. I peered through the plastic windows on the thick resin doors, a puff of cold air drifting around the floor. Carla and Doc Bob were already inside, standing next to the autopsy table with Dan Viken's body, which they'd work later in the day. Carla had added a splash of magenta to the top of her purple hair, giving it a rainbowish highlight. As she passed by the doors, the glimpse of color in the window reminded me of Dr. Swales, the moment catching me with a sad reminisce. To me, this would always be Terri Swales' morgue.

"Ready," I said, swinging the doors open, entering the morgue. I couldn't help but stare at Dan Viken's body while I walked by. His eyes were still open, the lifeless gray marbles bulging from their sockets.

"He can't hurt you," Jericho said, stepping between.

"I know," I whispered, my arm near his, touching indiscriminately, sharing an affection without being obvious. "He can't hurt anyone anymore."

"Shall we?" Doc Bob said when we reached the casket.

"Yes, sir." I gave the lid a tug. It didn't move. I jostled it, the metal clanking. The lid stayed tight. "Do caskets lock?"

"They do," Doc Bob replied. He looked toward Dr. Swales' old desk, asking, "Surely there is a key?"

I shook my head and searched Jericho's face, hoping to see recognition. He shook his head too and began to inspect the casket.

"Let's see if they're generic," Tracy said, her tablet in hand. "We could call Samantha too?"

"Let her rest." We all wanted to check in on Samantha, and there'd be plenty of time for that. I opened a drawer, the bottom of it covered in tools. "Jericho?"

He joined my side, browsing, picking each up, commenting, "Bone saw. Another saw. This one looks like it's used like a pry bar."

"None of these work without breaking into the thing," I said as he returned to the casket.

"Well, I've got my tools in my truck," Jericho offered while he slid his fingers along the edge of the casket. "Found where it goes."

"Says here we can use a hex driver," Tracy said, showing us the tablet with pictures of casket keys, the end of them with a hex-shaped post. "Which is definitely not a tool you'd find in a morgue."

"But you would in any standard toolset," Jericho said and turned to leave the room. "I've got that."

We stood in silence while we waited, the moment eerie, the

brother and sister of the Philadelphia Viken family lying in wait together, their lives ended. "Tracy, is there any remaining family?"

She knew what I meant and worked her tablet, lips moving as she read through the search results and shook her head. "The parents died years ago. He was the last," she said, tilting her head in his direction.

"This'll work," Jericho said as he shoved through the doors, breathless. He shined his phone's light into the slot where the casket key went, making contact with one of his tools. "I got it!" he exclaimed while turning a makeshift crank handle.

"Progress," I replied, glancing at my phone and cringing at the loss of time. Metal grinding on metal as the casket seal was released from the lock. When he stopped twisting the handle, I asked, "Is that it?"

"That's as far as it'll go." He put his tools away and leveled his fingertips on the lip of the casket. "You guys ready?"

"Uh-huh," I answered as Doc Bob and Carla returned, stepping closer. She dragged Dr. Swales' step stool closer, rising while sleeving a fresh pair of gloves over her fingers.

"There," he said with a huff, lifting the casket lid, its hinges rebelling, our muscles straining. The inside was a dingy white with old silk lining the casket. On the body was a shroud which had aged as if it had been moth-eaten, its color turning from contact with the corpse.

"May I?" Carla asked, her gloved hand appearing between us. She didn't wait for us to answer, her shoulder maneuvering next as purple fingers pinched the material. "I'll take the cover."

As the shroud slipped away, a charred smell rose from the casket, leading me to ask, "Wouldn't she have been embalmed?"

"It's not required," Doc Bob answered as he half leaned against the casket, his nose raised while watching Carla work. "Most states don't require it. A good mortuary can keep a body preserved up to a week before burial. There would have also been the state of her burns to consider."

"Could be the parents wanted a fast funeral too?" I asked. "Tracy, how soon after the accident was the service?"

She swiped her tablet, finding it. "Early morning on the fourth day after the fire."

Doc Bob snapped his fingers, replying, "There ya go." Like Carla, he moved in place of Jericho to help her remove the body. His hands were steady, the back of them covered in liver spots. He motioned to Carla to remove the remaining cover and reveal the remains, saying, "Let's see what we have here."

I had to blink. Had to refocus and try not to gasp. The woman's face was like a horror show. I'd seen the remains of a burn victim once before, the memory of it impossible to forget. But this was different. I tried to remain composed, my mouth shut tight, afraid to breathe the air. Jericho's hand brushed mine. I looked up to find shock. "She's completely unrecognizable."

"Jeez," Tracy said, mouth hung slack as she moved behind us. "Is that from her decomposing or is it from the fire?"

"Both," Doc Bob said without flinching. He shoved his hands beneath the woman's torso while I helped Jericho open the lower half of the casket. "Carla, could you move next to me?"

"We can help with the legs?" I offered, my mouth drying.

"That'd be splendid," Doc Bob answered. He studied Jericho, looking him up and down, adding, "I'm not expecting any weight. So, when we lift the body, would you roll the casket away?"

"Sure thing," Jericho said, the four of us working together to move the corpse onto the autopsy table. He repeated his countdown from earlier, "And one, two and three."

Doc Bob was right. There wasn't any weight, the bodily fluids evaporated by the fire. And with no embalming, it was like lifting a body made of papier mâché. "The height," I commented while placing her legs carefully onto the table.

"Come again?" Doc Bob asked, bending the top of his ear with his finger.

"Her height. Whoever this is, she's taller than Elizabeth Viken." I went to the other side of the autopsy table, assessing the remains. "At least by a few inches."

"I've got her arrest record," Tracy said, swiping her tablet while eyeing the body with a cringe. The skin was mottled black and brown, shriveled tight to the bone, its texture like a hard leather. Tracy glanced over her tablet as she gave the body a measure, shaking her head as she continued, "It says here that Elizabeth Viken was only five feet and two inches."

Doc Bob stepped back to assess the length of the body. "There's at least a four-inch difference. That'd be my guess," he said with a nod. "Good eye, Detective White. I'll confirm it with an exact measure."

"Is there any condition that would cause the body to appear longer?" Tracy asked, her stare fixed, shoulders rising in a shrug.

"Contraction," I answered, shaking my head and believing the heat of a fire along with decomposition would cause the opposite. "I'd think that the skin would shrink instead. Even more in this case since there was the fire."

Doc Bob's wiry eyebrows jumped with another nod. "The way a body burns is quite predictable when considering its makeup of soft tissue and bone. This includes contraction which helps us identify the burn patterns."

"You can see them?" I asked, the science of his explanation having me lean in closer.

"Certainly, look here," he began and ran his finger over the waist where there was an opening. "The outer layer of the skin splits open like you see here and exposes the subcutaneous fats."

"Which burns without the protection," I said, his losing

attention with a distraction. He lowered his head, his face inches above the chest. "What is it?"

"Carla, the bottle?" he asked, snapping his fingers with one hand while holding a spot on the corpse. "I see something here."

She rolled a tray to the table, metal instruments glinting under the overhead lights, bottles tipping slightly before they settled. Carla reached to pick up what he wanted, asking, "The water?" I flinched at the sound of her voice, turning sharply as I caught the pronunciation.

"What did you say?" I asked, my voice rising with alarm. I felt eyes on me like electricity before a storm, the tension in the room changing. Jericho blinked and regarded my tone with concern.

"I asked if he wanted the water," Carla answered slowly, her pronunciation of water changing. I found myself staring at her, trying to imagine her without the big glasses and thick lenses that made her eyes look small. I tried to see her with dark straight hair that touched her shoulders. I tried to find a likeness to the man we had in custody. But I couldn't see it. "Detective?"

"My apologies," I said. Embarrassment rushed with heat wafting from beneath my shirt. I was hearing what I wanted to hear, and eyed Dan Viken's body fifteen feet away. Even dead, I couldn't stand to be in the same room with him. "Please, don't mind me."

"Doctor, the water you asked for," Carla said, handing the bottle to Doc Bob and giving me a hard stare. The corner of her mouth tightened briefly, a sly grin appearing. I sucked in a breath to speak, the hair rising on the back of my neck. The look was gone in an instant, possibly a product of my imagination. Her concentration shifted to the work as she spoke to the group rather than to me, "If you need to step out, Detective, we can finish the examination without you."

"That's okay. I'm fine," I assured her. But I wasn't. Or was I? Was I seeing what I needed to see? Was I so desperate to find

Viken's sister that I was willing to pick anyone to be a candidate? I faced the autopsy table, seeing Doc Bob spray drops of water onto the chest bone. "What is it?"

"I believe there to be a puncture wound," he said, his voice low. "Forceps, Carla."

Carla obliged, handing him the forceps. He worked the area gently while motioning for Tracy to take pictures. "There! Do you see it? The circumference is the same size."

"I see it," she said as the mottled skin changed to an ash color when struck by her camera flash.

"Help me up," he asked, fists pressing hard against the table, a grunt slipping from my mouth. "On closer inspection, I suspect we will find a hole in the sternum, the heart muscle pierced. It is the same injury identified with the previous victims."

"She was dead before the fire," I said and began to understand who it was that was on the autopsy table. "Tracy, start pulling missing persons reports from that time period."

"Any in particular?" she asked.

Jericho read the tablet over her shoulder, adding, "Back in Philly?"

"Uh-huh. I want to be thorough. But I've got an old case we're going to concentrate on."

"Okay?" she said, gaze bouncing from the victim to me. "A week's time?"

I held up two fingers. "Two weeks," I answered, leaning over the body to see the puncture, my lungs cramped as I held my breath. As Doc Bob had said, it was like the others. I peered up at him, asking, "How was this missed during the original autopsy?"

"Let's see what we have here." Doc Bob flipped through the file, the corners of the pages colored by age. "Ahh. I might see why." He turned the folder enough for us to see a picture. The victim's skin was blackened by the fire, their body curled like a baby sleeping. I made the shape with my finger. The doctor explaining, "That is a pugilistic posture. It could account for the oversight on the height."

"Pugilistic posture?" Jericho asked, wrapping his arms close to his chest. "Used to guard yourself?"

"Somewhat, and also partially involuntary," the doctor replied. "The intense heat causes the muscles to contract. It is similar to a fetal position."

"What about the hands?" I asked. Tracy moved into position to take a picture. Although the hands were severely deformed by the fire, the placement of the bones indicated her hands were open. "Contraction from the heat, her fingers should be closed, like a fist. That means she was already dead."

"Interesting," Doc Bob muttered, his eyebrows busily moving while he regarded my question. He peered up from the body, giving me a surprised look. "That is a significant discrepancy."

Jericho closed his hand, balling it into a fist. "If she'd been alive during the fire, then yes, they would look like this."

"It's partially an involuntary response to ball up," Doc Bob explained, showing us. "But the fire would also tighten the muscles as well."

"Her hands are open because they may have staged her death, making the cause appear to have been from the fire," I said, a shiver running through me. They killed a girl to fake Elizabeth Viken's death. "They knew what was supposed to happen to the body, skin contracting and tightening, but they didn't close her hands."

"It didn't help to have had an overworked and underpaid city medical examiner on the case," Jericho added. He saw the look on my face and asked, "Who do you think she is?"

With a deep pain, my emotions finding Jenni Levor and Pauline Rydel, I answered, "If I'm right, she is the Midnight Killer's first victim."

TWENTY-SIX

This case felt like a paper cut. A hundred of them. My nerves were shot by the anxiety of it. Our main suspect was dead, his body on an autopsy table, chest filleted liked a fish, vital organs removed for inspection. Call it serendipitous luck to have the true Midnight Killer's first and latest victims in the morgue at the same time. Doc Bob had used Dan Viken's heart and sternum to produce measurements of the puncture wound, their showing at approximately four millimeters. He had used these to compare to what was discovered on the exhumed body, identifying a near exact match, the placements he called uncanny as though they'd be completed by a surgeon.

Adding to the weight of pressures, I had Steve calling, the Philadelphia District Attorney on his back about the case, along with our own DA. There was the FBI too, their fielding the same pressures as me. There were victims and evidence collected, along with everything else we'd need to present to a judge and a jury of the killer's peers. One problem, with Dan Viken dead, I had no other suspects to offer. The video of a fake FBI agent at the prison was our only lead.

Elizabeth Viken was our leading suspect. I could feel it in my bones that she'd killed her brother. But this too became complicated. She was presumed dead, which we disproved, leaving her whereabouts an unknown. How would the case be presented? Doc Bob's evidence proved the murders were done with skilled hands. However, I believed her brother did not perform the murders. I believed him to have been an accomplice in the abductions and the torture. It was a woman who'd come to me in the night and dressed my face with a teardrop. It was her brother's hand that both Samantha and I were survivors of, and could provide testimony to, his torture. But neither of us had seen who it was that had performed the murders.

If we caught Elizabeth Viken and had any evidence to make enough of a case and to go to trial, a good defense attorney could ask if anyone else was involved. Under oath, we'd have to answer yes. We knew Dan was involved but without sight, without our eyes, we could never testify exactly who had done what. Even with Doc Bob's testimony, it was circumstantial at best. Just like Dan, I was blind and so was Samantha. We were blind to all of it. In my head, I could already hear the closing arguments, the defense attorney explaining it was somebody else, that Elizabeth's brother, conveniently dead, must have done these horrendous things. The justice for the victims and all our work could evaporate in a whiff of credible doubt.

And though we knew Elizabeth Viken to be alive, our proving she'd faked her own death wouldn't help our case. I needed Dan alive so that both could be put on trial. But that wasn't going to happen. I picked at the scabs on my face, scratching the itch of it healing. I could smell the memory of that night she was on top of me. The faintness of the chlorine, the dust from the pump house floor coating my skin and hair. I cringed at the thought of her touching me. At how it was feminine and soft while evilly sinister.

In the deepest pit of my gut, I wanted to be certain it was Elizabeth Viken. I'd been made blind, as had Samantha. I'd never seen more than a woman's hand in the car when I was abducted. But Dan Viken's sister had disappeared, and a victim of the Midnight Killer was placed in her car. Where was she now? The Midnight Killer's murders had gone unsolved for more than a decade, and they'd remain unsolved, remain open like painful nerve endings until we had his accomplice in custody. Nerve endings can heal, which meant continuing. And that's what we'd do.

"Hey," Tracy said with a touch. Gentle as it might be, I nearly jumped out of my skin. She sat against my desk, her hands up. "I am so sorry. Are you okay?"

I nudged the folders on my desk, flipping open the cover of one, fanning the air which carried the smell of old paper. "Pauline Rydel's case file. These others are from ten years ago," I began to say and shook my head with a sulk. "If we find Viken's sister, they'll put me and Samantha on the stand to create doubt in the jury. We could end up losing all of the cases."

"How?" she asked, leafing through the pages. "You guys are witnesses."

"Are we? We'll have to testify that her brother was there." I pushed my chair back and squeezed my hair tight, frustration building. "They'll argue that Elizabeth is innocent. That it was Dan Viken that had murdered those girls. She might even walk free, if she tells a jury it was her brother's idea to fake her death. Coerced her into it."

"Let's just work on finding Elizabeth," Tracy said and gave my arm a squeeze. "Get her in custody."

"You're right," I said, knowing I tended to overthink at times. "What's up?"

"I just saw you staring at those folders," she answered, distracted as Nichelle walked by, the two trading a look. Tracy flashed her a smile that seemed forced. "I wanted to make sure you were okay."

"Thanks... A change of subject?" I asked, feeling the urge to talk about anything else. I lowered my face, my focus fixed with seriousness. "Tracy, I know your smiles. What was that?"

"You saw?" she asked, her voice expressing surprise. A slow nod. "You don't miss much, do you?"

"Is it about the move to Philadelphia, having some doubts?" I guessed, prying. When she didn't answer, I tapped her leg. Her lips pressed tight, she rocked her head and answered the question indirectly. "But I thought you were all set with finishing your degree at University of Pennsylvania?"

"Don't get me wrong. I am over the moon excited," she began to say, her lower lip trembling. "But I'm not sure I'm ready to move to a big city."

I took a breath, trying to think of what to say, siding with professional first. "As a lead, a mentor, let me start by saying that your work here is exemplary." A bashful smile. Her dimples appearing. "You're the type that can do well in anything you choose."

She dipped her head, the smile fading. "And?" She cocked her head, asking, "Or is it a *but*?"

"Neither. As your mother, and having just found you," I began, my voice shaking, "I'll tell you to follow your dreams. Follow your heart and the rest will always work out for you."

"That's just it," she said, staring around the station before her eyes met mine. With a slight shrug, she said, "My heart is here. I want to be with you guys. I don't want to lose you."

There are moments as a mom, as a parent, that can find a place in your heart and stay there forever. This was one of those. I took her hand, answering, "Tracy, you will never lose me."

She gazed around the station, starry eyed as she took it in. It was filled with the same wonderment I'd seen that first day I met her. "I guess I want it all."

"I get that, but when it comes to moves and careers—" I started to say, giving Nichelle a nod as she passed by us again. I lowered my voice, "—and love interests, you are one person and can't commit to it all."

"I do love her," Tracy said, following Nichelle as she made her way across the station where she stopped to chat with Jericho and the sheriff. Tracy turned back to me. "I can't imagine being without you and Jericho. Don't forget to talk about Philly, okay?"

"He knows that wherever you go, I'll want to stay close," I said, speaking from my heart without regarding the words, the implication of them. Her brow rose high with anticipation as she glanced at Nichelle and Jericho, and then back to me. I quickly added, "But that doesn't mean we've had a chance to talk about moving yet."

"How about the other thing?" she asked, batting her eyelids. She'd shifted the focus of our talk to me, something that she was good at doing. She mouthed the words, "Ya know... the proposal?"

I nodded slowly. Tracy's smile stretched from ear to ear. "I asked him to ask me again," I said as my heart thumped hard.

She clapped her hands silently and then placed her hand on my chest, "You have to follow your heart too."

I stood to stretch and to give Jericho a wave. With worry, I confessed to Tracy, "He hasn't let me out of his sight."

"Well duh, Casey," she replied, my phone ringing, her whispering as I answered it, "Of course he hasn't." She pitched her thumb toward her desk.

"Steve?" I said, answering. Detective Steve Sholes had left the Outer Banks to continue building the state of Pennsylvania's case against Dan Viken. Circumstances surrounding Viken's death meant he would continue working the case with me but do so from Philly. It also meant resurrecting the original case we'd worked a decade earlier.

"I'm on," he said, the background noise telling me he was at the station.

"Elizabeth Viken is alive," I blurted. I could have texted him the news but had to tell him. "The body we exhumed isn't her."

I heard a commotion, his phone jostling. "She's... what?" he said, raising his voice, the sound of it muffled. He was likely covering his mouth, keeping the conversation private. "Casey, that's a huge statement. Are you sure?"

"You'll see it in the report. There's no way the body in the grave can be Elizabeth Viken," I answered.

"Shit," he grunted. "You think she's your accomplice?" My stomach turned.

"Not just the accomplice, she's the Midnight Killer." I flipped on my computer, opening the documents I had on the previous cases. When the phone went quiet, I asked, "You still there?"

"Yeah. I'm still here. You know that the press is going to have a field day," he said, his voice turning flat, the enthusiasm lost. "Listen, I'll have to take this to the district attorney. Even if we find her, her brother is dead. That's gonna complicate the DA's case."

"Yeah, I know," I said with an ache for the women who'd been murdered. Even mine and Samantha's abduction, torture and imprisonment could slip with enough doubt. "Steve, we'll get her. We'll make the case that it was the two of them working together."

"I hope you're right. It'd be a real tragedy to have a case like this dismissed," he grumbled. "Sunny? Who was in Elizabeth Viken's grave?"

"You're at my desk?" There had been five unsolved murders, but now there was a possible sixth victim from Philadelphia, the exhumed body.

"I am," Steve answered, the sound of a desk drawer being opened. "You know who it was?"

"I think her name is Molly Jenkins," I said, the speaker grating, Steve holding his phone between his cheek and shoulder. "It's in the drawer where I'd pulled the other cases."

"Gotta hand it to you, Sunny," he began, my old chair groaning, the sound of him plopping into it behind my desk, "you have a heck of a memory when it comes to names."

"Did you find it?" I asked, papers rustling.

"Mm hmm," he muttered, his beard scratching the phone. "Yup, I got it here. Hmm..."

"What?" I swung my chair around to face Tracy. When she looked over, I wrote down *Molly Jenkins* and showed her the name. "What is it?"

"I think I remember this one," he answered, leafing through the pages, reading my notes, his words indiscriminate. "She went missing two weeks before Elizabeth Viken's death. I wouldn't have ever connected her disappearance to the Midnight Killer."

"Neither did I. The case went nowhere," I said with a pang of regret. It was a case that had zero leads. Nothing. No witnesses. No last whereabouts. The twenty-two-year-old single mother had simply disappeared. Her two-year-old had been in the care of the child's grandmother. "It's a thin file."

"What's got you thinking of this case?" Steve asked, a chair's backrest squeaking.

"There were some discrepancies," I told him, thinking of the victim's hands. "The body had the same puncture wound to the heart."

"And you think Molly Jenkins is the girl in Elizabeth Viken's grave?"

"I do. But we'll need a DNA match to confirm," I told him. I thought of the difference in height and added, "Send me pics of the case file. I want to see how tall Molly Jenkins was. It'll help with confirmation."

"How tall?" he asked, papers shuffling, his voice an echo. We were safe to speak, and he'd put me on speaker while working his phone's camera. "Was it the height that got you thinking it isn't Elizabeth Viken?"

"There's that. And there is also evidence of death before the fire. She was killed like the other victims, and then placed in Elizabeth Viken's car."

"Shorter or taller?" Steve asked, his emailed pictures beginning to arrive.

"The victim in the grave was taller by a couple of inches," I answered as I opened the first picture from the Molly Jenkins case file. It showed a picture of her apartment. A playpen in one corner. A futon couch, opened with bedsheets and a blanket that were mussed, one of the pillows lying on the floor. I recall believing there might have been a break-in, Molly taken while she was sleeping. But if she was a victim of the Midnight Killer, would he have followed his MO? Would his sister have helped?

"Okay, the new DA here is going to need some numbers for the height," Steve said, his voice returning. He'd taken me off speaker, the last of the emails arriving. "What's the height of the body in the grave?"

I flipped through my notes and realized I hadn't written it down. "Let me get back in a few minutes?"

"Don't leave me hanging, Sunny," Steve said with urgency. "Sunny?"

"Yeah, Steve," I said, my lips pressed tight while I searched my notes. "I'll get it and text it to you."

I hung up my phone and leaned into my chair and closed my eyelids. Tracy's chair wheels squealed as she slid from her cubicle to mine. "I heard."

"I figured you did," I said and shook my head. "He needs

the height of the exhumed body. And he knows we could lose the case against Dan Viken."

"I was thinking about that. What if you and Samantha didn't testify?" she asked, getting up to lean against the table.

"I wish it was up to us, but we'll have to testify." I sat up, opening my eyelids, feeling the heaviness in them. "Regardless of exhumation, a defense attorney will ask us to identify Dan Viken as the man who'd abducted us and who... well, you know —" I choked up thinking of what he'd done.

"Sorry, I didn't mean to bring that up," Tracy said, lips pouting. "But isn't it what he's done that is evidence too?"

"It's a large part of what our case hinged on," I said and fished out a picture of the pair of pliers. The image was from the motel room, the lineman pliers with the dark blue handle sitting on the nightstand. The FBI had them now, and with the help of their forensics team, they confirmed its bite was a perfect match to the injuries inflicted. "There wasn't a single print on them. Not one. Which means that we have no proof of who used them."

"There's the partial in the bathroom," she reminded me.

"Which is what led us to exhuming the body and discovering Elizabeth Viken wasn't buried in the casket," I said, rehashing what the defense team would use. "They only need to argue it was Elizabeth that had done everything."

Tracy lifted her head slowly with an understanding. "The jury can't convict anyone if there's reasonable doubt."

"I'll be under oath—" I had to look away, ashamed there were tears in my eyes. "I'll say what I know to be true."

"It's not fair." She wrapped her arms around me, her breath on my neck as she continued. "I'm sorry this happened. I love you."

"I love you too," I said. I wasn't used to the closeness, but warmed to it, welcoming it.

"What did I miss?" Nichelle asked, arriving with fast-food

bags, two in one hand and one in the other. "I ran out to grab food, thought we could eat?" When we didn't move, she asked again, "Seriously, what did I miss?"

"We need to find proof Elizabeth Viken is behind the murders," I said, rolling my seat while wiping my eyes. "If her defense attorney argues that it was her brother who did it, then we need the evidence to show it was her."

TWENTY-SEVEN

We ate in silence, my stomach growling, the girls making faces. I wasn't shy and ignored them as we watched the security footage from the holding cell. There was no recording of the audio, only the faint color images that stalled at times due to a bad connection we were told. On the screen, there was an FBI agent just as the patrolman had described. She'd entered the holding cell areas from the station, his greeting her with a polite smile, and then a discussion.

"Can you see her face?" I asked, rewinding and playing it back, but could only see the top of her FBI hat. "It's like she knows the camera is there."

"I'd say that's a certainty," Tracy replied. She raised a hand, pointing at the patrolman. "Look how she moves as the patrolman moves."

"She's making sure that she stays out of the camera's line of sight." I cranked up the brightness and lowered the contrast, hoping it'd reveal anything we could use. "Ten years ago, Elizabeth Viken had long hair. But that was ten years ago and it could have changed a dozen times since then."

"That outfit looks spot on." Nichelle's eyes showed the play-back, her pupils bright with the video as she moved closer to the screen. "Her hair looks pinned. Or it might be short these days. That outfit is really good. I wouldn't know that it wasn't the real thing."

"Here it is," I commented, heartbeat speeding up. The patrolman left her alone, the holding cell door open, Dan Viken stirring, turning his head with his ear toward the FBI agent. When he sat up, a smile forming, I belted, "See that! His expression. His body language. He knows her."

"He totally recognizes her voice." Tracy took a picture of the screen with her phone, gaze jumping from one screen to the other. "Is it admissible evidence?"

I shrugged, saying, "Let's gather still frames from the video for the district attorney." I paused the screen, snapping a picture and sent it to Steve. "The DA might be able to argue a brother and sister reunion. Maybe bring in a body language expert to testify to his reacting to her voice."

From the corner of my eye, doubt riddled Nichelle's face. "Could be he's just happy to have female company."

Tracy groaned, Dan Viken's penchant for younger women surely to be an argument used against any body language testimony. "Yeah, it could be. We'll leave it for the DA to decide." I pressed play.

"There she goes," Tracy said as we watched the FBI agent kneel onto the cot, her hand bracing his shoulder.

The three of us sucked in a sharp breath when seeing her lunge forward and drive her right hand into his chest. "That's it there!" I stopped the video again, taking another picture, Dan Viken's jaw slack, his eyes bugging from their sockets. "That's the moment she touched his heart."

"Literally," Nichelle commented. "He didn't fight it?"

I pressed play, Dan Viken's head slumping forward onto the FBI agent's chest. "He didn't expect it."

"I bet he thought she was going to release him," Tracy suggested.

"Possibly. She may have gotten close by saying she was there to free him." I took another picture, my phone dinging with text replies from Steve. "And she never looks up once."

"The other guy?" Tracy asked, a prisoner sleeping in the cell next to Dan Viken. We watched as the FBI agent left the body, Dan Viken sliding toward the rear of the cot, his head dipping until we could only see the top of it. The agent exited the holding cell, the prisoner in the adjacent cell moving. They sat up from their cot, looked around enough to have seen the door to the station open and close, and then went back to sleep. "Nothing there."

"He claims to have slept through it all." I turned back to my food, finishing what I had. When I was done, I began to pick at the fries Tracy hadn't touched, her scowl making me smile. I sat back with a deep breath, focus locked on the screen, on Dan Viken's dead body, trying to find anything we missed. Tilting my head back and studying the station's ceiling tiles, I pressed my mind hard with ideas of where Elizabeth Viken would go next. She could be anywhere. She could be across the country by now. Or maybe out of the country in Canada or Mexico. Maybe she was sitting right outside the station and watching us through the windows. Could she have gone back to Philadelphia to visit her old stomping grounds? There was simply no knowing where to go from here.

"What are you thinking?" Nichelle asked as she turned her face up to look at the ceiling.

"Maybe she'd stay near her brother?" I questioned, the idea striking out of nowhere. "That's where she would be."

"How does this help to locate her?" Nichelle asked, her face near her phone.

"Because she is linked to him beyond their being brother and sister." My eyelids sprang open as I scanned the station, centering on the corridor leading to the holding cells. "Elizabeth Viken will never leave her brother's side. Even in death. Even though she killed him. She's here in the Outer Banks."

"That's kinda creepy." Tracy stood to look around as if Elizabeth was still in the station. She wasn't, but if I was right, she wasn't far. "We've already got an all-points bulletin?"

"Since we first found the partial print." Nichelle held her phone for us to see. "It was issued from FBI headquarters; the broadcast has reached every station in the states between here and Philadelphia."

"I had one issued for Outer Banks already. Extending it makes sense." I sat back down and thought of Steve. "Shit, I completely forgot to send him what he asked for."

"The height?" Tracy asked.

"Uh-huh." I leafed through my notes but remembered not having it written. "Either of you get the height?"

"Not me," Nichelle answered and looked to Tracy.

"Uh-uh," she replied. "We can use the measuring tool on the video stream."

"Right!" Nichelle said and nudged her chin toward my computer. "All the security cameras were upgraded and have a boatload of analytical tools."

"You can measure with them?" I asked, logging on to our local county's website to access their pool of security cameras. "I didn't realize we had anything in the morgue."

"New directive from legal," Nichelle answered. "I helped set them up before I moved to the FBI."

I navigated the video camera names and links, clicking through five before we reached the morgue. Like the holding cell video, we saw Carla and Doc Bob continuing the work on the exhumed body along with Dan Viken's corpse, it's position unmoved. "They're still there. How about I just call?"

"Or you can use this—" Nichelle began, rolling close enough to reach my mouse, "this is cool. Lemme show you."

"By all means," I said, and sat back as she started to drive. Doc Bob lifted his head as if knowing we were on the other side of the security camera watching them. Perhaps he knew the municipal building's security systems had live video? His head leveled then as his focus shifted to the exit and he tore the gloves from his hands. "Look, he's leaving anyway. Carla could measure it for us—"

"Patience, Casey," Nichelle said with a huff. A tray of icons appeared, including one made to look like a ruler. She clicked it, and then selected two points, the first being the head of the exhumed body, Carla and Doc Bob having straightened the body from the pugilistic posture. A dashed line appeared while she dragged the mouse toward the feet. "See that. Now we just measure."

"Stop!" I yelled, my hand on hers, freezing the mouse. "What is she doing!"

"Carla?" Tracy asked, her face appearing over my shoulder as we moved around the screen. Carla stood on the step stool, her face inches from the burn victim, her purplish gloves removed, a finger extended as she brushed it down their cheek.

I gasped, Tracy and Nichelle's eyes jumping from me to the screen. "Carla?!"

"Maybe she's just looking for the teardrop mark?" Tracy questioned. "You know, to note in the autopsy findings."

"Possibly," I said, closing the distance to the screen. "It'd be difficult with this victim."

Carla lifted her head like Doc Bob, searching the corner of the morgue, seeing the camera, and sleeved the purple glove onto her fingers. She went back to work, the back of Doc Bob's head appearing again in the video frame. "I know I saw that!" Nichelle said, alarmed. "She touched the face like there was a cut on it."

"Then I'm not seeing things?" I asked, bile rising inside me, a spinning sickness threatening. I gulped water from my bottle, and then held it up, saying, "And I know she said water in a Philly accent... wooder!"

Tracy eased back. "I'm sure she can explain what she was doing?"

"Bring up that video from the holding cell," I said and opened a picture I'd sent Steve. On it, the FBI agent's hand clutched Dan Viken's shoulder, the FBI jacket sleeve long, but there were fingers. Purple fingers. Nichelle had the video frame on the screen as I dropped my phone to my lap and asked, "Look at the fingers! You guys know anyone else that uses purple gloves?"

"She's allergic to latex," Tracy commented. "That's what she told us."

"Oh my God," Nichelle gasped, zooming in, grabbing a still image, transferring the work to her laptop.

"Her picture?" I asked, taking the mouse to hurry through the files on my computer, finding the ones for Elizabeth Viken. When her mugshot surfaced, I zoomed in to cover most of my screen. "This is old, and it's the only one we've got."

Fingers tapping and sliding on phone screens, both Nichelle and Tracy searching. "Didn't we take a photo together?" Nichelle asked her.

"Yeah, I know we did. The night Samantha disappeared." Tracy swiped up a half dozen times and shook her head. "I could have sworn we did."

"She'd never let herself be photographed," I told them. "Not if she was hiding her identity."

"What if I got a picture of her in the background?" Nichelle asked, turning her phone around. On the screen, there was Tracy and Nichelle and Samantha, eyes half-lidded, the inside of K-Beatz disco bright with flying colors. "She's there."

"That's just the side of her face, and blurry." As I moved closer to the phone, my identification badge swung forward, the lanyard around my neck jumping. I lifted it. "She wouldn't have been able to avoid a county identification. We all have to use them for access to the buildings."

Nichelle's eyelids snapped open, her answering, "That was the second to last thing I worked on before moving to the FBI."

My heart skipped a beat with my asking, "Surely, security would have removed access when you left?"

"Probably," she replied. One brow lifted as she took over my keyboard, "Which is why it's a good thing that the ID photos are sitting on a shared drive."

"Which you keep around in case someone loses their badge," I exclaimed, Nichelle pressing the tip of her nose with a nod.

"I have access to the shared drive," Tracy said, her laptop open, its screen coming alive. "Send me the drive location, I can help."

"Shit, just numbers," Nichelle said with a groan, the folder on the screen listing more than a thousand image files. "They're not listed by employee name, just our employee ID number."

I held up my badge when seeing the dates to the right of the photographs. "That's the file name but look at the date of the files. They're ordered by the create date. Doc Bob and Carla would be the newest—"

"Found it!" Tracy yelled, her face turning red with excitement. "Like Casey said, they are the newest employees."

"The employee ID number?" Nichelle asked. Tracy showed her laptop to Nichelle. She copied the number and opened the file. We sat back to view the photographs side by side, a hush quieting us. "I don't know..."

"They'll be more than a decade apart," I said as I studied the mugshot and the county identification. They were two different people, but there was a likeness in the chin, the eyes and maybe the nose. "Let's take this apart. Subtract the differences first."

"Hair is first." Nichelle clicked through my list of apps. "It'd be the first thing anyone changes when they're hiding."

As she continued clicking, she began installing software with names I didn't recognize. "Shared drive?" I asked.

"I made sure all the good tools were out there," she answered while opening a photo app. A few clicks later, and the stray locks of Carla's wildly purplish hairdo were gone. The identification picture for a Carla Reynolds was altered. I squeezed my armrests, knuckles white when the hairline and color and style were copied from the mugshot. Nichelle mouthed a whisper, "Damn!"

"Get rid of those big glasses!" I said, voice hitching onto my heart in my throat.

"Can't be," Tracy said when the glasses were gone. Nichelle cloned the eyes from the mugshot, applying the skin tone to match the lighting. "It's her."

"The height?" I asked, chair rolling away as I stood. "The mugshot. It's cropped." I took the mouse and moved to the window, resizing until the full mugshot was in view. "Five feet two inches."

"That's about right," Nichelle said, standing with me, her hand level with my shoulder. "She's at least a head shorter than you."

I pulled my gun from my desk drawer as Tracy and Nichelle made room for me to work. There was ice in my blood, a chill racing through my arms and legs. But it wasn't fear. It was rage. When Tracy began to leave, her direction toward the station manager's desk, I grabbed her shoulder. "Not yet."

She frowned and pointed, saying, "But we want to call it in, get the patrols over to the morgue."

"Elizabeth Viken has stayed hidden for more than a decade." I opened the clip, checking the load, and holstered my weapon. I pointed to the screen, the streaming video where Doc Bob was working on one side of the room while Carla continued her work on the exhumed body. She wore a pair of earphones, their work shifting to the labor of their duties. "We don't know what she's listening to."

"It could be the radio dispatch," Tracy said with understanding. "I'll join you?"

"I need you guys to keep watching," I said, chest pounding as I pressed my badge against my heart. "Move to the conference room. Nichelle, bring up all the security cameras. I want to know when and where Carla goes next."

"Got it," Nichelle said as I turned to leave the station.

"Have patrols arrive after me." I glanced over my shoulder at them, and held up an earpiece, "I want to be in the parking lot before she leaves the building."

TWENTY-EIGHT

I wanted to be alone. There'd be backup coming soon enough, but I wanted to face Carla Reynolds by myself. It would be me and her, my surprising her with knowing who she was. A growing courage had me pressing hard on the gas pedal, nearly smashing it at times, my leg trembling with the mounting adrenaline. The metal of my gun was cool, the touch of it making me question how far I'd take this, question how courageous I was feeling. This was the person who'd assisted in my abduction. And who'd participated in the murder of seven women, possibly more.

"No. You won't die on my watch," I muttered, my hand returning to the steering wheel. "I'm bringing you in."

My car's front tire chirped against the curb when I took the turn too tight, the municipal building in front of me, its parking lot next to it. There were other cars, the Sunday afternoon's late hour being just another day in the life of a civil servant. After all, killers weren't known to take off on weekends.

Like the cops and detectives, that also included medical examiners, which meant Doc Bob and Carla too. Or should I call her Elizabeth? Whatever her name was, my heart leapt into my throat at the sight of purple hair, the top of her head bouncing as she came down the municipal building steps. Still wearing her lab coat, one of her hands dug into a black bag to fish out a set of keys. She paid me no mind as I passed her, parking in the first spot available, the space further than I wanted.

"Hey there," I said loud enough for her to hear me, and eased my car door close. I came around the rear bumper, shoes scraping the asphalt. She nudged her chin in my direction, smoothly playing the role she'd adopted.

With her thick glasses sliding down her nose, she turned back toward the entrance, asking, "Did you forget something?"

"It's for the Philly DA, they need more information about the exhumed body," I said, my focus jumping to her hand, the bulge in her bag. What else was in there besides her keys? The murder weapon? My tongue felt thick, the spit in my mouth drying like a dead creek bed. Her gaze fell to my gun and to my hand near it. She stepped sideways, making a cautious turn that took her closer to her car. I made a careful move to close the distance between us. She'd have a chance to escape if I didn't play it right. "Maybe you could help me collect the informa- tion? Ya know, like if I have to roll the body onto its side or something?"

Her hand appeared with keys from her bag, my breath short with relief. She shoved her glasses onto her face answering with a shake of her head, "Yeah, I can't. I've really got to go."

A step. Another. I took strides that stretched my calves and moved closer to her car. I glanced over my shoulder, chancing the distance back to car. "That's fine. I understand." Carla offered a short wave and went to her door, leaving only the top of her head for me to see over her car. Her keys rattled and fell, and her tinny voice cursed at them as she bent over. When she stood, her head and shoulders coming into view, I yelled, "Hey, Elizabeth!"

She flinched and spun to face me. It was a behavior we'd learned as children, and it betrayed her by exposing who she was. She didn't say anything but smiled. It was the sneer I'd seen earlier in the morgue. She squinted with a menacing look, the corner of her mouth rising. It was gone in a flash. She was gone too, her body disappearing into her car, the engine roaring to life as I ran with everything I had.

My shoes slapped against the parking lot as she ground the transmission into reverse. Through the rear window, her head bounced on her shoulders as she worked the steering wheel, the car rifling toward me, flying backward with white smoke spiraling from the tires. Brake lights fired in my eyes, bright red ellipses exploding when her car struck me and sent me flying onto my bottom, crushing my lungs with a heaving breath.

"Stop!" I wheezed, freeing my gun from its holster, cocking the hammer until it clicked into place. Her face appeared in the driver side mirror with a sinister smile. I aimed at the back of her head, the shot polluted by the car's side, its metal and glass blocking my shot. It would feel good to get one shot off though, but as I began to squeeze the trigger, I stopped and lowered my gun. Doc Bob appeared, his mouth gaping as he watched. Those eyes. Those evil eyes. Her face shined with delight as she shifted the transmission again, metal grinding, tires peeling as she gunned the motor.

"No!"

But I was too late. I was helpless to stop her. The car lurched forward with a ferocious appetite, the front of it chewing up the asphalt, chewing up everything in its path. That included Doc Bob. Her car slammed into him with a sickly thud, his body flying ten feet and crashing against the concrete steps. He lay motionless while I ran back to my car, an officer appearing at the entrance, a radio mouthpiece in hand to call in the need for an ambulance. "Dispatch," I yelled into the microphone, firing up the car's motor as Elizabeth drove wildly over a grassy median and narrowly missed a young couple with their baby in a stroller. "I am in pursuit of a late 1980s Oldsmobile with a faded white color and a black roof."

"Location!" the dispatcher asked, the voice on the other end squelching a reply that went unheard as I chased Elizabeth onto Route 12. She'd veered left after running over a row of sapling spruce trees, laying them flat, their bark split open with sap oozing from the green wood. "Heading north on Route 12. Warning high speed. Pedestrian is down! Municipal building—"

"An ambulance is on the way," dispatch replied.

"Have patrols intersect before Carova." I dropped the microphone onto my lap, yanking the visor down to show the flashing lights, a siren blaring from my car's grill.

Breathe, I told myself as we flew into the main stretch of Corolla, the miles becoming thin before there was no more road. I scratched at the cut on my face when the smell of the pump house seemed to fill my nose. It came with the taste of the dust and her voice in my ear. Fury burned in me as I belted a scream, "Fuck you!"

There were flashes of blue and red behind me, my rearview mirror covered by the bright colors. But they were of no help to me. The back of the Oldsmobile bounced over a hump in the road, the tires spewing white smoke. Her engine was smoking too, the car being old and threatening to quit the heavy pursuit. A gather of seagulls rocketed upward, two or three crushed as she sped over open ground, the rear of the car fishtailing and giving me hope this race would end in a crash.

It didn't though. Elizabeth regained control and wove through the hairpin turn on Route 12, taillights blinking as she slowed and sped up. We were nearing the end of Corolla, and where the town of Carova began. A mile ahead of us there was a cattle-stop in place, thick steel bars buried in the asphalt with nothing beneath them that kept the wild horses from exiting

Carova. My heart leapt when she sped up, pumping the gas pedal, gray exhaust fuming as she raced ahead. She had no idea it was there.

Her car jumped when it struck sand, crossing the cattle-stop with a bounce, the asphalt road ending and turning into nothing but beach access. I'd learned in a previous, unfortunate attempt that car tires have to be deflated to make them drivable on sand. Like my experience, Elizabeth's Oldsmobile stopped abruptly, the rear tires spitting sand fifteen feet into the air.

"Halt!" I shouted, jumping out of my car as she touched sand with her feet. She ran. The thick glasses were gone, along with her lab coat. And for her height, she was surprisingly fast as she made her way to the surf, to where the ocean water kept the sand packed tight. I had my handcuffs and made the decision to drop my gun inside my car, the beach packed with tourists. It thumped the car floor as I took off after her.

"I can't!" she shouted and stopped at the water's edge, the patrol cars following me, their tires established for beach access. She turned to face us, golden light bright on her face and turning her hair orange. It was dusk with daylight fading, the west bleeding pink across the horizon with the sun setting behind us. My shadow grew ten feet tall and reached her wet shoes as I moved into position. I crushed the nagging thoughts of having been her victim and stepped into the role of detective, lifting my badge and a pair of handcuffs. She shook her head. "Uh-uh! That's not going to happen!"

"I was hoping you'd say that." I slipped the cuffs behind me where I could easily gain access. I stepped into the sea but stopped short of reaching her. She had a black bag slung over her shoulder, her hand inside it.

"Put down the weapon!" the officers responded, their guns drawn, voices shouting around me.

"Officers," I shouted. I didn't want to see suicide by cop if that's what she was after. Was that her goal? In death, she'd join her brother, the two avoiding time in prison. She freed her hand of the bag as I kept my hands raised. I dug my feet into the sand, removing any chance of the looseness. It wasn't a gun she held. It wasn't even a knife. It was a spike with an odd point at one end that was less than an eighth of an inch wide. It was the murder weapon. "We're going to need that."

Elizabeth reared back to throw it into the ocean where the rough surf would steal it forever. I jumped into the deeper water, tackling my abductor. White foam circled around my head, bubbles running across my skin, ocean water splashing against my face with a sting as a wave rolled us end over end and Elizabeth fought my grip. There were yells and hollering from the shore, my hands tightening on hers, forcing her to keep the weapon in our possession. She was smaller than me, but strong, wielding the weapon above me, threatening to plunge it into my body. The ocean was my weapon as I shoved her into the water, plunging her face beneath the surface. Her eyes darted wildly, air bubbles blowing from her nose while I held her there, my anger rising with a threat to drown her. She batted her eyelids, trying to blink away the sting of salt water, and tapped my arms with alarm, pleading to breathe.

"That's enough," an officer yelled, legs splashing as he waded knee deep while Elizabeth continued to squirm, her lungs aching for a breath. "Detective!"

"Not yet!" I shouted back at him and nudged my chin toward the murder weapon. "Not until she lets go of it."

"This is torture—" he said.

"Oh yeah! Tell that to the women she killed." I shut him up with a hard glare, saying, "We need the murder weapon to prove—" My words ended abruptly, a scalpel appearing in her other hand, the end of it plunging into my shoulder. Fire raced down my arm as Elizabeth yanked the scalpel free, blood and metal shining in the beaming rays of sunsetting light.

"Jesus!" the officer yelled and lunged for her hand, gripping her wrist with enough strength to force her fingers open. A second officer peeled the scalpel from her fingers, holding it above his head while he backed away from us. Blood pulsed from my wound, spraying into the ocean, and dressing my sleeve and arm. But I wouldn't let up, wouldn't let her go until I had that murder weapon.

"Go, we got this," a third officer said, the group surrounding her with three pairs of hands.

"Uh-uh!" I spat, shaking water from my face. "Get that out of her hands!"

Elizabeth surprised me then, her mouth open and wide enough for me to see deep into the pit of her dark soul. She sucked in a lungful of seawater and convulsed immediately.

"There!" the officer yelled as Elizabeth's fingers loosened on the murder weapon.

I ripped it from her grip and lifted her face out of the ocean. She gasped and coughed and spit the sea from her mouth as I began to mirandize her, "Elizabeth Viken, you have the right to remain silent. Anything you say can and will be used against you in a court of law."

"You tried to kill me!" Elizabeth shouted, swinging her fist, her strength zapped. I motioned to the officer to restrain her while I held her above the water. We got to our feet, the cuffs closing with a satisfying click, her screaming, "No!"

"You have the right to an attorney. If you cannot afford an attorney, one will be provided for you. Do you understand the rights I have just read to you? With these rights in mind, do you wish to speak to me?"

She dipped her head, hair hanging limp and dripping, the water sparkling like diamonds. She didn't look at me as she answered, "No."

"I didn't think so."

TWENTY-NINE

We had the murder weapon. The setting sunlight glinted off the metal, which was old, the stainless steel tarnished, cleaned by the bath of saltwater. Bagged and tagged, I had no idea what it was I was looking at. But that didn't stop me from smiling. No less than four officers witnessed Elizabeth Viken attacking me with it.

"Ouch," I belted, a paramedic holding a gauzy swath against my shoulder, pressing it.

"Sorry," she said and made an apologetic face that was almost comical.

"Don't let it happen again," I joked, getting her to smile. I breathed in the sea air as Nichelle and Tracy joined me, Jericho following, the three of them kicking sand as they ran. "It's a beautiful day."

"You're in a really good mood," the paramedic said, pressing again. I winced and grunted, but she didn't let up. "I can't seem to get the bleeding to stop."

"Time takes time," I muttered, Jericho's scruffy cheek brushing against mine. It was one of his favorite sayings, which I like to borrow.

"What's that?" she asked.

"Is it serious?" he asked as I handed Nichelle the murder weapon.

"I don't think so..." the paramedic began, sounding unconvinced. She was joined by a second, his towering over all of us, peering down with narrow eyes. She lifted the bandaging which had started to soak through and showed the injury as a warm blood sprayed my neck.

"Does it hurt," Tracy asked with a look of concern.

I brought my finger and thumb together as if pinching the last of the sun like it was a raisin, a wave of giddiness flashing through me. "Just a little."

"We gave you something to manage the pain," the taller paramedic said as he covered the wound with a fresh batch of gauze. "I can't answer to how serious, but it's serious enough for a trip to the emergency room."

"No celebration dinner?" Tracy said, trying to lighten the seriousness of it.

"Oh there's going to be a celebration," I assured her, a chuckle slipping. "A couple of stitches and the night is ours!"

"You sound like the celebration already started," Jericho said, his hand on my side. He turned to face Elizabeth Viken, seeing her through a patrol car's rear window. The ocean hadn't been kind to her hair, the dye used in her disguise turning runny. It was a washable hair color and thick bands stained her neck and face. "No celebrating for her tonight."

"We have her," I said with conviction, the painkiller making my head light. With my good hand, I tapped my chest, pointing at the bloody gauze, adding, "We've got the murder weapon and charges of attempted murder."

"Vehicular homicide too," Nichelle said, the news putting a fresh ache in my heart.

"Doc Bob didn't make it?" I asked, my emotions on a sudden roller coaster. "I really liked him."

"I liked him too." Tracy asked while holding the murder weapon in the light, "What is this thing?"

"Wow, I've only ever seen them in books," the paramedic said. He motioned to the other to take over as he joined Tracy. He held out his hands, asking, "May I?"

Tracy looked to me for approval, my answering, "It's bagged."

When he had it in hand, he felt the weight, saying, "Heavier than I thought it would be."

"What's it called?" I asked, thinking it was a kind of ice pick.

"It's an orbitoclast, antique," he answered. He looked to us then with wide eyes, asking, "Do you have the mallet?"

"There's another part?" I asked with a frown. I leaned back and checked my wound. The flow had slowed, my trip to the emergency room possibly canceled.

"It works like this." The paramedic held up the instrument, the pointed end near one of his nostrils. Without warning, he made a swinging motion as if holding a hammer, striking the other end, the part I thought was a handle. "See?"

"You're saying that thing was used for lobotomies?" I asked.

"It's used to perform a lobotomy, or what's called, leucotomy," he answered, handing it back to Tracy. "Heck of a find for collectors. Especially if you have the mallet."

"Dan Viken was a surgeon," Jericho said. "It could be that he had a collection of antique medical instruments."

"Yeah," I said, getting to my feet. "Mind just wrapping that to go?"

"Wrap it to go?" the paramedic asked as she took hold of my arm.

Jericho smiled, answering, "What she means is that she won't be needing the emergency room."

The taller paramedic lifted the gauze, his brow rising. "Your bleeding stopped."

"Self-will," I joked. The last thing I wanted to do tonight was spend it waiting. My head spun a bit, the pain medication wearing thin as the ache returned to my arm. "I'll redress it every couple hours tonight. Along with a cocktail of Motrin and Tylenol."

The paramedics looked at me stunned, the taller one asking, "From experience?"

"You've no idea," Jericho answered, his hand on the lower part of my back, inviting me. Selfishly, I used him to lean against, the sand lying beneath my feet, shifting loose, my balance tipsy. "I'll take care of her."

"She's all yours," the paramedic said. They gave me a nod, saying in unison, "Ma'am."

"I'll file this?" Nichelle asked, taking the evidence bag. The orbitoclast was the murder weapon, the hard evidence needed to connect cold cases, along with the newer ones. That included Jenny Levor and Pauline Rydel, and even Dan Viken.

"I suppose the FBI will take custody first?" I asked, believing there'd be three hearings to begin with. The FBI coordinating the legal logistics at the federal level, as well as Philadelphia and the Outer Banks. "Whatever the outcome, I'm sure it will include many years in prison."

"For sure it will," Nichelle said, her hair brightened by a flash of red and blue, the patrol vehicles leaving. Elizabeth Viken's stare on us finally broke and she spun around. "We won't be seeing her again."

"No, we won't," I exclaimed, leaning heavily against Jericho, his chest rising with a deep breath.

"You know, we can celebrate tomorrow?" he asked, sensing the day's end included my crashing.

Nichelle and Tracy came closer, hands on my arms and shoulders with concerned looks, "Tomorrow," Nichelle suggested, nodding in agreement.

"You guys wouldn't mind?" I said, suddenly feeling old,

unable to keep up. "Not sure if it was the pain medication or tetanus shot, but I'm zonked."

"Tomorrow, fresh start," Jericho told us and put his arm around me, half carrying me as we walked toward the sunset.

"Tomorrow," I agreed, feeling drowsy. "A new day."

EPILOGUE

Beads of water glistened on Jericho's chest as he braced for a crashing wave, its spray pelting us before retreating across our feet. Seagulls gathered overhead, circling and calling, a glimpse of their flight reflecting in his sunglasses. Having lived in the Outer Banks his entire life, he had the body of a lifeguard and wore a tan that seemed to last year-round. I kicked the water playfully, looking ghostly pale next to him. That didn't stop me from wearing a bikini though, thankful that it still fit after the long winter. I loved that we had a place near the beach, loved the sand between my toes, the foamy surf rushing against my legs, and the heat across my shoulders. And I loved that Jericho never grew tired of wanting to hold my hand and walk barefoot along the ocean's edge.

The last of Dan Viken's horrific touch was nearly gone, the bruises on my legs faded. But that didn't mean I was healed. Not by a long shot. There were the deeper injuries that were beyond superficial, the ones I continuously buried but would have to face one day. I feared that those might never fade.

Nichelle and Tracy and Samantha sat nearby, their skin shining, Tracy sharing the same pale complexion as me. Their eyelids were shut tight, their ears plugged with music. Samantha wore a pair of spongey orange headphones, the sight of them making me smile. They'd been her aunt Terri's and we'd often find her singing along with Helen Reddy's "I Am Woman".

The memory of Terri made me smile, but it was seeing Samantha joining us for an afternoon lunch that made my day. We had to get her out of the house. She was still recovering from the abduction and torture and was slow to get back into the day to day. We'd lost Doc Bob, and Samantha had met all the qualifications for the medical examiner job if she wanted it. I hoped her being outside and being in the sea air with friends would help.

"Could we ever leave this?" Jericho asked and stared at a marine patrol boat as it raced across the horizon.

"Could you?" I asked, knowing I could live just about anywhere. He didn't answer, but continued to stare, and was probably wondering who was on shift. I nudged his arm and laced my fingers with his, deciding to stay in the moment. "Well, you can't ask for better than this."

"You're right about that." He lifted my hand, tilting his head to see me over his sunglasses, saying, "You can't do any better than this."

I turned back to face the ocean and thought of Elizabeth Viken. I didn't have a phone or watch to check the time, but this afternoon she would be arraigned on multiple counts of murder. We got lucky with the murder weapon. There were fingerprints on the orbitoclast, the antique spike used to separate brain matter. Mine was lifted from the shaft where I'd grabbed it while it was entering my shoulder. But it was the few lifted from the thick metal handle that told us the story. Three more fingerprints were recovered from it, along with two on the scalpel she'd used. And all of them were from Elizabeth Viken. She didn't argue or deny it. She didn't say much of anything to contest the charges. When I had a moment alone with her and saw her stare was fixed on the cut beneath my eye, I asked, "What?"

"One for the tears," she said, her voice soft, lips curling into a smile. "Like our mother used to say."

I wanted more and dared to ask, "And this one?" I touched the right side of my face, which had been spared, unblemished by her touch. The same couldn't be said for her victims though.

Her gaze drifted to my right cheek, "And one for the pain."

We also learned of the Viken family fortune, which would usually rightfully go to the last living heir, Elizabeth. But seeing how she'd been dead once before, which carried its own felony charges, the matter of estate inheritance wasn't straightforward. Without any means to hire an attorney, the state of North Carolina provided a defense attorney, just as I'd explained to her at the time of her arrest. North Carolina was only her first stop. She'd travel to Philadelphia as well, facing new charges. We also learned about the return of the original charges she'd avoided, and that they were being added to the pile of them she already had. But first, they had to bring her back from the dead. Not a small feat, which involved a mountain of paperwork to make happen.

Tonight, Elizabeth would sit in her cell while we celebrated with good food and drink and a beachside bonfire. I got a smile from Nichelle, her eyelids open, shading the sun, watching me and Jericho. I had to admit to liking the easy access and having her here. But she fit in well with the FBI, and with the move to their headquarters on Arch Street, she was going to do amazing things in Philadelphia.

"Guys," Tracy said, taking my hand as she kicked the surf. She fanned herself and knelt to splay water on her neck and chest. "It's getting hot."

"Yeah," I said and wove my fingers with hers as we kept quiet, saying a million things with a simple look. She pressed on, joining Nichelle again, stirring Samantha too, gathering them in a talk about tossing a frisbee or going for a swim. I tried to avoid it but couldn't help but think of following Nichelle and Tracy back home to Philly. "I love those girls."

"I know you do," Jericho said as I grabbed his arm, holding it, sad and happy by the sight of my daughter. The time was coming. I knew it. They were moving, and I knew it meant I had to make a hard decision. But that wasn't today. Today was ours and that meant dragging my man into the ocean to play.

"Where are we going?" Jericho asked. I tugged his arm, the surf rising to wet our middles, the water surprisingly colder than I expected. My teeth chattered as I laughed, a look of shock on his face.

"Wait up!" Nichelle said, following, holding Tracy's hand.

"We're coming in," Tracy said, eyeing the water, having just watched the seventies classic movie, *Jaws*. "You sure it's safe?"

"It's safe," Jericho told her with a laugh.

"Come on then!" I demanded and put weight into my grip. I was one arm down, the injury from Elizabeth Viken had needed to be stitched after all. It was the tetanus shot that hurt more than anything, turning my arm into a throbbing ache. The hospital gave me a white sling, and it was in there that my arm would stay until the pain was gone. Jericho stopped, reluctant to go any deeper. He wasn't afraid of the water but was a gentleman first and guarding against my sling getting wet. I turned around with a hard frown, saying, "I'll be fine. It's hot. Can we go a little deeper?"

"Fine," he said, lifting his sunglasses, the shine of his blue-green eyes making me smile. He mussed his hair, the length of it twice what it was when we'd first met.

I lifted my gaze to his hair, sunlight bouncing from it, and added, "I'm going to start calling you Fabio."

"Who?" he asked, missing the reference. Nichelle and

Tracy were close enough to have heard me, agreeing with a laugh at the name. "I'll get it cut."

I spun around, cold sand squishing beneath my feet as I ran my fingers through his hair. "Don't you dare." I wrinkled my nose, adding, "I think I kind of like it."

He played like he was a cover model, rocking his head back and forth, sea spray in the air while he swayed to an ocean-blown gust, asking, "Like this?"

"You go, Jericho!" Nichelle and Tracy chanted.

"So you *do* know who he is!" I laughed as he mocked the likeness. On the beach, Samantha waved to join us, Nichelle and Tracy leaving us for their friend. I turned serious then and took Jericho's hand and brought it to my chest, moving closer, my heart racing. We were deep enough to float, and I wrapped my legs around him, getting as close as I could. "I love you."

His breath was on my neck as he kissed my cheek, lifting his head to return the words, "I love you too." He saw there was concern and squeezed my hand, "What is it?"

"That thing you said the other day about home?" I asked as I bit my lip. He saw that I was nervous, my insides tingling. "Were you serious about that?"

Jericho braced my sides and put space between us. He cleared his throat, and answered, "Casey, my home is wherever you are."

"Well," I began, tears blurring, Tracy and Nichelle and Samantha who'd joined us again played nearby. "I think my home is wherever Tracy is," I said, hating how it sounded, hating how the words were like an ultimatum.

Jericho blinked slowly and turned away, my heart stopping, our bodies rising with an ocean swell. I kissed his lips, our bodies drifting, the taste of salt on my tongue. He must have tasted it too and said, "Philly's soft pretzels and cherry Wishniak soda?"

"Go on," I said, tearing up with bated breath.

"The Phillies. The Eagles," he continued, sweeping me into his arms as I let out a giddy cry. "How about hoagies and cheese steaks with whiz?"

"You'll come with me?" I asked, knowing the answer but wanting to hear it. "A move to Philly?"

"I did say home is where you are," he answered and held me tight. "How else am I going to ask again?"

"You can ask me any time," I said, my lips on his.

"Really?" he asked, the whites of his eyes growing.

"Of course!" I told him, a warm flush rising in me.

"Casey White," he said. I stopped breathing, his taking my comment literally. I grabbed his stubbly cheeks, my eyes inches from his. "Will you marry me!"

A LETTER FROM B.R. SPANGLER

Thank you so much for reading *Taken Before Dawn*, Detective Casey White book 7. As with the previous Casey White books, the Outer Banks setting, the technology, and science used in crime scenes, and the police procedures have been fun researching. There's the growth of the characters and the addition of new characters in the stories too.

I hope you have enjoyed reading them as much as I have enjoyed writing them. If you did enjoy it, and want to keep up to date with all my latest releases, just sign up at the following link. Your email address will never be shared and you can unsubscribe at any time.

www.bookouture.com/br-spangler

Want to help with the Detective Casey White series and book 7? I would be very grateful if you could write a review, and it also makes such a difference helping new readers to discover one of my books for the first time.

Do you have a question or comment? I'd be happy to answer. You can reach me on my Facebook page, through Twitter, or my website. I've included the links below.

Happy Reading,

B.R. Spangler

KEEP IN TOUCH WITH B.R. SPANGLER

www.brspangler.com

 facebook.com/authorbrianspangler
twitter.com/BR_Spangler

Made in United States
North Haven, CT
17 February 2023

32734792R00157